and the
SWINDLED SOIL-SOLES

and the
SWINDLED SOIL-SOLES

Peter Nelson & Rohitash Rao

Balzer + Bray
An Imprint of HarperCollins*Publishers*

Balzer + Bray is an imprint of HarperCollins Publishers.

Library of Congress Cataloging-in-Publication Data
Nelson, Peter.
    Creature Keepers and the swindled soil-soles / Peter Nelson,
Rohitash Rao. — First edition.
        pages   cm. — (Creature keepers ; 2)
    Summary: "Jordan, Abbie, and the rest of the Creature Keepers
investigate a case involving Bigfoot and the Chupacabra"—
Provided by publisher.
    ISBN 978-0-06-223645-6 (hardback)
    [1. Animals, Mythical—Fiction. 2. Secret societies—Fiction.
3. Chupacabras—Fiction. 4. Sasquatch—Fiction. 5. Humorous
stories.] I. Rao, Rohitash, illustrator. II. Title.
PZ7.N43583Crm 2015   2014048049
[Fic]—dc23   CIP
                                                              AC

Typography by Alison Klapthor
15 16 17 18 19   CG/RRDH   10 9 8 7 6 5 4 3 2 1
❖
First Edition

To Dad, who's still leaving me big footprints to follow.—P. N.

To Dinesh—my brother and very first fan.—R. R.

1

Jordan Grimsley wasn't running away from what had him so terrified. He was running toward it. And he was running faster than he'd ever run in his life.

He could almost taste the fear in his throat as he ducked and leaped through the thick, dark jungle, racing frantically to face the creature he knew was waiting for him. It was the fear that drove him. Because it wasn't a fear for his own life. It was a fear he wouldn't arrive in time to save someone else's.

The strange thing was, Jordan couldn't recall who exactly it was he was rushing to save. He knew he *knew* the person. It was someone he loved very much. He could feel it. But this person's name, their face, their identity, was hidden in the shadowy jungle of his memory, just out of reach.

Jordan burst out of the jungle and tore across a moonlit field toward a group of small, crumbling stone houses. Standing beside a stone wall was a frail-looking old man with a short, white beard. The man looked familiar, and didn't seem nearly as frightened as Jordan was—in fact, he casually raised an old camera and pointed it at Jordan. Jordan wondered why this old man would want his picture.

CRACK! The ground suddenly split open. It formed a fiery red line that separated the two of them. The glow nearly blinded Jordan as he skidded to a stop to keep from tumbling in. He looked down. Orange lava bubbled inside the deep, wide crack. Jordan felt the intense heat hit his face and looked up to see that the man was safe. As he did, something suddenly leaped out of the crack between them and landed on the old man's side of the chasm. It was tall and lanky, and stood on long hind legs dripping with the hot, red goo. The terrible doglike creature's glowing red eyes were immediately familiar to Jordan. He realized this was who he was rushing to face—Chupacabra.

The creature growled loudly as it towered over the little old man. Jordan looked down again and was afraid to leap over the magma-filled crack. Feeling helpless, he tried to yell for the old man to run. But no sound came from his chest.

FLASH! The old man's camera blasted white light in Chupacabra's face, blinding it for a second. As the beast recovered, it raised its claw to strike the little old man, who lowered his camera and simply smiled at Jordan. And that's when Jordan recognized him.

He was a man Jordan had never met, but whom he knew very well and cared a great deal about—his grandfather George Grimsley. He nodded to Jordan, then shut his eyes. In a panic, Jordan looked down, picked up a large stone, and hurled it as hard as he could. *WUMP!* The stone struck Chupacabra in its snout. It snapped its head toward Jordan. In an instant, the creature sprang into the air, leaping over the chasm. In the next instant, it had Jordan pinned to the ground.

Chupacabra's red eyes seemed to burn into Jordan's. He could feel its hot, horrible breath on his face. Jordan shut his eyes and tried to scream—

"Aaaaah!" Jordan's eyes popped open. His sister's bored-looking lizard stared at him, just inches from his nose. Jordan kicked and squirmed beneath the fat, scaly reptile and fell out of his bed, tumbling onto his bedroom floor. Then he heard his sister's laughter.

Abbie was holding Chunk, her pet iguana, over him. She wore her typical outfit of all black, and her

black-eyelined eyes twinkled through her jet-black hair. She smiled down at her brother. He must have looked funny, because Abbie didn't smile very often.

"Why'd you do that?" Jordan asked angrily.

"To wake you up," she said. "You were having a nightmare. Hope I was in it."

Abbie scanned Jordan's bed and nightstand. Both were cluttered with books on cryptids, mythological creatures, and mysterious monsters. There were also multiple copies of *Weekly Weird News*, a newspaper that blared such headlines as *HALF BOY, HALF POSSUM SPOTTED IN PIZZA PARLOR!* and *BIGFOOT PART OF ANCIENT ALIEN RACE?* and *GLOBAL WARMING CAUSED BY LEPRECHAUNS!*

"You've gotta stop reading this stuff before you go to sleep," she said. She dropped Chunk on Jordan's bed and picked up an old, leather-bound book sticking out from under his pillow. "Including this old relic." She flipped through it. "Is this Grampa Grimsley's actual handwriting?"

"Yes. But it's not a vampire book, so you wouldn't be interested in it. It's his research journal. Pretty dry stuff. Grampa Grimsley was technical. Like me."

"You mean boring. I bet he was creative. Judging by his handwriting, I'd say he was a little of both."

Jordan snatched the journal from her. "His hand-writing isn't important. It's what he wrote that matters." He flipped to another page. "See? Here's a passage about *cryptosapiens*. He says that in his travels he came across folktales about creatures who could change from their animal form into human form, and back."

"Sounds cool. I'd totally be a lizard."

"That's just it. Grampa Grimsley didn't care if it 'sounded cool.' He was all about research and discovery.

And what he discovered was they were pure myth. He didn't let the fantasy get in the way of the facts. Like I said—technical. Like me."

Jordan got up off the floor, turned on the computer on his desk, and pulled out a small collar-like object with an even smaller antenna wired to it.

"It'd still be cool to be a lizard-girl," Abbie said, looking down at Chunk.

Even though Jordan and his fourteen-year-old sister disagreed on practically everything, they were both equally excited for their summer vacation—and not for the normal reasons. In fact, not much had been "normal" for either of them ever since their last vacation, just a few months ago. Their spring break began horribly when their parents drove them to southern Florida to help fix up a run-down house they'd inherited from Jordan's long-lost grandfather, George J. Grimsley, and turn it into a retirement home. It was located in an old folks' community, newly renamed *Eternal Acres*, and sat at the end of a street that dead-ended on the edge of a vast, smelly swamp in the middle of nowhere.

The Okeeyuckachokee Swamp, as Jordan discovered, served as the perfect hiding place for a command center of a secret organization known to nearly nobody as the Creature Keepers. Before he died, Jordan's grandfather had founded the Creature

Keepers to protect and keep safe all the cryptids of the world—at least the ones he was able to track down and befriend during the course of his life's work. These were creatures that some people believed in, but whose existence had never been proven. As Jordan learned, it was the Creature Keepers' duty to maintain George Grimsley's legacy and make sure it stayed that way. The sacred vow of this secret society was to help, hide, and hoax—a vow Jordan and Abbie took at the end of their spring break, when they were made honorary Creature Keepers themselves.

"Hey," Abbie said. "What do you think you're doing?"

Jordan was putting the small electronic collar around Chunk's neck. "Relax. This is the same Global Cryptid Positioning System tracking device I had Doris deliver to all the Creature Keepers to put on *their* beasts," Jordan said. He turned the device on and then turned to his computer. "After Nessie's kidnapping, it became clear to me that we could use a more technologically advanced tracking system. With these tracking devices, central command can know the whereabouts of all the creatures, anywhere in the world. This particular one will help me sleep easier in my own bedroom."

Their last adventure involved a kidnapped cryptid, which turned the entire Creature Keepers operation upside down. Not helping was the fact that the cryptid in question was one of the best-known, relatively speaking: the Loch Ness Monster. Jordan and his sister ended up finding Nessie and rescuing her from a mysterious, sinister man named Señor Areck Gusto. But Gusto was able to make off with Nessie's special coat of scales, her Hydro-Hide, which allowed her to control and keep the world's bodies of water in balance. Luckily, she grew them back. Luckier still, Gusto was blasted out of a volcano and met a very unpleasant landing somewhere in the mountains of southern Mexico.

Jordan hit some keys on his computer and pulled up a program showing a map of the world. He typed in "Chunk." The screen zoomed in on a map of his country, then his state, then his city, and finally his room. There was a small, blinking dot representing Abbie's iguana, who'd apparently crawled under his bed.

"Bingo," Jordan said. "Target identified."

Abbie pulled Chunk out from under the bed and took off the collar. "Chunk's not a runaway cryptid, you dork. He's family."

This struck Jordan as an odd thing to say. He'd come to think of the Creature Keepers and the cryptids he'd met as family. A really weird, super-top-secret family, but family. In addition to Nessie, Jordan and Abbie were introduced to creatures they wouldn't have dreamed in a million years they'd get to see, never mind meet and hang out with. There was Bernard, a Florida Skunk Ape who despite his foul stench was really great to be around. And Peggy, a Giant Desert Jackalope with a tendency to slip into a catatonic daze when presented with any shiny object. Lou was a tough, good-natured demon-like creature known as the New Jersey Devil. And Kriss was the shy, legendary West Virginian Mothman, whom Abbie may or may not have developed a slight crush on.

But the two creatures Jordan found to be the most unique of this extended family were, surprisingly, human. Doris wasn't a cryptid at all, but rather a very nice old lady who had more curiosity, life, and adventure in her little pinkie toe than most people an eighth of her age. This may have had something to do with the fact that up until very recently, she *was* an eighth of her age. Like nearly all the Creature Keepers, Doris was magically kept at about the same age as Jordan and Abbie—twelve or fourteen years old—by an elixir taken from the waters of the Fountain of Youth. But the supply was wiped out because of a mistake Jordan had made—a mistake he still felt horrible about, and would do just about anything to go back and make right, if only he could.

Eldon Pecone, on the other hand, was just a few

years older than Jordan and Abbie, yet had an old-school way about him that was more like a grown-up—a slightly dorky grown-up. Eldon was a proud Badger Badge–wearing, by-the-book, First-Class Badger Ranger, which made him the perfect person to run a large-scale, top-secret, international operation like the Creature Keepers, with Doris's help, of course. He was also one of Jordan's very best friends, and although they had little in common, they'd been through a lot together. Of all the amazing creatures and characters he'd met last spring, it was Eldon who Jordan was most looking forward to seeing again.

DORIS

NESSIE

KRISS

PEGGY

LOU

BERNARD

ELDON

Eldon had been on Jordan's mind more than usual
lately, ever since he'd received a postcard from him a
few weeks ago. The postmark was from Brazil, and it
had a picture of a little cantina called El Encantado
on it. There was a blurb describing the place as a
"charming and colorful cantina located on the small,
remote floating village of Palafito, anchored to the
banks of the Amazon River." Jordan agreed it looked
charming and colorful enough. But what really
interested him was what Eldon had written on the
back of the card:

> *Howdy, Jordan!*
> *Hope this finds you swell. Spooring isn't easy*

down here in the Amazon, but I'm counting on my
Badger Ranger training to serve me well in my con-
tinuing search. Wish me luck, and hope to see you
soon!

Your pal, Eldon.

Spooring was
an ancient tracking technique that
Eldon swore by and excelled at, and he had a First-
Class Badger Badge to prove it. In Jordan's opinion it
was a lame, outdated method for both tracking and
keeping track of the cryptids the Creature Keepers
were responsible for. It certainly couldn't compare to
the GCPS devices he'd gotten Doris to distribute to
all the cryptids for him, one of which Abbie had just
tossed on his desk.

"Does Eldon know about your little critter trackers?" Abbie pulled Eldon's postcard off a map of South America pinned to Jordan's wall. "Seems like you and Doris slipped that little upgrade in while Eldon was out of town. He's not gonna like it when he gets back."

"He'll love it, once he sees how well it works."

"Uh-huh."

"C'mon. You know as well as I do that for the Creature Keepers to be effective, we have to move into the modern age. Especially if—" Jordan stopped short. He and Abbie shared a look, and she pinned the postcard back on the map.

"Especially if Gusto's still out there," she said. "I know."

They both got very quiet for a moment, remembering the terrible things Areck Gusto had done. In order to kidnap and steal Nessie's powerful Hydro-Hide, Gusto had somehow managed to form an alliance with the only bad cryptid Jordan was aware of—Chupacabra. This was the creature in Jordan's nightmare, but over spring break he had been all too real. Chupacabra had a vendetta against Jordan's grandfather, and for some reason, he and Gusto were convinced that Jordan was actually his Grampa Grimsley, disguised with the help of the Fountain of Youth elixir. It wasn't true, but that hardly mattered. Chupacabra wanted Jordan dead, and

Gusto agreed to help him in return for sacred information: the whereabouts of some of the cryptids. With the help of Jordan's sister and their brave new friends, the evil duo didn't kill Jordan. In fact, Chupacabra was swallowed up in a pool of fiery lava. As for Gusto, he got the Hydro-Hide he wanted but was blasted out of a volcano. Everyone was hoping they'd soon hear from Eldon that he didn't survive.

"Hey, kids! Come for breakfast!" The sound of their father's voice from down the hall startled them both. "Your mom and I have a surprise for you!"

They opened the door to the hallway and were immediately smacked in the face by an oddly pungent and rather unpleasant odor.

"Ew," Abbie said.

"Smells like Dad's 'surprise' might be that he discovered an omelet recipe that uses onions, liver, and ripe cheese," Jordan added.

They followed the wafting stench down the short bedroom hallway to the kitchen/breakfast nook/den/living-room area of their city apartment and stopped short at what they saw.

Standing awkwardly between Jordan and Abbie's grinning parents was Bernard, the Florida Skunk Ape. He was crudely shaved, with patches of black fur jutting out of his otherwise pink, stubbly skin that had been nicked in some unfortunate spots. And he was dressed in a familiar disguise: a way-too-small, super-uncomfortable-looking Badger Ranger uniform.

"Surprise!" Mrs. Grimsley squealed. "It's Ranger Master Bernie!"

"Hey!" Jordan said. Standing there in his pajamas, he felt the very odd sensation of déjà vu. He wanted to hug his big, stinky friend, but knew better than to blow Bernard's cover in front of his parents. "Uh, what on earth could possibly ever bring you here, Ranger Master Bernie?"

"He came all the way up from Florida," Mr. Grimsley said. "Just to deliver some very exciting news!"

Abbie covered her mouth and tried her best not to laugh, while holding her nose from Bernard's skunky odor. Bernard fidgeted in his wedgie-inducing under-sized khaki shorts. "Yes! Hello, Badger Rangers!" Bernard blurted awkwardly. "I personally came to personally invite you as my personal guests to the Badger Rangers' Forty-Seventh Annual International Badgeroobilee!"

"Hooray!" Mrs. Grimsley burst like contents under pressure. "So exciting!"

"Yes sirree," Mr. Grimsley said proudly. "You two must've done something right on your Badger Ranger campout last spring, because you've been chosen to represent South Florida Badger Clan Seventy-Four— on the international stage!"

"Well, Canada," Mrs. Grimsley said, suddenly more sober.

"It's another country, Betsy. It counts." Mr. Grimsley handed Jordan a slick, four-color brochure. "We know how unfair it was to ask you both to give up your spring break to help us with your grandfather's house. So when this opportunity came along, we figured, heck, you deserve it! But we told Ranger Master Bernie the only way we'd agree to let you go is if he personally came and surprised you with the good news!"

"Surprise," Bernard said.

"All the arrangements are made," Mrs. Grimsley said, holding up two plane tickets. "You leave today!"

"Leave for where, exactly?" Abbie snatched the plane tickets from her. Jordan flipped through the brochure. It had photos of clean-cut rangers enjoying camping, hiking, fishing, and roasting marshmallows by an open fire. It described all these exciting activities, plus the big finale—building and torching a massive "Bonding Bonfire Beach Badger," whatever that was.

"Canada?" Abbie said, staring daggers at Bernard, who was beginning to get itchy. "You want us to go to *Canada*?"

"That's right," Bernard said. He began winking awkwardly. "You and your brother have been *handpicked* to come to the heart of *the Pacific Northwest*, where you will meet *new and interesting individuals*." His winking grew spastic, and was beginning to look more like something that might require medical attention.

"Are you all right, Ranger Master Bernie?" Mrs. Grimsley said. "Can we get you a glass of water or something?"

"Uh, no, thank you, ma'am. I'm just not used to

being in the big city. I think I just need to get some fresh air. If you don't mind, I'll wait downstairs. I'm parked right out front of your building, whenever you two are ready to go."

Jordan and Abbie looked at each other. Even though they disagreed on practically everything, in this moment they were both thinking the same thing:

Jordan and Abbie each packed up their backpacks, thanked their mother and father for letting them attend the Forty-Seventh Annual International Badgeroobilee, and kissed them good-bye. They took the elevator down to the lobby, stepped out of their apartment building, and stopped. Bernard had parked the car *directly* in front of their building. On the sidewalk. The usual stream of people speedwalking along, talking on their cell phones and paying attention only to the space directly in front of them moved in mindless unison, hardly noticing the Florida Skunk Ape dressed in a Badger Ranger uniform sitting in a bright red convertible rent-a-car, waving madly—as if Jordan and Abbie wouldn't have noticed him otherwise.

The car was sporty and small, and quite economical from the looks of it. Whether it was practical for an eight-foot, unlicensed nonhuman driver was a whole other question.

"I know what you're thinking, guys," Bernard said as Jordan and Abbie approached. "Red's a bit flashy. But I didn't expect to get such a sweet parking spot right in front of your building, and I was worried I'd have trouble finding it."

"Nope," Abbie said as she got in the back. "Not what I was thinking."

Jordan hopped in the passenger seat and the two of them observed Bernard on the driver's side of the tiny automobile. He could barely move the wheel, his big belly was so packed in against it. He turned the ignition and put on his turn signal.

The tiny red car jerked to a start, and a dozen or so pedestrians leaped out of the way. *HONK-HONK!* Bernard tooted the horn. The car jerked again as it lurched into traffic. *BEEEEP!* Six or seven taxis assaulted the little red car with their horns, weaving around it and yelling not-very-nice things. Bernard waved politely to them as he puttered down the busy avenue.

Once they were moving, Jordan and Abbie quickly got over their initial shock and began asking questions. They had a lot of them.

"Bernard, what is this all about?" Jordan asked.

He turned to them. "We're in crisis mode, guys." The little red car screeched across three lanes. Bernard yanked the wheel, jerking the car back. He stared straight ahead as he continued. "We really need your help. It's Eldon. After helping Doris set up the Creature Keeper central command deep beneath the retirement house, he left it under her and my control, then headed down to Mexico to see if he could find whatever remained of Gusto. Him being blasted out of that volcano, we assumed he didn't survive, but Eldon wanted to make sure there was no evidence of a cryptid lying around, and to get the Hydro-Hide back. He also mentioned something about your grandfather's ring."

Jordan felt a pang of anger as he remembered how the ring Eldon had given him, once belonging to his Grampa Grimsley, had been taken from him.

Bernard continued. "We've learned that he found only a scorched area where Gusto landed, but no Gusto. He did pick up some sort of tracks, and followed that trail south, into Central America. Nobody's heard from him since."

"I have," Jordan said, looking through his bag. "I got a postcard from just south of there, in Brazil, a couple of weeks ago." He pulled it out and handed it to Bernard.

Bernard's stubbly, poorly shaved lip began trembling a bit as he read it. *HONK!* He nearly sideswiped a limousine, then handed the card back, returning his glassy eyes to the road. "Well, we know he made it that far," he sniffled. "That's something. But we still don't know where he is now. I'm really worried about him."

Eldon was technically Bernard's Keeper, but it often seemed to Jordan like it was the other way around. This was not the first time Bernard had come to him with concerns over Eldon's safety.

"I'm sure he's okay," Jordan said. "It's probably just really remote down there. Hard to make contact. We'll hear from him soon. It'll be all right."

"It's not just that," the Skunk Ape continued as he

cut off a city bus to take an illegal left turn. "We need Eldon back to get the whole operation under control."

"Why?" Abbie asked. "What's happened?"

"We're getting reports in from all over. Cryptids are getting spooked, and their Keepers are getting anxious."

"Over what?" Jordan said.

"We sent out a number of emissaries from CKCC to deliver your electronic homing devices for the creatures. The emissaries were also instructed to quietly deliver some news to the Keepers—that there would be no more Fountain of Youth elixir."

A second pang hit Jordan, this one more like a knot in his stomach. He'd almost gone a whole morning without recalling the horrible mistake he'd made that resulted in the destruction of the lifeblood that kept the Keepers young.

"Our messengers came back with varied reactions from the Keepers. Many were worried they wouldn't be able to continue if they couldn't stay young. And some were afraid their creatures wouldn't accept them once they'd aged."

"Didn't the creatures know about the elixir?" Abbie asked.

"Not all of them, no. Not to be snooty, but there are different levels of sophistication among us cryptids. This is why some of us can speak, or master driving a car as I am right now, while others simply can't. Depending on how evolved a cryptid is, he or she might be able to handle that information. But the more wild cryptids usually have a history that includes terrible experiences being hunted by men. For them it's not only necessary for their Keepers to be young in order to keep their trust, it's also crucial that the source of that youth be kept secret."

"And now that's all been ruined," Jordan said. "By me."

"Nothing's ruined yet," Bernard said. "For one thing, the Keepers don't age overnight. It will happen slightly more rapidly than the natural process, as the elixir gets out of their systems and their bodies begin to naturally catch up to their biological age. But for now it's barely noticeable."

"You said the cryptids were spooked, too?" Abbie said.

"This is something we're still trying to figure out. A few of our field members came back and reported that some cryptids were claiming to have been visited in the middle of the night. By a shadowy figure. Whispering to them as they slept."

"Could it just be nightmares?" Jordan said.

"We thought that, too. Except each of them reported hearing the same thing."

"What did it whisper to them?"

"Horrible stories, almost all tales of Gusto. How this powerful human was able to capture and nearly kill Nessie. The voice warned each of them that Gusto will come for them next—and that the Creature Keepers can no longer protect them."

An eerie pall hung over the little red sports car as they approached the airport and pulled up to the curb. "It's Gusto," he said. "It has to be. He survived the accident, probably thanks to the Hydro-Hide, which he's now using to swim around the world, visiting cryptids in the night and spreading rumors about himself."

"That doesn't make sense," Abbie said. "If he

wanted to hurt them, he could just do it while they slept, instead of warning them about himself," Abbie said. "Why would he do that?"

"More important to the CKCC is *how* he would do that," Bernard said. "He doesn't know where these creatures are. No one but the cryptids themselves and those at the highest levels at CKCC has that information."

"So this whole Canadian Badgeroobilee is just a cover," Jordan said. "We're actually flying down to Brazil to help find Eldon, right? Very sneaky, Ranger Master Bernie."

"Uh, no," he said. "Those tickets are real, and you're on the next flight to Vancouver. It boards in thirty minutes. You'd better get moving."

"You just finished explaining how you need us down in South America," Jordan said. "But you're sending us up to North America?"

"We have your tracking devices to keep tabs on the cryptids. The Keepers are far more unpredictable. Because they're human." He tossed Abbie's bag to her. "When you land, you two will get to Harrison Lake, a few hours north of Vancouver. You'll meet Hap Cooperdock. He's Syd's Keeper.

"Syd. I know that name. . . ." Jordan suddenly remembered. "You mean Bigfoot!"

"I wouldn't call him that when you meet him. He's

a little sensitive about it. If you need to get formal, go with Sasquatch."

"We're going to see Bigfoot," Abbie repeated, letting that thought sink in.

"Yes," Bernard continued. "But you're also going to see Hap. He's put in a request for a couple of interns to help deal with an increase in local traffic near Syd's hideaway. Not an unheard-of request, but strange for him. He does things his own way. You're officially going as interns, but we secretly want you to see that everything's okay."

"So you want us to be spies," Abbie said. "Cool . . ."

"It'll also be a good chance for you to see firsthand what a real Creature Keeper does. Even though he's a bit of a loon, Hap's one of the best. Think you can handle all that?"

Jordan was staring wide-eyed, with a goofy grin on his face. He'd hadn't heard anything Bernard had said after the word *Sasquatch*.

The flight on Maple Leaf Airlines from the east coast of the United States to the west coast of Canada was about five and a half hours, but to Jordan it felt like an eternity. He couldn't get over the fact that he was going to actually meet Bigfoot. Of all the cryptids that he'd studied, Bigfoot was by far Jordan's favorite. He was obviously a mystery, but at the same time he was such a part of popular culture—like a superhero or a rock star. Meeting Bigfoot would be a moment to remember. So long as in that moment he remembered not to call him Bigfoot. Sasquatch? Mr. Squatch? The Squatchmeister? *What?* Stick with Syd. Syd would be fine.

His excitement was almost enough to make him forget the worry he now shared with Bernard over their friend Eldon. That would be the hardest part of this amazing adventure—sitting somewhere out in the woods observing Syd's Creature Keeper, while wondering where Eldon might be, and hoping that he was okay.

"May I offer you some complimentary syrup?" A flight attendant smiled down at him from the aisle. She was pushing a maple syrup cart, filled with dozens of tiny little bottles, all different shades of brown.

"Oh, no thank you," Jordan said. They both glanced at Abbie, who had a black eye mask pulled over her face. "She's good, too, thanks." The flight attendant smiled and moved on.

Jordan looked out the window and took a deep breath. He told himself that Eldon would be all right because there were good people who would find him. If there was one thing he'd learned from his horrible mistake last spring, it was that the Creature Keepers worked because they were a team. Every member of that team had a job to do. When each member did his or her job, everything worked out all right.

Jordan and his sister had been asked to do a very big, very exciting job. And Jordan was determined to do it perfectly. Starting with calling Bigfoot "Syd."

Once they'd landed, Jordan and Abbie got off the plane and made their way through the Vancouver airport. They realized they had no idea who this Creature Keeper Hap Cooperdock was, what he looked like, or where to find him.

"I guess we stand around and wait for him to make contact."

"Great. So the plan is to hang out in an airport in Canada, waiting for a kid named Hap Cooperdock to notice us."

"Well, do you have a better plan?"

"Maybe ask them."

She pointed out the window to the curb. Standing in perfect formation was a line of young Badger Rangers outside a large bus. At the end of the line, two rangers held a small banner: *47th Annual International Badgeroobilee or Bust!* As Jordan and Abbie looked on, a Ranger Master stepped off the bus with a clipboard. He saluted the young group. They saluted back, and began filing on board.

"C'mon!" Jordan burst toward the airport exit. "That could be our ride!"

Abbie picked up her bag and slowly followed. "It better not be."

Jordan ran up to the two rangers at the end of the line holding the banner. "Hey! Are either of you guys Hap Cooperdock, by any chance?"

They both saluted him, and waited. Jordan saluted

back. "Badger Ranger Tommy and Badger Ranger Sinclair!" one of them chirped. "At your service, sir!"

"Are you here for the Badgeroobilee?" the other one asked. "It's gonna be Badgeriffic!"

"Uh, well, that depends," Jordan said. "Is there a Hap Cooperdock on that bus that you know of?"

"Not that I'm aware of, sir," Badger Ranger Tommy said.

"Doesn't ring a bell, sir," Badger Ranger Sinclair added.

"'Sir'? I'm maybe a year or two older than you guys, at the most."

"We're trained to treat fellow citizens with respect, sir," Badger Ranger Tommy said.

"It's the Badger Ranger way, sir," Badger Ranger Sinclair added.

Jordan turned to Abbie. "Aw," he said. "They're like little mini Eldons."

"This is my nightmare," Abbie said. "No way am I getting on that bus with those miniaturized dorks."

"Hang on, I've got an idea." As Tommy and Sinclair got on the bus, Jordan confronted the Ranger Master, who was checking off a clipboard. Jordan leaned in to read his name tag.

"Ranger Master . . . MacInerney! Can I ask if there's

a Hap Cooperdock on board, or checked in at the Bad-geroobilee, or anything?"

"Sure! And welcome to the Forty-Seventh Annual International Badgeroobilee!" Ranger Master Mac-Inerney flipped through his clipboard. It reminded Jordan of his dad when he had a list of do-it-yourself fix-it items to get through.

"Uhhhhh . . . nope! Sorry, but I'm afraid there's no one by that name registered for this year's Forty-Seventh Annual International Badgeroobilee!"

"Stop saying that," Abbie said from the curb as she checked her phone.

"Sure thing!" Ranger Master MacInerney shouted back.

"Sorry," Jordan said. "She's a little grumpy because we just got off a long flight and our friend Hap Cooper-dock was supposed to pick us up here and take us to Harrison Lake, and also she's just generally like that all the time, so—"

"Harrison Lake? Say, that's where we're headed!"

"It is?"

"Sure! That's the site of the Forty-Seventh Annual—" He stopped and glanced over at Abbie. "That's where we're going," he whispered. "We'd be happy to give you a lift!"

"That would be great! Thanks!" Jordan rushed over to Abbie and grabbed his bag. "C'mon! I got us a ride! Grab your stuff!"

Abbie didn't move. "I told you, I'm not getting on that bus. I'm allergic to dorks in khaki."

"Abbie, we have to get on that bus!"

"No."

"Yes!"

"You get on."

"Maybe I will!"

"Fine."

"FINE!"

Ranger Master MacInerney watched the two Grimsleys fighting. He slowly backed onto the bus, slid into a seat, and gestured for the driver to go. Quickly.

"I'm not going to blow this mission," Jordan said. "And that's our only ride!"

"Well, what are you waiting for?" Abbie said, looking up. "Oh, no. Too late."

Jordan saw the Badger Bus pull away from the curb. "Wait!" He took a few steps, then stopped and stared across the street. Abbie stepped up to join him.

As the Badger Bus drove off, it revealed what was parked on the other side of it: a beat-up old orange Volkswagen microbus. Mounted atop the bus was a large, crudely made brown furry foot. A bedsheet duct-taped to the side of the VW had a spray-painted message: *Shuttle to Harrison Lake—Cheap!* Leaning against the bus was a skinny old guy wearing sandals,

grubby shorts, a tie-dyed T-shirt, and shades. His head was mostly bald except for the sides, which were grown out and pulled back and tied in a gray ponytail. He held a sign that read, *Jordan/Abbie.*

Abbie picked up her bag. "I'm thinking maybe we go with that dude."

After patting the both of them down and checking to make sure they weren't wired with microphones, their strange driver steered the microbus onto the Trans-Canada Highway. Abbie and Jordan sat crammed together in the tiny front seat, sizing up the odd old dude behind the wheel. Ever since they'd gotten on the road, he'd been jittery.

"Uh, you all right, there, Mr. . . . uh—"

The man glanced at Jordan, then turned the radio up, LOUD. Then he whispered, "Cooperdock. Hap Cooperdock." He winked, and turned down the radio.

Jordan and Abbie shared a glance. "Excuse me?" she said.

"Not to be rude," Jordan said. "But you're way too

old to be Hap Cooperdo—"

"*SHHH!*" The old man cranked up the radio again. He glanced in his rearview mirror, then his side mirrors. "If that's true, then I feel awful," he whispered. "'Cause I been wearing the guy's underwear for, like, eighty-six years."

"I don't know what this is all about," Jordan said. "But we're here on real business, and we need to meet the *real* Hap Cooperdock. He's an important person with important responsibilities and he's, well, he's younger than you. About seventy-five years younger. So if you can't take us to see him, I suggest you just—"

"Cram it, Grimsley!" The old man cut him off. "I figured Bernard would send me a couple of stiffs, but if you wanna learn how to be a Creature Keeper, you gotta do more listenin' and less yappin', man!"

Jordan was confused. "But—you *can't* be Hap Cooperdock. According to the CKCC Handbook, all Keepers must be between the ages of eleven and fifteen. . . ."

"Man, you're just like your grandfather—all about the rules. Well, at least you'll have that much in common with Syd—" He suddenly slapped his hand over his mouth as if he'd said too much, and looked up at the sky again.

"You seem paranoid all of a sudden," Abbie said.

"Everything okay?"

"No, no, everything's fine. Just fine. It's all gonna be fine."

Jordan and Abbie traded glances. Jordan came to a terrible realization. He felt shame and embarrassment rise up in him like a cold sweat. "Mr. Cooperdock, I think I owe you an apology. This is hard for me to say, but it's my fault you're so old."

"Why, because you destroyed the entire secret stash of Fountain of Youth elixir that kept all us Creature Keepers young and able to do our sacred work? Forget it, kid."

Jordan's mouth hung open as Hap suspiciously eyed a field of cows, then glanced back at Jordan. "Listen. Whatever you did, it was no lint on my baloney. I ain't old because I quit taking that elixir. I'm old because I *never* took that elixir. Ingesting some weird liquid that keeps you in a childlike state? Too far out, even for me, man. Unnatural. Not to mention dishonest."

"And your—er, *large-footed* roommate—he's okay with that?" Abbie whispered. "He didn't freak out when you turned into a grown-up?"

Hap glanced in the rearview mirror. "You'll have plenty of time to ask him yourself." Hap turned the radio back up. "Enough talking. Never know who could be listening."

It was midafternoon when they pulled into the Harrison Lake area. After a long, tense, silent drive, both Jordan and Abbie were relieved to see clusters of tents, campers, and other recreational vehicles in the vast space. They passed a sign at the entrance to the lot that read:

"This must be the place," Jordan said, reading the sign.

"Sasquatch Park?" Abbie said. "Subtle."

They parked and stepped out of the Volkswagen. Jordan and Abbie immediately noticed, less than ten feet away, a large, hairy bigfoot lumbering past. Another one, about twenty feet away, stepped into a port-a-potty holding a magazine. A shorter one, carrying a big red cooler and a bag of chips, stepped in front of them as he headed for a nearby picnic table. "'Sup, guys," he said.

The place was crawling with bigfeet. Every fifth person or so was in some sort of homemade Sasquatch costume.

"Is this a convention?" Jordan asked. "Why's everyone dressed like Syd?"

Hap crawled into the back of the bus and slid open the side door. He tossed out Jordan's backpack, then Abbie's. "This is a government-operated park. But lately it's morphed into something different. A tourist attraction. For BuckHeads."

"BuckHeads?" Abbie said.

"Fans of that TV show, where the host searches for"— he shifted to a whisper—"*Syd*." Hap suddenly grinned

at a few passing oddballs, one in a poorly stitched costume, two others in bigfoot-themed T-shirts.

"What TV show?" Abbie said. "World's Weirdest Weirdos?"

"That Buck Wilde guy's show. *Searchin' for Squatchy*, or something."

"*Buck Wilde: Squatch-Seeker!*" Jordan said. Abbie looked at him. "I watch it for research. It's bogus. Every episode the guy finds some faked evidence, then nothing."

"Buck and his crew work out of a big broadcasting RV parked at the entrance to the forest area," Hap said. He seemed more comfortable in an open, public place. "They go deep into the wilderness back there, film themselves with night-vision cameras, root around for Syd, then beam it out live all over the place, including to a coupla jumbo screens set up for the die-hard BuckHeads. Folks dress like Syd to show their pride, I guess. It's Squatchstock. Kind of a groovy, Squatchy vibe, actually."

"This is a lot of people," Abbie said. "Is Syd close by?"

Hap stepped out of the VW bus. "NO," he yelled in a super-loud voice, like he wanted others within a ten-mile radius to hear him. "THE ONE YOU CALL SYD IS NOT HERE, NOR ANYWHERE IN THIS VICINITY, RANDOM HITCHHIKING CHILDREN! BUT I

SHALL SOON LEAVE AND RETURN TO HIM, ON MY OWN, IN THIS BRIGHTLY COLORED, EASILY TRACKABLE VOLKSWAGEN BUS WITH A BIG FOOT ON TOP!"

Hap glanced around, then sidled up to Jordan and slipped him a stack of books and maps. "Take these," he whispered out of the side of his mouth.

"Okay," Jordan whispered back. "But why are we whispering?"

"And why are you so crazy?" Abbie also whispered, mocking them both.

Hap climbed into the driver's seat and slowly scanned the perimeter. Then he waved the two of them over. Abbie and Jordan stood at the driver's-side window.

"Okay. It's safe to tell you guys now, for your own protection," Hap said.

"Tell us what?" Jordan asked. "If Syd's not here, why are we here?"

"Because this is as close as I can get you to him. And this is where I leave you."

"What?" Jordan said. "What are you talking about?"

Hap spoke in hushed tones. "The word among the Creature Keepers is that Gusto survived. We all heard about how Gusto got to Quisling, the Jackalope's Keeper, a few months back. And then how he stole Nessie right out from under her Keeper's nose! Alistair MacAlister!

One of the best there is!" Hap tried to calm down. He was sweating a bit as he glanced around the parking lot. "And now, the word is, he wants to get to others. Now the word is, Gusto's coming for me."

"You?" Abbie said.

"Yeah," he said softly. "To get to Syd."

"Who told you this?" Jordan said.

"We Keepers are rarely able to communicate, but news gets passed along through the CKCC emissaries. They used to come regularly, to deliver the elixir—"

"I thought you said you didn't get the elixir," Abbie said suspiciously.

"I said I didn't take it," Hap whispered. "Never said I didn't get it." He looked at Jordan. "The Global Cryptid Positioning System devices. We all got them, and they were delivered by the CKCC delivery folks."

"And they were your source for this information," Jordan said.

"When you've got no one but a big furry creature to talk to for years on end, any bit of news from the outside is like serving up a double cheeseburger to a starving man."

"So it could be a rumor," Abbie said. "You don't know it's true."

"I don't know that it ain't. As Syd's Keeper, I can't take any chances."

"Alert the CKCC," Jordan said. "They'll send you whatever you need."

"No one's too confident about the CKCC right now. Besides failing to protect Quisling and Mac, they let some kid destroy the entire elixir supply!" He glanced at Jordan. "No offense, kid." Jordan looked down at the ground as Hap continued. "There was even a rumor that Eldon's gone missing, and joined the other side, man!"

"That's not true," Jordan said. "He'd never abandon a creature. Or the CKCC."

"Maybe you're right." Hap shook his head. "But I'm just not sure I trust 'em."

"But you trust us?" Abbie said. "We've never done this before!"

"But I know who you are. You're George Grimsley's grandkids. That don't make you full-fledged Creature Keepers, but I know I can trust you guys. 'Course, the one I'm really trusting to watch over Syd is right up there. . . ."

He pointed off past the lake. Jordan and Abbie saw a distant mountain peak rising above the tree line. "Old Man Breakenridge. That's where Syd lives. And as long as he stays on that mountain, he's safe. All I need is for you guys to make sure that he does."

"I can't believe this," Abbie said. "How do we even get up there?"

"First step, find
Guy and Andre. They're a couple
of French-Canadian brothers. Local businessmen.
They run a paddleboat rental shack by the lake. They
make a little on the side selling T-shirts to the Buck-
Heads. You'll find 'em over with the rest of the Squatch
freaks. Once you get up the north end of Harrison Lake,
consult the map I gave you. It's all in there."

"But I don't know the first thing about caring for a
Sasquatch," Jordan said.

"That's what the book is for, man! You're a rule
freak. There you go!" Jordan looked down at the stack
of books. On top was a well-worn copy of a book titled:
Raising and Caring for Your Sasquatch. "You've got to
be kidding me."

VROOM! The VW bus started with a rattle. Jordan and Abbie took a step back as Hap stuck his head
out the window and hollered again. "OKAY, HERE I

GO, OFF TO MY SECRET DESTINATION, WHICH IS QUITE A LONG WAYS FROM HERE! I SURE HOPE NO ONE FOLLOWS ME AND MY *BIG FOOT-MOBILE*!" He winked at Jordan and Abbie.

"Don't worry," he whispered. "Just make sure he sticks to his schedule, and he'll be fine. That's in there, too."

"Don't worry, Hap," Jordan said. "We'll take good care of him."

Hap pulled out slowly, passed the *Sasquatch Provincial Park* sign, turned south, and headed in the opposite direction from Mount Breakenridge. Jordan and Abbie watched until the bright-orange Volkswagen bus with the crudely made brown furry foot on the roof disappear around the bend.

Crunch-crunch. Munch.

A pudgy guy in a snugly fitting bigfoot costume was suddenly standing beside them, eating from a bag of chips. He nodded toward the road. "Sweet ride."

The path into Sasquatch Provincial Park led to a large clearing with picnic tables and fire pits. Beyond that, parked at the edge of the park's thick wooded area, was a massive RV. A banner hanging across it proudly displayed the TV show logo for *Buck Wilde: Squatch-Seeker!* There was a makeshift front porch attached to the side of the RV that seemed to serve as some kind of stage, and a large gathering of excited fans, some in bigfoot costumes, some not, packed up against it. Hanging on trees above the crowd to the right and left of the stage were a pair of jumbo television screens. They were showing clips and highlights from Buck Wilde's show. Jiggly action-camera shots of Buck running through the woods, night-vision goggle shots of the shadowy forest, and close-ups of Buck pointing to vague footprints in the mud were set to high-energy electric guitar riffs. It was doing a good job of getting the BuckHeads pumped up.

As the afternoon wore on, Jordan and Abbie made their way through the rowdy crowd, searching for any French-Canadian-looking brothers selling T-shirts.

Suddenly, the crowd began to cheer louder. They squeezed closer to the stage, catching Jordan and Abbie up with them. Abbie's face was smushed against a rather large and furry fanny belonging to someone in a homemade Sasquatch costume. Jordan looked up at the large televisions and saw the montage had ended.

In its place, a fancy 3-D logo for *Buck Wilde: Squatch-Seeker!* rotated onscreen. And then, there was Buck. Live and in the flesh.

"Now what's all this noise all about, huh?"

"*YEEEEEEAAAAAAAHHHHHHH!*" The crowd went berserk at the sight of the heavyset, potbellied Buck Wilde as he stepped out of his RV and onto his porch-stage. He soaked it in with a grit-eatin' grin, then tipped his signature catchphrase-printed trucker hat as a thank-you. He wore a plaid, sleeveless shirt and a pair of blue-jean cutoffs with muddy old boots and mismatching socks on his feet. Buck strutted up and down the stage, high-fiving all the hands and paws that reached up to touch him. Then he stood back, pulled a lasso off his belt, and swung it over his head impressively.

"Me an' my Buckaroo Crew came out here into nature to git me some peace and quiet! Ain't that what y'all are here for, too?"

"*NOOOOO!*" The crowd yelled back.

"Ya don't say! Well then what'd we all come out here to git, I wonder?"

He put a hand to his ear.

Everyone in the crowd except Abbie and Jordan screamed back as one: "TO GIT! OUR! SQUATCH! ON!"

"Ohh . . . that's right! Thanks for remindin' me! We're broadcasting live right here in the heart of Sasquatch central to catch that big, ugly critter!" Buck turned to two barrel-chested men standing just offstage. One wore a T-shirt that read, *I Got My Squatch On with Buck Wilde!*," while the other's read, "*My French-Canadian Brother Got His Squatch On and All I Got Was This Awesome T-Shirt!*"

"Andre! Guy! My French-Canadian brohams! Give the people somethin' for helpin' me remember why we're here!"

The barrel-chested men raised large-tubed cannonguns and pointed them out over the crowd. *BLAM! BLAM! BLAM!* They fired the cannons, blasting official Buck Wilde T-shirts at the fans, who went crazy diving for them.

"Mercy cowpoops, fellas!" Buck turned from Andre and Guy back to the crowd. "Now, y'all keep yer eyes peeled on them supersize TVs! Yer gonna see some top-notch, professional, turbo-powered super Squatch-searchin', tell you what!" He grabbed his lasso and swung it out at the crowd, snagged a sign, and pulled it back in, catching it with his other hand. It read: *We ♥ Buck Wilde!*

The crowd cheered louder as Buck waved them kisses. "I heart you guys, too! Don't go anywhere, now—I got a feelin' tonight's the night we catch that Squatch!" He waved one more time to the erupting crowd, then disappeared inside his RV.

The crowd spread out and dispersed, allowing Abbie to pull her face away from the furry fanny in front of her. Jordan was already cutting through the crowd. "Those are our guys!" he said. "C'mon, we've got to get to them!"

"Good," Abbie said. "That guy's costume smelled like wet dog and corn chips."

They followed as Andre and Guy made their way along the side of the crowd, heading back toward the path down to Harrison Lake, where Jordan and Abbie intercepted them. "Excuse me, Andre? Guy?" Jordan said.

"No more free shirts," Andre said in a French accent.

"You'll have to wait until tomorrow's show, eh?" Guy added.

"No, we're interested in a couple of paddleboats," Jordan said. "Hap sent us."

The brothers turned around. "You two know Hap?" Andre said.

"Uh, yeah! I mean, *oui!*" Jordan said. "He said you could help us."

"Hap owes us money," Guy said. "For zee Volksy bus we sold him, eh?"

"We don't know anything about that," Abbie said. "So can you help us or not?"

"You know where he is, *non*?" Andre said.

Something told Jordan it would not be helpful to explain that Hap may be on the run for some time. "Tell you what," he said. "You lend us the boats and if we see him, we'll let him know you're looking for him. Okay?"

Andre eyed the two of them sternly. His brother whispered something in his ear. The two of them grinned. Then giggled. And not in a good way. "Okay," Andre said. "You need paddleboats, eh? We've got just zee ones for you. . . ."

Jordan and Abbie followed the brothers down to a dock. Out over the water, some people were paddling around in large, plastic swan-shaped boats.

"Nope," Abbie said. "Definitely not getting into a pretty white swan."

Guy reached down into some reeds and yanked a moldy old tarp with a flourish.

"Voilà!" Andre said. Bobbing there in the reeds were a pair of banged-up, water-damaged, completely unsafe-looking paddleboats, both in the shape of the ugliest black geese Jordan or Abbie had ever seen. Their gray and black paint was chipped, both had a layer of smelly slime on the floors, and one of their eyes was poked through, leaving a grotesque, gaping hole.

"Eez good, no?" Guy said. "Only zee best for friends of our pal Hap."

"Ugh," Jordan said as the two brothers laughed.

Abbie grinned. "I can work with this," she said. "Au revoir, dudes."

The two-person paddle-geese were perfect in one respect—Jordan and Abbie could each operate one, with room in each passenger seat for their gear. They loaded up quickly and were soon paddling past the tourists floating around the bay in their pretty white swans.

A little farther up the lake they passed a small island. The map said this was Echo Island, and as they approached it, they spotted canoes beached along its shore. The Badger Rangers they'd seen in the airport were disembarking, setting up identical tents on the sand. A sign strung up in the small grove of trees in the center of the island announced that this was the site of the Forty-Seventh Annual International Badgeroobilee. They could see Ranger Master MacInerney giving orders, as well as various young Badger Rangers gathering driftwood, as others began constructing

53

what Jordan assumed would become the official Bonding Bonfire Beach Badger. Abbie and Jordan ducked down low in their geese and kept paddling north.

The coastline surrounding the lake became more remote and rugged the closer they got to the base of Mount Breakenridge. The waters of Harrison Lake wrapped around the mighty mountain, and as they approached, the sun was beginning to set behind the trees. Jordan and Abbie were having a hard time spotting a place they could make land and ditch their geese.

Drifting there in the shadow of the mountain, Jordan studied the map that Hap had given them. It showed a small, strange outcropping of rocks along a patch of shoreline. There was an arrow pointing to them.

"C'mon," Abbie said. "The sun's going down. It's getting chilly out here. Let's just park the geese and start climbing."

"I think we should consult the map," Jordan said. "If you'd keep quiet a moment, I might be able to figure out which of these rocks it's pointing to."

"You do that, map boy. I'm paddling over to those giant toe boulders."

Jordan looked up. In the distance were five roundish rocks sitting in a row, each one a little smaller than the next. They looked exactly like massive toes, and matched exactly the rocks drawn on the map. Jordan tucked it away, then paddled to catch up with Abbie. "I was just about to suggest that, per the map's instructions."

They ditched their geese between the first and second toe boulders and gathered up their gear. There was a small, pebbly beach hidden behind the wall of toes, and a steep trail leading behind that into the thick trees covering the mountain. Jordan and Abbie threw their backpacks on and began hiking up the trail.

7

The path leading up Mount Breakenridge was easy to follow, but tough to climb. It cut back and forth across the face of the mountain, growing steeper as it went higher. Every so often they would get a glimpse through the trees at the lake below. At the first vista they could see their little goose boats stashed between the toe boulders. At the second lookout point they could make out Echo Island in the distance.

As it grew darker, the forest trail began to grow fainter. Jordan and Abbie were thankful to reach a plateau where the mountainside leveled out before rising up again. The flat ground in this area was a tapestry of grayish solid rock and rich, dark-brown soil. Where there was dirt, giant sequoia trees stretched toward the sky, looming so high that Jordan and Abbie couldn't see their tops.

Jordan sat down at the base of one of these thick trees. It was near pitch-black now, as the moon had not yet risen high in the sky. He pulled out his flashlight and studied Hap's map, while Abbie glanced around the peaceful resting spot.

"I can't find where the trail continues up," Abbie said.

"That's because it doesn't." Jordan looked up from the map. "We're here."

"We're where?"

"Syd's place. According to the map, it should be right here."

Abbie looked around again. "I don't see anything. What does the map say?"

"It just marks this area in a grove of trees, with a big red X."

Jordan and Abbie both immediately started looking around on the ground. Abbie stopped, looked up, and smiled. Jordan looked up at her.

"What's funny?" he said.

She giggled. "Like there'd be an actual X on the ground."

Jordan smiled, then started giggling, too. They were both so exhausted from such a long day, they were soon rolling in laughter.

BOOM! A deep, loud thud shook the ground beneath them.

"What was that?" Abbie whispered.

"Probably a small earthquake. They're kinda common around here—"

BOOM! RRRRUUUUMMMMBLLLLE! This thud was followed by a short tremor. But this time they felt where it came from. They both looked over to their left. Something large and dark moved in the distance, disappearing into the shadows.

"C'mon!" Jordan turned to chase after it. Abbie held back.

"Jordan—what if it's Gusto?"

He took a step toward her. "We're official Creature Keepers now. If it's Gusto, that's all the more reason to go after him."

She nodded. "Let's go."

They ran to a thick patch of underbrush beneath a grove of trees and stopped. "Right here," Abbie said. "Whatever it was, it disappeared right—"

BOOM! CRACK! HISSSSSSS! Another thud sounded directly behind them. Jordan and Abbie spun around. A wall of steam was blasting out of a large split in the solid rock floor—a split that had not been there a moment before. The steam caused them to stumble back into the underbrush. The moon had begun to rise and was shining its silver light across the plateau, through the dissipating steam.

A shadowy form appeared within the steam. Backlit by the moon, it had a ghostly look. But this was no ghost. It was not Gusto, either.

"*Sasquatch*," Abbie whispered.

The hulking silhouette loomed at least eight feet high. Its long, dangling arms hung at its sides, and its thick legs stood anchored by incredibly enormous feet.

Jordan mustered his courage and stood up. The steam felt warm and wet as he reached his hand toward the figure in the moonlit mist. "Hi. We, uh, we come in peace. My name's Jordan, and this is my sister, Abigail."

Abbie stood beside her brother. "Hey," she said softly.

"We're your new Creature Keepers. It's an honor to meet you, Mr. Bigfoot."

The steam faded, leaving just the creature standing before them in the moonlight. They could hear it breathing, its massive chest heaving up and down

"My name's Syd." It slowly lifted a giant leg. "NOT BIGFOOT!"

BOOM! His gigantic foot thundered down on the ground just in front of Jordan and Abbie, shaking the earth so hard that the two of them bounced a foot in the air. It also caused a new split in the rock beneath them, a crack that crossed the first, forming a large, deep X in the stone.

An X that swallowed Jordan and Abbie whole.

"*AAAHH!*" The two of them plummeted into the rock crevice for just a few seconds. Their screams were suddenly met by a louder sound rising up beneath them.

HISSSSSSSSSSSSSSSS! The burst of steam caught them and blasted them back up and out of the X-shaped chasm, pushing them high above the ground. Tumbling in the warm rush of moist air, Jordan looked down at the ground a hundred feet below. He could see the Sasquatch in the moonlight, staring up at them.

The force of the steam lifted them higher and higher, until they hit a large, dark green tarp camouflaged in the high branches. It stopped them like a soft ceiling, and they dropped into a netting system that stretched like a huge hammock across the trees above the forest floor. Jordan and Abbie bounced at an angle off the uneven netting, then tumbled into a series of wide, split, hollowed-out logs connected to form a long slide. They skidded down the logs, zigzagging through the trees, until they were finally dumped onto a great wooden platform.

Jordan was shaken and bruised but otherwise okay, and still warm and moist from his thermal steam shower. He pulled himself up and found himself standing on a deck. He stepped to the railing and looked over the side. They were hundreds of feet in the air, securely cradled among the branches of the towering sequoia trees, and completely hidden from the ground below. Jordan turned around slowly. He looked across the vast wooden deck, and faced a perfect secret tree house.

The structure was simple, modest, and incredibly beautiful. Its construction looked to be exclusively of logs, trunks, bark, and branches, as if the trees themselves had created the house in their image, or given birth to it, and were now supporting, protecting, and watching over it.

"Should we go in?" Abbie's voice was quiet. She stood facing Jordan, with her back to a doorway. She seemed to be as awestruck as he was, and he understood exactly why she was asking. He felt the same hesitation—not out of fear, but respect. This was a sacred place. To barge in uninvited somehow didn't feel right.

On the other hand, they were Creature Keepers.

The heavy pine door creaked as they pushed it open. Jordan and Abbie stepped inside to find a clean and cozy living space, warmly lit with scented candles.

Just inside the door was a small kitchen with a wooden counter separating it from the bigger part of the room, which looked to be a den. Along one side wall was a bay window looking out onto the trees. A small table and two matching wooden chairs beautifully carved out of tree stumps were positioned at the window. Near the back wall was a heavy coffee table that sat before a large couch upholstered in soft, worn buckskin and adorned with a wool blanket draped over one arm. Near the corner was a doorway leading into another room.

Against the other side wall was a bookshelf, which held no books but had framed pictures, posters, and what looked like toys and figurines. Beside this was a small table on which sat an old television. It seemed slightly out of place, but only in that this was Bigfoot's home in a treetop tree house halfway up a mountain in the middle of the wilderness. Other than that, the TV was a charming relic that fit in with the cozy decor quite nicely.

"Do you think he even has electricity up here?" Jordan asked, eyeing the TV.

Click. A small lamp answered his question, lighting up the room and scaring them both. Jordan and Abbie spun around to see the same hulking figure as before, standing perfectly still just outside the open doorway.

Jordan couldn't help but notice something peculiar: the Sasquatch's front door looked too short for him. He and Abbie watched as the silhouetted cryptid moved to the corner of the deck and seemed to slip off a pair of high-heeled boots, stepping down out of them. Suddenly he could fit through his door, with room to spare overhead.

"You guys almost made me miss my favorite show," he said as he entered.

Jordan and Abbie got their first good look at the Sasquatch. Syd didn't look any different from what they and the rest of the world had come to know in all the hoaxed photos, bad movies, faked videos, and *Weekly Weird News* covers they'd seen: a broad-shouldered, big-bellied, fur-covered apelike creature with a smaller, almost human-sized head. But he did seem a lot shorter. Looking down at his feet, they quickly saw why.

Syd flopped himself onto the couch, clicked on the TV and put his feet up on the coffee table. The ground-shuddering clodhoppers that had cracked open solid rock were now pale-pink little tootsies at the ends of his thick, furry trunk-like legs. Syd noticed them staring, tossed a blanket over his feet, then pointed to theirs.

"House rule number one: leave your shoes outside. You won't believe the forest crud that you'll track in here. Go on. Just put 'em next to mine."

Jordan and Abbie removed their sneakers and placed them outside the door beside Syd's gigantic, furry, muddy foot-boots. They rushed back in to find Syd watching TV. He reached for a bowl on the coffee table. It was filled with what looked like greenish-white gummy worms. He popped a few in his mouth.

Jordan swallowed hard, glanced over at Abbie, and stepped forward. He cleared his throat, then opened his mouth to speak. Syd held up a large, furry hand. "House rule two: no talking when my show's on."

Jordan and Abbie turned their heads from the mighty Sasquatch relaxing on the couch, his little pink feet all warm and cozy somewhere under his blankie, and joined him in gazing at a familiar face on the television.

"Stay tuned, there, Squatch-Watchers! Coming up next is me, Buck Wilde, live from the heart of Sasquatch central! Don't go anywhere 'cause it's time to . . ."

8

Abbie was standing at the bookshelf looking at the pictures, posters, and paraphernalia that filled Syd's den. It was a Sasquatch shrine, complete with toys, coffee mugs, action figures, and even a lunchbox. "Jeez," Abbie muttered to herself. "Self-obsess much?"

Buck's voice blared from the television. *"All right, all right, all right!* You Squatch-Watchers at home keep your eyes peeled, 'cause tonight we're gonna catch that overgrown varmint! My infrared thermomolecular night-sensor goggles have picked up something big and nasty out in these woods, and I got a strong feeling it's that stinky ol' freak of nature, the Sasquatch! C'mon!"

"HAW-HAW!" Syd let out a deep belly laugh. He was totally enjoying *Buck Wilde: Squatch-Seeker!* "Yeah, Buck! Come and get me! Man, this guy's the best."

"Mr. Bigfoo—er, *Syd*," Jordan quickly self-corrected. He was still standing in the same spot, staring at the chuckling cryptid. "Uh, do you know who we are, and why we're here? Y'see, Hap asked us to come hang out with you, while he's away. . . ."

Syd looked up from the TV at Jordan. Then he looked over at Abbie standing in front of his portrait gallery. Then he shrugged. "Yeah, he told me." He moved a pillow on the couch to make room. "Now sit down, will ya? Your dogs must be barking—that was no easy hike up here, and you two made pretty good time."

Abbie sat down on the end of the couch. "Wait. You watched us?"

"More like felt you." Syd said, staring at the TV. "Nothing moves on this mountain without me feeling it. I can tell you when a grub farts. Oh, that reminds me"— he held out his bowl of the greenish gummies—"care for a grub?"

"Ew," Abbie said.

Jordan spotted a good opportunity to bond with

Syd and seized it. "Don't mind if I do!" He plopped himself down on the couch and picked up the bowl. Not only were these actual grubby-grubs rather than gummy-grubs, they were, in fact, alive. The plump little worms squirmed under Jordan's nose. Syd glanced sideways at him. Jordan picked one up and forced a smile.

"Don't mind if you do," Abbie said.

Jordan shut his eyes and popped the slimy grub into his mouth. He felt it squirming on his tongue and bit down hard to stop the horrible sensation. This only replaced that sensation with a way worse one—grub guts exploding inside his mouth. He turned pale as he swallowed, then turned to Syd and gave a trembling thumbs-up.

Syd wasn't watching. His attention was back on the television, where Buck Wilde had dramatically discovered a nest of raccoons.

"Ooh, close call!" Syd hollered. "Better luck next time, Buck!"

Abbie looked at Syd, trying to figure out if he was being sarcastic or not. She hoped he was. "Yeah," she said. "He should change the name of his show to *Buck Wilde: Raccoon Wrangler.*"

"HAW!" Syd snarfed a laugh so hard, a grub flew out of his nose. Jordan felt his stomach turn, as Abbie giggled. Meanwhile, Buck went to a commercial.

"You watch this show every night?" Abbie said.

"Never miss it," Syd said. "Mostly because it's the only thing I can get. Buck does his show just down the other end of the lake. I'm kinda famous on it. Hap set up a special satellite dish to catch the show out of the air. I love it."

"What else do you like to do, Syd?" Jordan asked as he tried to wipe off his tongue.

"That's easy. My schedule is sleep all day, get up, eat, walk the fault line to prevent global seismic catastrophe, come home, eat, watch TV, go to bed, repeat."

Abbie glanced at Jordan. "Uh, what was that one in the middle?"

Syd thought for a second. "Eat, probably. Okay, quiet—Buck's back on!"

Hours later, the cozy wooden room was filled with white noise as the television static cast a dull, gray light on Jordan, Abbie, and Syd. Of the three creatures sitting on the couch, only one was still awake.

Even though this had felt like the longest day of his

life, Jordan couldn't sleep. He sat beside Syd and stared at him as he snored loudly. Jordan reached out and gently touched the fur on Syd's arm. It felt softer than he thought it would—for some reason, he'd expected a pricklier coat.

He turned and looked on Syd's other side. Abbie had her head on his shoulder, dreaming peacefully. Jordan didn't understand how she could sleep, knowing that for the time being, at least, they were Bigfoot's Creature Keepers. Jordan was pretty sure that if Bernard and Doris back at the CKCC knew what Hap had asked them to do, they'd send someone more qualified immediately. But Bernard hadn't given any instructions on how to contact the home base, or if it was safe to do so. And if what Hap said was true, that he didn't have faith in the CKCC and wasn't planning on alerting them, who knew how long it'd be before someone came.

That meant that he and his sister would have to stay on the lookout for Gusto. It sounded to Jordan like Hap's Gusto paranoia was just rumor. But Jordan also knew that Gusto should never be underestimated. He knew he had to keep Syd safe.

Jordan looked back up at the snoring cryptid. He was going to be the best Creature Keeper Syd had ever had. *Help, hide, and hoax,* he thought to himself. It occurred to him that Syd's strict routine could be dangerous. He knew what Hap said about sticking to it, but Hap didn't know Gusto. He'd have to do something about that schedule.

Jordan thought about his strong need to prove something, and not just to make up for his horrible mistake that destroyed the Fountain of Youth elixir. Deep down, the thing he felt he had to prove was for himself—that he had what it took to be a real Creature Keeper.

This was his chance.

"*SNORT!*" Syd's buzz-saw snore suddenly shifted gears. His great body jerked, and he mumbled something in his sleep about being chased by a giant raccoon. His arm flopped over onto Jordan's lap, landing on him like a big bag of wet sand.

Jordan winced in pain, but he didn't mind. He smiled up at his creature, then shut his eyes tightly, wishing with all his might that the sun would hurry up and rise. This was going to be the longest night of his life, too.

"Jordan. Jordan, wake up . . ."

Jordan opened his eyes. Abbie was hovering over him. His sister's face was not the first thing he especially liked to see in the morning, but he preferred it slightly over her fat, scaly lizard, Chunk. He rubbed his eyes and looked around his room. Then he remembered he wasn't in his room.

He sat up on the couch and glanced around the tree house. Sunlight streamed in through the windows, and he could hear birds chirp from the branches outside. It was beautiful and peaceful—and Jordan couldn't care less.

"Where is he?" he asked. "Abbie, where's Syd?"

"Sleeping," she said, nodding at the doorway beside the couch.

Jordan got up and peeked into the next room. A huge pine sleigh bed took up nearly the entire space. Lying in the middle of it was a massive lump of fur, snoring away like a giant baby.

"All right," Jordan whispered. "You'd better wake him up."

"Pff," Abbie scoffed. "And why would I do that, exactly?"

"Because you're his Creature Keeper, and he can't just sleep all morning."

"First, you're his Creature Keeper too, so *you* can wake him up. Second, morning came and went hours ago. It's, like, three in the afternoon. And third, sleeping all day is number one on his schedule, remember?"

Jordan remembered. He rushed to his backpack in the den. He filed through the stack of stuff Hap had given him and found a handwritten list: *Syd's Schedule.* He read from it. "'Sleep all day, get up, eat, walk the fault line to prevent global seismic catastrophe, come home, eat, watch TV, go to bed, repeat.' No, no. See, this is bad. This is *so* bad."

"What?" Abbie said. "Step one, sleep all day. Check. This is gonna be easy. And wait 'til you see outside. It's awesome. Relax, dude. We're right on schedule."

"Yeah! That's the problem—*it's a schedule!*"

"So?"

"So it gives Gusto a perfect opportunity to attack him! You know in the movies when there's a guy who someone's after? The good guys always tell that guy to switch up his schedule—take a different way to work every day! Don't eat lunch in the same place twice! That sorta thing!"

"Syd lives in a tree, miles away from anyone."

Jordan shook the schedule again in her face. "And from five to eight every night he's scheduled to go out stomping all over a mountain, saving us from seismic catastrophe, whatever that means—"

"Don't overthink this. It's your first day. You've *got* to calm down. Come with me."

She opened the door to the deck for Jordan. He stepped outside.

Syd's tree house deck felt completely different in the daytime. Nestled in the lush, ancient sequoias, the solid wood structure reminded Jordan of an old sailing ship floating on a sea of green. He stepped to the railing and looked out at the thick tree trunks surrounding the house in all directions, like the outer walls of a secret fortress. It made him feel safe, hidden and protected from the rest of the world.

He looked up. The towering trees stretched up and

away, their branches crisscrossing overhead in an endless patchwork, allowing only broken sunlight to stream down, like a cathedral ceiling formed from stick and sky.

Jordan closed his eyes and took a deep breath. The soft breeze carried the rich, fresh scent of wood, earth . . . *and chocolate*. He opened his eyes. Abbie set a steaming cup of hot cocoa on the railing. He took a big sip and a deep breath.

"Okay, I get it," Jordan said in a much calmer tone. "But I can't mess this up. Hap has never dealt with Gusto. We have. We know how shrewd and dangerous he is. It's only a matter of time before he catches on to Syd's schedule and puts two and two together—"

"*Four*," a voice said from behind them.

Syd stood behind them, holding up four fingers, looking a little strained at having to add so early in the afternoon. Shoved up around his forehead were makeshift eyeshades like Abbie's, but these were homemade from an old sock and a strap. Under his arm was a small, furry stuffed animal. On his dinky little feet were fuzzy little bunny rabbit slippers.

He rubbed his eyes, stretched, and shuffled back inside. "Any hot chocolate left? I'm useless 'til I get my first cup of cocoa in me."

Jordan watched him, shot his sister a look, then followed.

Inside, Syd sat munching from a bowlful of grubs. His little stuffed animal was sitting next to him on the counter.

"Who's that little fella, Syd?" Jordan smiled at the fluffy toy.

"Teddy Squatch. Hap got him for me down at the park. They sell a lot of stuff down where Buck does his TV show." Syd got up, grabbed Teddy Squatch, and scratched his butt as he shuffled back toward his bedroom. "C'mon, Teddy. Daddy's gotta go to work."

Jordan got up and followed Syd again. "Hold up, Syd. We need to talk."

"Okay, but make it quick. I've got a schedule to keep. Gotta walk the fault line."

"That's what I wanted to talk to you about. You can't go outside. Not today."

Syd stared at him blankly.

Jordan stood between Syd and his bedroom doorway, blocking him. "As your Creature Keeper, I'm putting my foot down. We'll figure out a new schedule, okay?"

Syd looked at Jordan. "You're funny." He turned and grinned at Abbie, standing by the kitchen. "He's funny." He lifted Jordan and set him aside like he was a small piece of furniture. Then he entered his bedroom and slammed the door.

"SYD!" Jordan pounded on the door. "YOU OPEN THIS DOOR RIGHT NOW!"

"Somebody needs more deck time, I think," Abbie said.

"What I need is for this stubborn Sasquatch to understand that I'm in charge now, he's my responsibility, and I'm not going to let anything go wrong on my watch!"

Syd swung open his door and stepped out. He'd removed his bunny slippers and left Teddy Squatch in his room. His eyeshades were still shoved up over his enormous forehead. "You're throwing me off, messing up my schedule," he said. "Not cool."

"Hey," Jordan said. "Where do you think you're going?" He followed Syd outside.

Syd spun around to face him. "Look. I've been doing this a long time. I don't need someone to watch over me. Hap knew that. He stayed out of my way. He trusted me to stick to my schedule."

"Well, Hap doesn't know what we know. And what we know is there's someone out there, looking for you. His name is Gusto, and he's no good. We've dealt with him before. He's dangerous, Syd."

"You don't have to worry about me getting spotted or caught. I want nothing to do with the outside world, and I know how to stay out of it."

"Well, you sure have a nice collection of proof that the world knows you're in it." Abbie pushed a framed photo at Syd's belly as she stepped outside to join them.

Syd looked down at the photograph. "Yeah, okay. So I keep this stuff around. But only as a reminder of how curious people are. Humans are super curious. Stuff like this keeps me one step ahead of humans. See?" He turned the picture around. Jordan and Abbie had seen it before. *Everyone* had seen it before. Syd struck the famous pose for them. "See? One-Step-Ahead Syd. That's me."

"But you're not stepping at all—you're stomping around," Jordan exclaimed. "And you're doing it less than twenty miles from a park that's named after you, where a guy dedicated to hunting you down films his live television show, which by the way is titled *Buck Wilde: Squatch-Seeker!*"

Syd thought about this for a second. "Okay, I'll give you that. But see, by searching for me, Buck Wilde is my best protection from being seen."

Jordan put his hand over his face. "That's so insane, on so many levels."

"Think about it! Thanks to Buck and his show, anyone who's curious about me only has to flip on their TVs. I mean, why get off your butt and hike up some big ol' mountain to try to get a glimpse of little ol' me when you can sit at home on your couch and watch Buck Wilde every night! I know what I would do!"

Jordan looked confused. Either he was going crazy, or Syd was starting to make sense.

"Look," Abbie said. "As fun as this is to watch you two, here's a suggestion. What if Syd sticks to his schedule for now, but we tag along, keep an eye out for Gusto, and make sure everything's cool. Cool?"

Jordan and Syd stared at each other. Syd shrugged. "I guess that's cool."

"All right," Jordan said. He suddenly thought of something. "Wait. Where's your GCPS tracking device? You should've had a custom wristband delivered to you, from headquarters. Didn't Hap give it to you to wear?"

"Oh, you mean this thing." Syd pulled the homemade eyeshade off his head and held it up. It was the homing bracelet, taped to an old sock. "It works great."

Jordan grabbed it. "It's not a headband, Syd! It's an advanced technological tracking device, so the CKCC can know where you are at all times." He checked that it worked, turned it on, and clicked it around Syd's wrist. "In case anything happens to you, or if Gusto ever got up here and tried to get ahold of you."

Syd looked at his wrist. "Okay. But I told you guys, nobody sets a pinkie toe on this rock without me feeling it, so long as I have my Soil-Soles. Also, this pinches."

"Your what?" Jordan said.

"Soil-Soles. You must've noticed my feet don't exactly live up to the legend."

"I so wanted to ask," Abbie said. "But we were told you're sensitive."

"The Soil-Soles are my version of technology," Syd said. "They're an alarm system, intruder tracker, weapon, and world saver, all rolled into one. Or two, really. Comes in pairs. Let me show you."

Syd stood with his soft little feet facing the backs of the Soil-Soles, which sat docked on the deck like a pair of giant empty vessels—with toes. He looked back at Jordan and Abbie, and smiled. "Ready?" he said. "This is so cool." Then he stepped up and into them, slipping his feet inside.

Instantly, the massive foot-boots added two or three feet to Syd's height. Syd shifted his feet inside, undoubtedly wiggling his tiny toes, too, as he settled in. Jordan noticed that as he did, the Soil-Soles began to pulse, like they were waking up or coming to life. Either way, they seemed to be breathing. Syd turned around and grinned again at him and his sister. "This part tickles a little," he said.

Jordan and Abbie watched in amazement as the toes, arch, and heel of the Soil-Soles began to shift their shape very slightly, as if searching for Syd's matching features within and melding with them. All at once they seemed to lock in, as the pulsing material seized up, tightening around his feet. Syd looked down at the giant tennis-ball-sized toes, watching them wiggle. The way he was smiling, Jordan could tell he was controlling them.

As the lower part of Syd's new feet tightened and solidified, the upper-ankle part gripped and wrapped itself around Syd's actual ankles, meshing with his thick, furry calves, completely sealing his feet within the Soil-Soles.

Syd turned and stepped carefully to face Jordan and Abbie. His feet were completely natural-looking, as if he'd always been a size-ninety-seven shoe. He smiled at them and lifted one foot up on its tippy-toes with a flourish. He grinned at them.

TA-DA!!!!

"Instant Soil-Soles. All the technology I need."

"Okay, I have to admit," Jordan said. "That's a pretty cool upgrade."

Getting down from Syd's tree house was almost as dangerous as getting up to it, but slightly less terrifying, and therefore a little more fun.

A trapdoor in the floor of the deck opened to reveal a very long rope ladder, coiled up like a garden hose on a large wheel attached to the underside of the tree house. "This is what Hap always used to get up and down," Syd said. "I think you just spin this thingy, here." He spun the wheel, and the rope ladder whizzed down, hundreds of feet to the forest floor below. "Yeah, there you go."

Syd took his own way down, by stepping off the deck and grabbing hold of a pair of sequoia trees. These two younger trees grew about five feet apart and were oddly bare of any bark on the sides that faced each other. Syd jammed a foot against each tree, wedging himself in a spread-eagle pose. He grinned as he slid down the trees feetfirst, crossing his arms as patiently as if he were riding in an elevator.

Jordan and Abbie watched him as he reached the ground far below. He waved up to them to join him.

Jordan peered down at the flimsy ladder swinging and swaying beneath him. He looked at his sister. "Ladies first," he said.

* * *

As the sun began to set, the giant sequoias cast long, dark shadows across the forest floor. Jordan and Abbie watched the woods carefully as they followed Syd. The Sasquatch plodded along over the ground with his massive feet, then suddenly stopped, planted them firmly in the dirt, closed his eyes, and stood perfectly still.

Jordan had remembered Eldon telling him that of all the cryptids, three of them were given special gifts that allowed them some control over the earth's elements. Nessie's sparkling green Hydro-Hide controlled water. The Yeti (whom, like nearly all humans, Jordan had not yet had the pleasure of meeting) had some way of controlling the wind and weather. And Syd, he recalled, used his great feet to manipulate the earth. He wasn't sure what that meant exactly, but it looked at that moment like he was just standing in the dirt, dozing off.

Abbie rolled her eyes. She had little patience for this kind of "one with the earth" meditation stuff. On top of that, she and Jordan both felt vulnerable standing outside as the sun went down, watching Syd nap standing up.

"Okay, Syd," Jordan said. "C'mon, that's enough. We should really get back."

Syd took a deep breath. "Shhhhhhh . . ."

"Dude, what are you even doing?" Abbie said.

"I'm feeling the earth," Syd said, his eyes still closed. "Listening to it."

"Oh, brother." Abbie sat down on a log. Jordan approached Syd and tapped him on the shoulder. "It's getting dark. Being outside like this might not be safe."

"We're safe. There's no one around us for miles. Fourteen point two miles, to be exact. Female, hundred-ten pounds, hiking due south of here. With a slight limp."

Jordan looked down at Syd's foot in the soil. "You can feel all that?"

"And a lot more," Syd said. "The underlying rock formations that run through Mount Breakenridge are unique—they run deep into the earth's upper crust, touching the plates below this area, picking up and transferring any low-wave vibrations, like a giant tuning fork."

"Dude, if you're about to say the earth sings to you, I swear . . . ," Abbie said.

"Not sings, just vibrates. Thermal energy beneath the rock builds up seismic pressure, causing the vibrations to get louder and higher. And that's when it gets bad." He stepped over to another area, a few feet from his first spot. "Right . . . here."

BOOM! CRACK! RUMMMMMBLE! He stomped on the ground, which shook beneath the three of them. Under the soil, a large slab of rock cracked open. *HISSSSSSS* . . . Steam seeped out, and Syd smiled. "Oh, yeah. That was a good one."

Abbie stood up. "Wait. All that steam was in the rocks?"

"Not in the rocks. Deep beneath them, near the earth's upper crust. The rocks are kinda bottling it. When there's a dangerous buildup of pressure, I crack 'em, and release a bit of it."

"Okay," she said. "That's kinda cool."

"I read that little earthquakes are common in this area," Jordan said. "Is that you?"

"Better a bunch of little ones than one big one." Syd walked a few yards. Jordan and Abbie followed. He stopped and smushed his big foot into the soil. They watched him, waiting eagerly with eyes wide. "Nope, all clear," he said, walking on. "That last crack cleared out this area pretty good." He continued walking. Jordan looked down at the perfect Sasquatch print left behind and immediately began kicking dirt in it, filling it up.

"Hey!" He ran to catch up. "You've gotta be more careful about leaving your footprints lying around. People find these, y'know!"

"I know," Syd said. "People collect the weirdest stuff. I say let 'em. Doesn't mean anything to me."

"Right," Abbie said. Jordan and Syd turned to look at her. She shrugged. "I'm sorry, I don't buy it. I think you kinda like being famous."

BOOM! CRACK! HISSSSSSSSS! Syd slammed his foot down. A burst of steam rose out of the ground and shot into the air in front of Abbie. The earth rumbled for a second. "Another good one," he said, smiling at her. Then he looked up at the sky. "Uh-oh, getting late. Almost time for my show. Let's keep moving."

As it grew darker, Jordan grew more nervous. "Syd, listen. I get that your job is important. But earthquakes are natural things that happen. Would it be so bad if you took some time off, even if pressure did build up? Let the earth blow off steam on its own. How bad could that be?"

"Have you guys ever heard of Pangaea?"

"They're a hard-rock metal band," Abbie said. "From Cucamonga, I think."

"You're right on the hard rock part," Syd said. "It's the name of the supercontinent that existed during the late Paleozoic and early Mesozoic eras, when all the continents were smushed together as one. It formed approximately three hundred million years ago and then began to break apart after about one hundred million years."

"Oh, yeah," Abbie said. "It's also that."

"Continental drift," Jordan said. "We learned about it in science. Pangaea split up into the seven continents we know today, right?"

"Six if you count Europe and Asia as one," Syd said. "Anyway, they drifted apart, until they each came to rest."

"Rest?" Abbie asked. "Rest on what?"

"Well," Syd said. "The continent you're currently

standing on rests upon the Pacific Oceanic crust, way beneath our feet."

"It isn't attached?" she said.

"Nope. Just really heavy," Syd said. "Take a big disruption to break free."

Abbie was beginning to get it. "Like, maybe a super earthquake?"

"It's called a megathrust," Syd said. "Quick. What's the biggest fault line?"

"I know this," Jordan said. "San Andreas Fault, in Southern California."

Syd smiled. "Americans always think their stuff's the biggest. Nope. It's called the Cascadia Subduction Zone. Biggest earthquake machine in the world. Huge."

"I've never heard of it," Jordan said. "Where is it?"

"Also under your feet. Directly below us, actually."

Jordan and Abbie looked down.

"It starts here," Syd said, "beneath Harrison Lake and Mount Breakenridge. Then it runs about six hundred miles all the way down the coast to California. It's where the North American tectonic plate sits atop the Pacific Oceanic crust."

Syd started walking again. Jordan and Abbie followed, tiptoeing lightly. "C'mon," Syd said. "One more stop. I've got someone I want you to meet."

They made their way to the far side of the flat part of the mountain, where a solid rock floor bigger than the area of Syd's tree house extended all the way to the edge, forming a cliff overlooking Harrison Lake.

"Meet Roxanne," Syd said, smiling down at the exposed-stone surface. "She's mostly gneissic granodiorite, cored by a younger porphyritic quartz diorite."

"Wow, she's a real looker, Syd." Abbie shot Jordan a surprised look.

"Yep," he said. "Not too bad for a gal born in the Upper Cretaceous period. Hefty, too! Probably a good million times deep as she is wide. She's the main vein to the Cascadia Subduction Zone. Cracking Roxanne open would be pulling the emergency cord, if the pressure ever built to megathrust earthquake level. She's special. And I sure hope I never have to crack her."

"Why is that?" Abbie asked. "Aside from the personal connection, I mean."

"Because she also makes up a nasty shear zone—see how she runs to the edge and forms a cliff over the water? A major Soil-Sole fracture would break off her entire cliff, setting off a mini-tsunami across Harrison Lake. Would take out Echo Island, Sasquatch Provincial Park . . . wouldn't be pretty."

Abbie stared down at Syd's huge feet. "Syd, would you mind stepping down off Roxanne's face, please? Like, verrry slooooowwwly . . ."

Syd hopped onto the ground. It trembled, but only slightly. "Don't worry, Roxanne's a tough old gal. It'd take a very hard, very solid direct hit to crack her."

"Let's say the pressure beneath Mount Breaken-ridge built to a super-high level, and you *didn't* crack her open?" Jordan said. "What then?"

"It'd likely cause a megathrust. Probably break the North American tectonic plate free from the Pacific Oceanic crust."

"And form a new supercontinent?" Abbie asked.

"Re-create Pangaea?" Syd shook his head. "Nah. All the continents would have to be broken free, and something very powerful would have to push them back together. It took hundreds of millions of years for them to drift and settle where they are today. More likely, North America would sink, or break apart like a saltine cracker, along every fault line it has. Or some combo of the two."

Jordan and Abbie stared at Syd. "Anyway, that's kinda why it's important I walk the fault line every day." He looked up at the sun in the sky. "Shoot! I'm gonna miss my show! Race you guys back—time to get our Squatch on!"

BOOM! BOOM! BOOM! BOOM! He thundered off in his Soil-Soles. Abbie tiptoed after him, trying to get him to stop. Jordan was about to run, but suddenly froze. He heard a rustling in the bushes, and peered into the shadows. The hair stood up on the back of his neck as he thought of Gusto. He readied himself for anything.

"That's just a black-tailed deer, Jordan!" Syd's voice boomed from across the plateau. "Feels like a male, probably about a hundred eighty pounds!"

A large buck popped out of the bushes, looked at Jordan, and trotted silently off. Jordan shook his head. "Those are some shoes," he said to himself. Then he ran across the side of Mount Breakenridge, toward the waiting rope ladder.

Up on the tree house deck, Jordan and Abbie watched as Syd stepped to the corner by the door and closed his eyes in concentration. *Tsssssss* . . . The ankle sheaths opened like a blooming flower, although the fragrance was a little different. They unwrapped from his ankles and Syd stepped out, a couple of feet shorter. He walked through the door, grabbed some grubs on his way past the kitchen, plopped himself on the couch, and switched on the television. Abbie followed him in as Jordan lingered outside. He crouched down and peered at the empty Soil-Soles.

Jordan entered the den to find Syd and Abbie settling in to watch Buck Wilde's show. On TV, Buck was going through his usual dramatics, creeping through the dark woods, looking back to whisper to his audience his every thought and observation. "I'm picking up a very strong scent here," he murmured tensely. "It's a foul odor that I would definitely describe as *Stank de Squatch*!" He pulled his lasso off his belt. "We better be ready—I think we're getting close to something!"

"If it was the inside of Syd's Stank-Soles, you'd know it, dude!" Abbie yelled.

"HAW! HAW!" Syd laughed loudly. Abbie smiled up at him.

"What's with the lasso, anyway?" she asked. "What's he gonna do, try and rustle you?"

"That's Buck's thing," Syd said. "He's really good with it."

Jordan sat down and looked at Syd and Abbie. He felt worried, and anxious, and trapped. He understood now how important it was for Syd to go out and do what he did, but he still had a bad feeling about Gusto. Jordan couldn't let anything happen to Syd. Not on his watch.

There was another thing bothering him. Watching Abbie and Syd, he worried once again that maybe he didn't have what it took to be a Creature Keeper. If this was what creature keeping was all about, basically creature-sitting, Jordan wasn't sure he could do it. There had to be a better way for him to help.

Buck was spouting off after hitting another dead end on his show. "That Squatch barely got away from us again, folks," he said. "But don't you worry, as long as that varmint is out there, I'll keep looking for him! He can't hide from ol' Buck Wilde forever! And so long as you keep watchin', I'll keep searchin'! And together we'll *GIT! OUR! SQUATCH! ON!*"

"*NO!*" Jordan found himself standing in front of the television, sweating and breathing heavily. Syd and Abbie stared up at him.

"Dude, are you all right?" Abbie said.

"Maybe we should all get some shut-eye," Syd said. "Got a schedule to keep."

Jordan woke a little before dawn. He quietly slithered out of his sleeping bag so as not to wake his sister and peeked in on Syd, who was snoring away in his big bed. Then he tiptoed out onto the deck.

He stood there, barefoot, staring down at the Soil-Soles. Jordan considered carefully what he was about to do. Sure, it might be a little extreme, but desperate times called for desperate measures. This was just the kind of bold action that a truly great Creature Keeper should take, he thought. His cryptid was in danger if he ventured out, but his work was important to the safety of the world. Yes, this was bravery at its best—the kind that would be recognized, rewarded, and respected.

Jordan hoped that once the Soil-Soles were on his feet and his feet were on the ground, he'd be able to feel what Syd had felt. He'd watched carefully where and how Syd stomped on the ground at the various pressure points. *I can do this*, he told himself.

He took a deep breath and closed his eyes, then stepped up and into them.

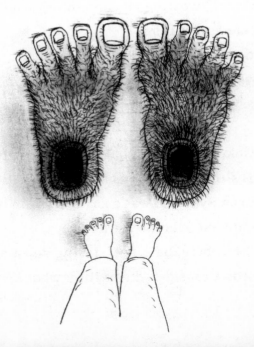

He felt a coolness surround his feet, then ooze between his toes. It felt alive, and Jordan had to fight the urge to pull his feet out. What stopped him was the strange sensation of them probing and tightening, as if the Soil-Soles were connecting to him. He looked down and wiggled his toes. The large, brown, meatball-like toes wiggled in sync. He watched as the sheath part climbed his ankles, wrapping around his calves. There was a slight pinch as it sealed tightly around his lower calf, then it was over. Jordan was wearing Syd's Soil-Soles.

He lifted his leg and felt the odd sensation of wearing something dense and unwieldy, yet at the same time light and completely in his control. It wasn't a struggle to lift his enormous new feet. They felt like they were filled with helium, as if they were responding to his effort, helping him. He stepped carefully to the center of the deck, then walked to the railing.

Jordan looked out at the twin sequoias with the scraped-off bark. He remembered how Syd had slid down feetfirst, and knew he had to try. He stepped off the deck, pushing just a bit with his anchored foot. He found that the Soil-Soles gave him more leaping strength, and he reached the tree easily. Not only that, his new feet gripped the bare, barkless trunk tightly. Jordan brought his other foot over and placed it on the other tree. The effect of his feet gripping the trees felt strange, especially as he loosened that grip. It was like a new muscle he'd never used before. Trusting his foothold, he pulled his arms away and steadily slid downward, in complete control of his speed. Reaching the bottom, Jordan gently stepped onto the ground. As soon as he did, a sensation overcame him like nothing he'd ever felt before.

The earth was alive, and Jordan was connected to it. It was a surge that came through his feet like electricity, shooting up his body, entering his mind. It wasn't just feeling vibrations and movements in the ground. It was more instinctive than that. Like a sixth sense, he could almost *see* what he was feeling, which meant he could separate all the different impulses he was receiving. He quickly understood how, with a little time and practice, he could learn to identify what each vibration was, from a lady with a limp fifteen miles away to a deer hiding in the nearby brush.

Jordan made his way to the places Syd had stopped. Each step was an incredible experience, introducing new impulses, as some signals faded and others got stronger. He would have been happy standing in one spot with his eyes closed for hours, just feeling everything, but the sun was coming up and he had a job to do.

He reached a rock outcropping where Syd had tested and planted his massive foot. He felt a slight pressure, almost like a dull pain, which made its way into his mind, like a light headache. He lifted his foot and put it in another spot on the rock. The pressure immediately returned, but in this spot it felt sharper. He actually winced when the throbbing reached his brain. A few more tests revealed the highest pressure point, and Jordan opened his eyes. "Here," he said.

He lifted his foot, took a second to concentrate, then slammed the Soil-Sole down on the stone floor. *BOOM! CRACK! RUMMMMBLE!*

He looked down. There was a thin fissure beneath his big brown Soil-Sole. He heard a faint hissing, which got louder. He stepped back. *HISSSSSSSS!* The steam seeped out of the crack he'd made. He placed his foot near the crack. There was no pressure, no dull pain. He stomped off, giggling to himself. "This is so cool. . . ."

He repeated this exercise at just a few more spots, careful not to get too excited or to overdo it. He remembered what Syd said about Mount Breakenridge being a double threat—not only the tip of one of the biggest fault lines in the world, but also the host of "Roxanne," a very dangerous sheer cliff that could fall into Harrison Lake and cause some very unpleasant consequences. Before he headed back, Jordan had to check out the massive rock.

He stood in the center of Roxanne, staring out at the lake that could be turned into a mini-tsunami with just a stomp of his foot. It was an incredibly powerful sensation, so much destruction in his control. Jordan shuddered to think what could happen if that power were in the wrong hands—or in this case, on the wrong feet.

Everything was still and peaceful as the sky above Harrison Lake began to lighten from dark blue to deep orange. Jordan was about to tear himself away from the beautiful sunrise when he spotted a falling star. As the fiery red streak cut across the sky at an angle over the lake, Jordan realized it must be a meteorite.

He couldn't see where it hit the water, but a bright green light flashed across the surface of the lake. Jordan thought he'd better check it out. Beside the ridge was a sloping descent made up mostly of boulders and other large rocks—terrain that would be far too rough and treacherous had he been wearing his sneakers. But with the Soil-Soles on his feet, Jordan felt confident jumping right in and sliding straight toward the water far below.

He leaped like a snowboarder hopping into a pipe-line, and landed on a small boulder. It immediately crumbled under the weight of his mammoth feet, and the rubble caused him to slide down the hill. He skidded faster and faster as the slope grew steeper, pulverizing the loose rocks and rolling along the debris as he struggled to stay on his feet.

Jordan carved and dredged his way down the mountainside toward a patch of thick trees waiting at the bottom. Caught in a direct collision course with some thick tree trunks, Jordan pushed off with his powerful feet. He soared over the small grove, then hit what was waiting for him on the other side.

SPLASH! Jordan hit Harrison Lake feetfirst and felt the cold chill of the water surround him as he went under. He kicked his big feet and pumped his arms in an attempt to swim toward the surface. It was no use. The Soil-Soles made his kicking more powerful, but their weight seemed to be pulling him deeper toward the bottom of the lake. He was sinking like a stone.

Jordan reached down and yanked at the dense, deadly anchors encasing his feet. He clawed at the Soil-Soles in a desperate attempt to free himself.

Thrashing around, it felt as if the tugging on his feet was growing stronger as he sank. He was losing air quickly, and getting light-headed. Was he imagining the water pulling at his shoes, or was he just sinking more rapidly? It didn't matter. If he didn't get them off, he would drown. He remembered how he'd controlled the grip of the Soil-Soles when he slid down the tree trunks, that feeling of a new set of muscles. He tried to relax those muscles. In his mind he pictured the Soil-Soles opening, releasing his feet. Suddenly, he felt the chill of the lake water filling the heavy boots. They had opened, and the water was pouring in. Jordan slipped his feet out, and kicked to reach the surface as the Soil-Soles sank beneath him, into the dark depths of Harrison Lake.

Jordan burst through the glassy surface and gulped at the cool morning air. As soon as he'd recovered, a horrible feeling overtook him. He took a deep breath and dived back down, swimming as deep as he could, trying to reach the bottom—and hoping to reach the Soil-Soles. But some force was pushing him back up. The more he fought it, the more it was like he had on an invisible flotation device. He was too buoyant, and each time he ran out of breath and gave in, floating to the surface. Exhausted after countless tries, Jordan finally had to give up. He needed to get help, and quickly. He swam back toward the shore with a heavy heart. He'd lost Syd's Soil-Soles.

It felt like hours later when Jordan reached the top of the trail. He was wet and shivering and completely wiped out from hiking as fast as he could back up to the flat plateau. Once he got to the top, he couldn't rest. He used what little energy he had left to sprint across the flat land to the grove of giant sequoias that held Syd's tree house. He had to let Syd know what he'd done as fast as possible.

He saw the hanging rope ladder, unrolled from the deck above. He stopped and looked around. Abbie, and possibly Syd, must have come down looking for him.

"Abbie!" he yelled out. "Syd!" There was no answer. He couldn't go looking for them. He needed dry clothes, and he needed to tend to his aching bare feet. They'd return soon enough. And when they did, he'd explain everything. Jordan reached out for the bottom rung of the hanging ladder and began climbing.

The ladder jerked. Jordan looked up. He could see Abbie peering over the deck rail. He could make out Syd's big furry arms, slowly turning the crank. As he was lifted, Jordan clung to the ladder. His body slumped with exhaustion. The higher he rose, the closer he got to Syd, and the worse he began to feel.

He'd done it again, he thought. Rather than figure out a way to work with the others, he recklessly went about it on his own, just as he did when his recklessness led Gusto to destroy the Fountain of Youth elixir. It seemed no matter what he did, no matter how hard he tried to be a Creature Keeper, he always found a way to mess things up.

As he reached the top, Syd lifted him through the trapdoor. The look on his face made Jordan's heart sink.

"Jordan," he said softly. "What have you done with my Soil-Soles?"

13

"Syd. I don't know what to say. I'm sorry."

Syd looked a little scared, a little confused, and very concerned. "Just tell me where they are, Jordan. Where you last saw them. So I can get back on schedule."

"In the lake," he said. "Just south of Roxanne's cliff. But listen. There was something strange. About the water—"

"I'm going out to get them," Syd said, stepping toward the trapdoor. "And you two are staying here."

Before Jordan and Abbie could react, Syd dropped through the trapdoor, grabbing hold of the bottom rung of the rolled-up rope ladder. *WHIZZZZZZ!* He flew down, the ladder slowing his landing a bit, but still slamming him hard on the forest floor. The impact also pulled the upper end of the ladder right off the wheel. It sailed down after him, landing in a pile on the forest floor hundreds of feet below. Jordan and Abbie were stranded in the tree house.

They watched helplessly as Syd ran off across the forest floor, toward the cliff overlooking Harrison Lake. Jordan also noticed something about Syd's tiny feet.

"Was he . . . wearing my sneakers?"

"Jordan, do you know how dangerous that was? What were you thinking?"

Jordan stormed into the den. Abbie followed him inside and watched as he grabbed his backpack and began cramming his things into it. "I screwed up again," Jordan said.

"So you're leaving? We're Creature Keepers! We can't leave our creature!"

"*We* aren't doing anything. I'm leaving; you're staying. I watched you with him. You're good at this. I'll just mess things up. The sooner I'm out of here, the better."

"This is crazy. Where will you even go?"

"I have to find Eldon. He's the one we need to fix everything."

"So you're off to Brazil. With no shoes. Great plan."

Jordan looked down, then back up at his sister. "What size foot are you?"

"Forget it."

WUMP! BUMP-BUMP!

A clamor on the roof grabbed their attention. They ran out onto the deck and looked up. A lanky, gray, slightly furry winged creature was fluttering overhead. In his arms he held a portly old woman wearing a motorcycle helmet.

"Doris!" Jordan exclaimed.

"Kriss?" Abbie blushed.

"Your landings are terrible!" the old woman yelled at the winged cryptid. "Three thousand miles, easy as pie, then you nearly kill us trying to land on a roof? Set me down! Gently, now."

Kriss dropped her the few feet onto the deck. *WUMP!* Doris landed on her plump fanny, but wasn't amused. She glared up at the Mothman. "You did that on purpose. Don't make me write you up, 'cause I will." She pulled off her helmet. Her hair was sticking out in all different directions.

Jordan and Abbie rushed to help her up as Kriss fluttered awkwardly.

"Doris? What are you doing here?" Jordan said.

The old woman beamed, her cheeks red and windswept. "Boy, am I glad to see you two! Official CKCC business. Kriss carried me all the way across the country without stopping to rest—never gone so fast in all my life!"

FLUTTER-FLUTTER-WUMP! Abbie turned. The West Virginia Mothman was flopped facedown on the deck behind her, exhausted. "Hi, Kriss," she said. The cryptid raised a hand and made a soft squeaking noise.

SQUEAK

"Bernard wanted me to come check on how our two 'interns' are holding up with Hap and Syd!" She winked at them. "Where is the hippie and the hairball? Get 'em out here!"

"It's really good to see you again," Jordan said quietly. "But I'm afraid we've got a bit of an emergency going on up here."

Although they'd met the past spring and known each other for only a short time, Doris and Jordan had a strong connection and were very close. And as difficult as it was for Jordan to have to relive all the disastrous details, he filled her in on everything—from Hap hearing rumors of Gusto and making them replacement Creature Keepers, to losing the Soil-Soles, to Syd going AWOL.

When Jordan had finished, the old woman nodded her head and put a hand on Jordan's shoulder. "All right, dearie," she said softly. If Doris was angry or disappointed, she didn't let it show. She turned to Kriss. "Change of plans. This is our new priority." The Mothman nodded.

"A runaway cryptid is serious business," Doris said to Jordan and Abbie. "HR-four-seven-dash-three situation. And if Gusto's out there, oh, that could be bad. *So bad.*"

"Plus the missing Soil-Soles," Abbie said. "Don't forget that."

"Thanks a lot," Jordan said sharply. "For the reminder."

"Actually, that could work to our slight advantage," Doris said. "Syd without Soil-Soles won't get very far. He doesn't do too well on those little tootsies of his."

"He has my sneakers on," Jordan said morosely.

"And I'm sure they're very nice tennis shoes, dearie. But he's gonna want his special footwear back. Now where do we think he's gone looking for them?"

"To the lake," Abbie said. "We saw him head toward Harrison Lake."

Doris turned to Kriss. "Take Abbie with you. She'll show you the direction—and she can interface with any locals you come across and may need to question."

Kriss nodded. Before Abbie knew what was happening, the Mothman had her by the waist, and was leaping off the side of the deck, swooping through the trees over the forest floor below.

"*Woooooo!*" Jordan heard her excited screams echo off the side of Mount Breakenridge. He sat and put his head in his hands. Doris approached him.

"We all make mistakes, dearie," she said softly.

"Not like mine," Jordan said.

"You *have* pulled some stinkers, I'll grant you that. But the only truly unforgiveable act is to walk away from a mistake rather than work to make it right."

"What can I do?" Jordan said. "I'm no good at anything except messing up."

"Is that so? Oh, I'm sorry, I must have you mixed up with another Jordan Grimsley—the Jordan Grimsley who designed, planned, and equipped the wonderful new secret underground command center I work at back in Florida!"

"You got the stuff I sent," Jordan said.

"Wait 'til you see it! We're becoming a real state-of-the-art, twenty-first-century Creature Keeping operation, all thanks to you and your *techspertise*."

"My what?"

"Techspertise. I mashed up 'tech' with 'expertise.' I'm trying to get it to catch on, make it a thing with your generation. Techspertise. Cool, right?"

"Uh, yeah. Real cool." He smiled at his old friend. She always made him feel better.

Doris leaned in closer. "And you know what my favorite thing is about all the new stuff? Eldon doesn't understand how to use any of it!" She cackled loudly and slapped Jordan hard on the back. He couldn't help but laugh, too.

"Okay," she said. "Let's quit sulking and put some of that *techspertise* of yours to work. Does Syd still have that old telly I got him for his birthday years ago?"

"*You* gave him that ancient crate of tubes and wires?"

"Hey, it was top of the line the year I bought it for him. Think you can rejigger it into something more useful? We need to contact CKCC, and I haven't gotten the device you gave me to work since Kriss and I flew over the Rockies."

"It's a cell phone, Doris. Let me see it." She reached into her fanny pack and handed him her smartphone. Jordan inspected it, and gave her a look.

"I told you, it needs to be charged once in a while. But I'm not sure there's any reception way up here, anyway. Syd told us Hap set the TV up to a receiver dish to catch the live feed of Buck Wilde's show. I should be able to reverse that to transmit. I'll connect your cell phone so it charges, and I can probably use its GPS history to pinpoint the coordinates of the CKCC. With a little luck and clear weather, we might be able to reach them."

"I didn't understand a word you just said. But it's good to have you back."

Abbie felt the wind in her hair as they swooped low over the treetops, out over the lake, just inches from the surface. Held tightly in Kriss's arms, she could see their reflection in the clear, still water, and couldn't help but smile.

Her view was replaced by rocks and sand as Kriss flew south along the shoreline. Abbie spotted something fly by, and tugged on his fur and pointed. "There!"

The Mothman banked sharply, circling back, landing on a muddy part of the lakeshore. She crouched. They both stared at a pair of enormous footprints in the mud. Bigfoot prints. *Soil-Sole prints.*

"He must've found them!" Abbie grinned, then suddenly looked puzzled, looking off down the lake in the direction of the tracks. "But why would Syd head south, rather than north, back toward home?"

Kriss fluttered, and lifted Abbie into the air again. They followed the prints along the rocky beach, until they came dangerously close to Echo Island and the Sasquatch Provincial Park just around the bend. Kriss flew them up to a tree, where they perched and looked down at the prints heading into the thick forest, directly toward the park.

Abbie shook her head. "Syd would never go in there. He knows it's swarming with Sasquatch fanatics. He'd be mobbed, and maybe even meet up with Buck Wilde—" She stopped and shared a look with Kriss.

"Oh, no," she said. "Syd would *totally* go in there."

Jordan had taken Syd's television apart out on the deck and done his best to reassemble it into a crude but operational receiver and transmission console. He stepped back and proudly admired his work. It felt nice to be useful again.

"Great job," Doris said. "Now, how do I use it?" Her cell phone was charged and wired to the TV, so Jordan had her pull up the coordinates to Creature Keeper central command as he fiddled with the small satellite dish Hap had installed on the roof. They stared at the fuzzy white screen and listened to the static. And waited.

"Once we establish a connection," Doris said, "I can ask Ed to pinpoint Syd's whereabouts using your Global Cryptid Positioning System collar thingy."

Jordan couldn't believe he hadn't thought of that. "Doris, you're a genius."

"Me? It's all your *techspertise*, dearie."

Jordan smiled. The static on the TV screen suddenly sputtered, intermittently showing a man's looming face. His voice was choppy, interrupted by white noise.

"Ed!" Doris yelled into her cell phone. "Ed, come in, for Pete's sake!"

"This isn't Pete," a voice crackled. "It's Ed. Who in the heckfire is Pete?"

On the screen, the static gave way to an elderly man's looming bald head. "Hello? Who's there? Hello?" Ed seemed confused.

"Ed! It's me, Denmother Doris! Can you hear me?

Step away from the camera on your computer! You're sitting too close to the screen again, Ed! We talked about this!"

Ed sat back, and Jordan got a good look at him: late eighties, short-sleeved dress shirt, tie, a nametag that said *Ed*, and a coffee mug that read, *#1 BOSS*. He grinned into the camera. "Doris! Is that you?"

"Yes, Ed, it's me. How are things back at the CKCC? Everything okay?"

"Just the way you left it, Doris," Ed said. "Everything A-OK, under control!"

"Well, that's about to change. I'm afraid we have an HR-four-seven-dash-three situation on our hands." They watched as Ed set down his coffee mug, pulled out a manual, and started flipping through it. Doris interrupted him. "It means we have a cryptid on the loose, Ed. Is that my coffee mug, by the way?"

Ed looked up guiltily. He held it up. "Oh, uh, is this one yours?"

"Yes. It is. Listen carefully now. Go to the Global Cryptid Positioning System monitor and type in Syd's passcode. It should locate Syd's homing device and give us his exact whereabouts. Ask Gene to help you, if you're not sure. Got it?"

"Easy-peasy, Denmother. We're on it!" Ed then stepped out of frame. *"GENE!"*

As they waited, with Ed out of the way, Jordan got a glimpse of the layout of the new CKCC secret base beneath Eternal Acres. He could see the terminals and workstations, with elderly people in ill-fitting Badger Ranger suits hustling about and working away. Suddenly, an enormous white rabbit with antlers hopped into view, wearing a tiny hardhat. "Hey, there's Peggy!" Jordan said, smiling at the sight of the Texas Jackalope he'd befriended last spring. "She looks good. Is she helping?"

"She's our top tunnel digger," Doris said. "Antlers make a nice forklift, too." Doris checked her watch. "Probably on her lunch break right now." Peggy scratched her nose, stared off into space, then hopped out of view.

Suddenly Ed was looming in the camera again. "I got it!" he yelled excitedly.

"Great, Ed, but again, take a step back from the camera, please. We can see what you had for breakfast on your dentures."

"Sorry." Ed stepped back and read from a small bit of paper. "Okay. The GCPS system traced Syd to these exact coordinates—forty-nine degrees, forty-three minutes, twelve seconds north latitude, one hundred twenty-one degrees, fifty-six minutes, two seconds west longitude!"

"What does that mean? That doesn't help us, Ed. I need an address. An area."

"Hold on, Doris," Jordan said. "Let me see your phone." Jordan punched the coordinates into a mapping function on the device. A map of North America came up. It zoomed in on the Pacific Northwest, then Canada, then British Columbia, then Mount Breakenridge, and then . . . Jordan looked up. "Wait. This can't be right."

"What? Where is he? Is he close?" Doris said.

"Yeah," Jordan said. He got up and walked toward Syd's bedroom. A moment later he came out with something in his hands. "Tell Ed and Gene they nailed it. We located Syd's tracking device. The system worked perfectly." He held up what was in his hands. Teddy Squatch was wearing a decorative collar around his furry little neck—Syd's GCPS wristband.

Doris looked at him, then turned to the transmitter. "Thanks, guys. Looks like we've hit a dead end. But keep this channel open. Let us know if you hear anything. We'll be in touch soon. Over." She turned to Jordan, who was staring out over the railing, toward Harrison Lake.

"It was my responsibility to make sure Syd had his wristband on. Looks like I blew that, too." He turned to face her. "We need Eldon. He'd know what to do. He'd have gone out spooring for Syd, and already have him back by now."

"We'll get Eldon back in no time. That postcard information you gave Bernard will help Kriss track him down, once he gets to the Amazon."

"Kriss is supposed to be looking for Eldon? You never told me that!"

"He was giving me a lift, dearie, then flying on to South America."

"Great. So it's my fault he's being kept from doing that, because he's here fixing my mistakes. What if Eldon's in trouble?"

"Don't you worry about Eldon. Bernard tends to overreact when it comes to his Keeper. I'm sure Eldon's fine. He's probably out researching jungle spoor samples or something, trying to get himself another Badger Badge." Jordan could tell that Doris was just trying to make him feel better. It wasn't working.

FLUTTER-FLUTTER-FLAP-WUMP! Kriss and Abbie made a less-than-graceful landing on the deck, nearly tumbling into the TV-turned-transmitter.

"Well?" Doris said.

"Good news, bad news," Abbie said breathlessly. "Which do you want first?"

Once again Doris calmly took in all the information, then once again she began giving everyone assignments. "Okay. First thing is we need to get down to that park right away and make sure Syd's not in any danger, or doing anything stupid."

"I spotted our two goose boats when we were flying back," Abbie said. "They're both still stashed by the giant toe boulders down at the shoreline. Each seats two."

"We'll only need to take one, then," Doris said. "For

you and me. Jordan, I want you to stay here in case Syd turns up or Ed calls in with any information."

Jordan turned and stormed into the tree house.

Once Jordan was out of earshot, Doris turned to Kriss. "It's time for you to fly down to the Amazon. We need Eldon."

The Mothman nodded. He glanced at Abbie, then stepped toward the railing.

"Wait." Jordan stood in the doorway. He had his backpack on his back, Syd's fuzzy bunny slippers on his feet, and a determined look on his face. "I'm going with Kriss. I'm going to help find Eldon."

"What in heaven's name are you talking about?" Doris said. "And what are those things on your feet?"

"I know why you want me to stay—so I don't mess anything else up. I don't trust myself to help with Syd, either. But I can't sit around here. What we need more than anything right now is Eldon's help. So I'm going to find him."

"Jordan," Abbie said. "You can't just run off and save the day."

"Look. Eldon sent that postcard to me. Maybe it's me he wants to come find him. Besides, there'll be people there. Human people. It's not like Kriss can just flutter down and chat it up with the locals. You need someone to—how did you put it?—'interface with any

125

locals you come across.'"

Doris stepped toward Jordan. "Now you listen here. I wasn't keeping you here because I thought you'd mess up. I have confidence in you. In fact, I couldn't be more confident that you'll find Eldon and get him back safely."

She tossed him her motorcycle helmet. Jordan grinned and took a step toward Kriss. Abbie approached them. "Well, if you're going, I suppose you'll need a kiss. For luck."

This was a first for Jordan, but he figured he needed to be brave. As his sister puckered up and leaned in, Jordan shut his eyes. Nothing happened. He opened his eyes and saw Abbie smooch Kriss on the cheek. As the cryptid blushed, she pulled back and looked at Jordan.

"What?"

"Uh, nothin'," he said. He quickly put on his helmet. Abbie picked something up and stuffed it in his backpack. "There. A good-luck charm for you, too. Don't mess this up."

Jordan tightened Doris's helmet. "Good advice. Thanks."

Kriss suddenly grabbed Jordan by the waist and leaped off the edge of the tree house deck. They dived straight down and swooped across the forest floor.

Jordan grabbed one end of the rope ladder lying bundled on the ground. Kriss fluttered awkwardly back up to the deck, and Jordan tossed the end of the ladder over the railing. He smiled at Doris and Abbie, then he and Kriss went soaring off across Mount Breakenridge.

Kriss carried Jordan far out over the Pacific Ocean before turning south. Flying low, close to the rolling waves, Jordan noticed the way Kriss used the strong winds that blew across the sea. The Mothman had an erratic, almost embarrassing way of fluttering about crazily when he had to fly slowly, or hover, or land. But when he wanted to go fast, he could zip through the air at alarming speeds. As his passenger, Jordan could feel Kriss picking up the air patterns around him, and with those same erratic movements that looked so awkward when he was fluttering, quickly adjust and lock in to the invisible currents all around him as they glided southward.

The only sound Jordan could hear was the wind whooshing by, and the occasional flapping of Kriss's wings in the strong winds. There was a powerful odor of salt air and sea, with just a touch of Mothman's natural smell, which reminded Jordan of his great aunt Diane's musty old winter coat.

Once they passed the equator and entered the South Pacific, Jordan began to feel the air currents getting warmer. Kriss banked eastward, and Jordan spotted the coast of South America in the distance. Kriss climbed as they approached land to avoid being detected, and soon they were peering down through the clouds over the jungle mountains of Colombia.

They spotted the Amazon River next, and followed it from above as it curled into Brazil, twisting and turning, cutting through the bright green jungle like a dark anaconda. Finally, where the Amazon slithered through the dense jungle, there was one last outpost of civilization: the last place Eldon had been heard from, the floating village of Palafito. Kriss dived, heading straight for it.

The tiny village of Palafito was much like Eldon's postcard described—it wasn't just located on the banks of the Amazon River, it was actually floating in it. Anchored to the thick jungle shore, the cluster of ramps, docks, and small buildings bobbed gently on the murky green water.

In the center of the rickety riverside outpost sat El Encantado—a small cantina with a patio that hung out over the water, and an inside bar and café. It was one of the few structures along the bank that also accessed the land it was tied to. A series of short paths ran from the land side of the cantina about a hundred feet toward the tree line, to a few cabana-style huts.

The sun was beginning to set as Jordan sat beside Kriss atop a tall Brazil-nut tree, looking down at the little cantina with its cabanas.

"I'll go down and have a look before it gets too dark," Jordan said. Kriss whispered quietly, indicating the deeper part of the rainforest. Jordan got that he was going to go look for Eldon in the jungle.

"Okay," Jordan said. "It looks like they have rooms to rent at El Encantado. See what you can find in the jungle, and I'll ask around here if anyone has seen or heard from Eldon. We'll meet under this tree around nightfall tomorrow, okay?"

Kriss nodded, dived from the top of his perch, and swooped off around the riverbed, leaving Jordan sitting alone, high in the tree. He watched the Mothman disappear into the jungle, then looked down. "Would it have killed you to give me a lift outta this tree?" he grumbled as he began climbing down.

Jordan made his way along the riverside dock that

served as the main street of Palafito. Barefoot locals ducked into small residential shacks, and a few fishermen sat with their poles dangling over the slow-moving waters of the Amazon. There were boats tied along this rickety lane offering river cruises or fishing expeditions. There was also a small warehouse of some kind, where, inside, Jordan could see a number of Brazilian workers packing into boxes what looked to be toys or clothing.

Jordan stood before El Encantado and pulled out his postcard. It was the same place, but in real life it was a bit shabbier and more worn looking.

Jordan walked through the river patio section into an open-air juice bar area and immediately noticed a unique theme: there was dolphin or porpoise art everywhere—murals painted on the walls, sculptures hanging from the ceiling, wood carvings on the tables and bar. And nearly all of them were pink. A few guests and locals sipped brightly colored fruit smoothies at the tables, while off to the side someone operated a loud blender behind the bar.

"Greetings, my friend, and welcome to El Encantado!" a robust voice called out over the grinding noise of the blender. "You are new here, are you not?"

Jordan looked over and saw the brightest smile he'd ever seen. The man behind the bar was very handsome, with a bronze complexion and bushy black moustache.

He was dressed in a white suit and a matching fedora hat with a pink trim ribbon around it. His eyes twinkled almost as brightly as his teeth gleamed.

He poured a bright orange concoction from his blender into a glass and offered it to Jordan. "Be my guest! First-timers to El Encantado get a free smoothie, on the house!"

Jordan sat down and took a sip of the smoothie. "Wow," he said. "That's good."

"HAHAHAHA—*squonk!*" The handsome man's laugh ended with a strange noise. He covered his mouth and then smiled at Jordan again.

"Allow me to introduce myself. I am Manuel Boto. At your service."

"Pleased to meet you. I'm—"

"NO!" Manuel stopped him. Jordan glanced around. The other patrons were all staring at them. Manuel leaned in and spoke low and serious. "Here at El Encantado, we have a strict *no-names policy.*"

"But—you just told me yours. Mr. Boto, right?"

The bartender broke into a grin again. "Please! Call me Manuel!"

"Okay, Manuel. And you can call me Jor—"

"*SILENCIO!*" This time Manuel slammed a large hunting knife into the bar, skewering a chunk of guava. "Again. I must insist. No names, if you please."

"Uh, okay," Jordan said. He opened his backpack and pulled out a photograph. "I'm hoping you can help me. I'm looking for a friend of mine. He was here a few weeks ago."

Manuel took the picture from Jordan and studied it. "Yes. I have seen this person."

"You have? That's great! When did you see him? Where did he go?"

Manuel's grin disappeared. "I'm afraid that I cannot tell you."

"Why not?"

"This is a remote place. It is hard to find, and even harder to get to. Many come here to never get found. Drifters, outlaws, retired librarians. This is why we have a strict house rule respecting the privacy of all our guests—no names are used in this place."

"Please," Jordan said. "I'm very tired. And my friend isn't any of those things. He was just passing through, and now I need to find him. He sent me a postcard from your wonderful cantina here. He said it was the finest he'd ever seen."

Manuel smiled at this. He caressed his bushy moustache. "And did he, by any chance, mention anything else?"

Jordan studied this strange man for a moment. "Uh, yeah. He *loved* the porpoises you've got here. They're his favorites."

"Dolphins. The rare, pink Amazon river dolphin. Not porpoises. Porpoises are the swine of the sea. Are we clear on this, senhor?"

"Of course, of course! Dolphins. That's what he said. Not porpoises, no. Ew. It was the rare, pink Amazon river dolphin he spoke so highly of. Forgive me."

"You are forgiven. And your friend, did he mention . . . anything else?" Manuel was now adjusting his hat and raising his chin to catch the light just so.

"Oh, uh . . . he definitely commented on how, uh, *handsome* the bartender was."

"Ah! Yes, I remember him now. He was quite . . . observant." Manuel leaned in and spoke in a hushed tone. "Your friend came here after a long journey. He was in very bad shape. He needed rest—and many smoothies—to feel better. He stayed as my guest for a few nights, then once he was stronger he asked me if there was someone who could take him upriver, into the deep jungle."

"Please," Jordan said. "Do you know who might've taken him?"

"I certainly do, senhor." Manuel smiled. "The most dashingly handsome—"

"Okay. It was you."

"—charming, suave—"

"Manuel, I get it. You're referring to yourself."

"—dazzlingly attractive—"

"*MANUEL!*" The bartender shot a surprised look at Jordan.

"It was you, Manuel. I get it. You're describing yourself."

"That is correct! Such a smart boy!" Manuel poured Jordan a fresh smoothie. "Here, another icy fruit beverage for the smart boy! On the house!"

"Thank you, but what I want is for you to take me to the exact spot where you dropped off my friend Eldon. Right now. Please."

"Of course, of course! But I cannot take you now—it is too dark. The river is dangerous at night. We will go in the morning. You will stay the night, as my guest."

Jordan turned and looked out over the patio. The sky above the jungle had grown a deep shade of dark orange. The sun had set, and night was falling fast.

"All right," Jordan said. "That would be great, Manuel. Thank you."

"Please, senhor. It is my pleasure. And again . . . welcome to El Encantado."

16

Jordan was given a small towel and bar of soap and made his way out the back of the cantina onto the river bank, through a narrow path that led into the jungle. Just behind the tree line was his cabana—a very small but very cozy little hut with a sink, toilet, and single cot. There were no windows or doors, and the thatched roof was worn thin in spots, allowing Jordan to stare up at the stars through the jungle canopy.

He thought about how these were the same stars Abbie might be looking up at from Syd's tree house deck, and he hoped she was with Syd. If any-thing happened to her or Doris or Syd because of his carelessness, he'd never forgive himself.

The sounds of the jungle at night were different from anything he'd ever heard. Lying there in the dark hut, Jordan couldn't begin to imagine what the crea-tures making all those chirps and squawks and clicks and squeaks might look like. In this place, he thought, a cryptid might actually walk around unnoticed. The exotic symphony soon had his eyes growing heavy, and he drifted off to sleep.

SMASH! Jordan woke to the sound of shattering glass. He didn't know the time or how long he'd been out, but it was still pitch-dark in his cabana.

CRASH! Another burst of noise told Jordan that whatever was happening, it was happening in the can-tina. He heard muffled voices, but couldn't make out what they were saying. Jordan slid off his cot and out of his cabana and tiptoed down the path to the open back window of the cantina.

Inside, on the same barstool where Jordan had been sitting earlier, sat a tall figure in a dark hooded robe. The figure was facing Manuel, who was behind the bar as before. But Manuel didn't look his usual cheerful, confident self. He looked scared.

"You are acting crazy," he said nervously. "What I gave you was—"

"What you gave me was no good, Boto. And I don't like to be cheated." The hooded figure spoke in a deep, croaky whisper. Jordan couldn't see any features other than the back of its head, which was covered in the dark, tarp-like hood.

"I would never cheat you," Manuel protested. "We had a deal, and I delivered my part of the bargain. . . ."

"THE DEAL IS DEAD!" The hooded stranger shot back. "What you gave me wore off, as you can see. Now, I'm going to ask you again—will you give me more, or am I going to have to squeeze your eyeballs until I get what I want?"

"Listen to me! I told you when I gave it to you! Once taken, the transformation can be made at will, but if the subject is exposed to his natural element, he will permanently return to his natural state! Now, as I heard it, you had a recent conflict in which you—uh, how shall I say this—*got into a little hot water. . . .*"

In a flash, the hooded figure reached out and grabbed Manuel by the throat, knocking off his fedora. "Whatever you heard isn't relevant to this conversation, BOTO."

"Please." Manuel panicked. "My hat! Give me my hat, I beg you! I'll give you anything you want! Just cover my head, quickly!"

Jordan strained to see where the hat landed, and what was so special about it. Here this odd, violent figure had him by the throat, but all Manuel cared about was his hat? Jordan couldn't believe it when Manuel started to sob—over his hat.

"Please, senhor, show mercy and return my hat, before someone sees!"

The figure reached under the bar and picked up Manuel's fedora. He pulled the sobbing man's face even closer.

"Thank you, oh, thank you." Manuel was still crying but had calmed down at the sight of his beloved hat.

The figure set the hat just out of Manuel's reach, and pulled something out of his robes. He placed it against Manuel's cheek.

Jordan couldn't make out what it was, but a chill shot down his spine as he noticed the figure's hand. It was brown and scabby, with long, gnarled fingers and nails, like a claw. Jordan caught his breath as he watched the figure's talon-like hand push whatever he had against Manuel's trembling cheek. A knife?

"Now, that wasn't so hard, was it?" The raspy voice whispered from inside the hood. Jordan's eyes went wide at what happened next—the figure's long, nasty tongue extended from the dark void of the hood and licked Manuel's cheek. He then slipped whatever he'd pressed against his cheek into his robe pocket, picked up the fedora, and dropped the hat on Manuel's head, releasing his neck.

Jordan had to put his hand over his mouth to muffle a small squeal from the shock at what he'd just seen. Manuel looked up at the window, and the hooded figure spun around. Jordan ducked down just in time. He crouched in the jungle bushes outside the window, trying to be as still and as quiet as he could, hoping they hadn't seen him.

When he heard their voices resume, he decided it was safe to peek in again.

"Try to relax," Manuel said calmly. "Soon you will feel like a new man." The hooded figure was breathing heavily, but had calmed considerably. "And of course I am happy to give you what I have, as a symbol of my allegiance to you. And, I trust, to reestablish our bargain." Manuel wrote something on a napkin as he spoke.

"I will consider it," the hooded figure said. His voice sounded suddenly clearer and less strained.

"Well then, please, accept also this token to show my loyalty." He slid the napkin over to the hooded stranger. "I think you may find it informative."

"*WHAT?*" As soon as the hooded figure read the napkin, he leaped to his feet. "Why didn't you tell me this sooner? Where is he?" He knocked over his stool and spun around. Jordan ducked down again as he heard the crashing of chairs and the smashing of glass. "Never mind! I will find him myself!"

Jordan crouched in the dark bushes as the figure rushed out of the back doorway of the cantina and ran past him down the narrow path into the jungle. Manuel tore out, chasing behind him.

Jordan looked back at the two of them disappearing into the dark jungle, then quickly climbed into the cantina. He rummaged through the broken glass and furniture on the floor until he found what he was looking for. There, under the bar, was the napkin. He picked it up and read it. Written on it was a simple message:

G. WAS HERE.

The hooded stranger's raspy screech echoed through the jungle, and Jordan heard more smashing and crashing—this time from the cabanas.

He quickly pocketed the napkin, jumped out the window, and ran along the riverside, back to the Brazil-nut tree, where he hid between its wide roots. He decided it was safer sleeping among whatever was making all those chirps and squawks in the jungle than facing whoever was making all that noise back at El Encantado.

17

In the morning light, Jordan's cabana looked as if a meteorite had crashed into it. The thatched roof was torn off, the cot ripped to shreds, and some contents of his backpack were strewn all over the dirt floor of the tiny hut. He immediately began rummaging through his things, and a panicked realization quickly set in— his grandfather's journal was missing.

"HAHAHA—*squonk!*" A familiar laugh echoed behind him, from the cantina.

OH
NO.

Jordan stood up, and before he realized it, he found himself running through the path, bursting into the cantina, and confronting Manuel in a very loud voice.

"Where is he?" Jordan yelled. "Where's the psycho who trashed my room and stole my stuff?"

Manuel glanced nervously around at the few customers in his juice bar, then tried his best to calm Jordan down. "Senhor, please. I assure you, I have no idea what you're talking about. . . ."

"You're lying! I heard you two! You told him I was here! You slipped him this note!" Jordan pulled out the napkin and held it in Manuel's face. "See? 'G. WAS HERE'! Now who is he?"

A flash of worry crossed Manuel's face. Then his expression warmed into a sly smile. "I told you," he said. "El Encantado house rule—no names, no questions asked. You are a smart boy. Think, senhor. How could I tell anyone you were here if I do not know your name?"

Jordan thought about this for a second. Then he thought of something else. He jumped up and grabbed Manuel's fedora off his head.

"WHAT ARE YOU DOING? GIVE THAT BACK!" Manuel covered the top of his head with his hands, and glanced around at the other people in the room. "Give it to me this instant! Please! I beg of you!"

Jordan jumped up onto the bar and walked over to the blender. He turned it on and held the fancy hat over the spinning blades. "Not 'til you give me some answers! If the G on that napkin isn't me, then who is it? Who did you mean?"

As Manuel reached to grab a bar rag to throw over the patch of scalp atop his head, Jordan caught a quick glimpse of something strange. The pink bald spot wasn't just skin—there seemed to be some sort of hole there. Jordan wasn't quite sure what he saw, and before he could look closer, Manuel had covered it up.

"Please!" Manuel yelled. He held out a trembling hand. "I cannot give you the name of the stranger, because of El Encantado policy."

"It's your policy or your hat!" Jordan pushed it toward the blades. "CHOOSE!"

"*WAIT!*" Manuel suddenly whispered. "All right, I will tell you only this." Jordan could tell he was thinking quickly, trying to figure out a lie. "The initial on the napkin, senhor—it was not for you—it was for . . . *Gusto*. The G was for Gusto."

"Gusto?" Jordan tossed Manuel his hat and jumped down off the bar. "Areck Gusto was here? Where is he now? Tell me!"

The other customers immediately filed out of the cantina as Manuel frantically pulled his fedora over his head. He suddenly seemed very frightened. Jordan approached him.

"Manuel. You have to bring me to him. Where is Gusto?"

"It is complicated, senhor," he whispered again. "And very dangerous. He is—"

CRASH! Tables and chairs outside on the patio suddenly toppled and flew against the cantina as a strong gust of wind blasted off the river. A loud whirring sound accompanied the chaos. Jordan fought his way out onto the patio.

Outside, a white flying machine hovered over the river. It was a futuristic aircraft, with the rotors of a helicopter but also armed with massive jet thrusters on the side. The rotors spun, but were nearly silent. Over the quiet whirring, a horrible voice called out.

"Looking for someone, Grimsley?" Jordan stared up at the aircraft. A side cargo door slid open. Gusto stepped out onto the running board. He was covered head to toe in the sparkling Hydro-Hide bodysuit, formed from the scales of the Loch Ness Monster, made from properties that could control water. His left hand gripped a side rail, and Jordan spotted something on his finger, catching the sunlight. It was his grandfather's clear, crystal ring. The one Eldon had given him, and he'd lost.

"Well, here I am, once again, working right under the noses of the noble, vigilant Creature Keepers! Tell me something, Georgie boy—did you miss me?"

"I'M NOT MY GRANDFATHER!" Jordan yelled back at him. He blocked his eyes from the debris blowing around in the air as the Heli-Jet maneuvered closer to the dock. Gusto stood over a number of workers from the warehouse next to El Encantado. They ran pallets filled with boxes marked *MADE IN BRAZIL* out to the dock, loading them into the sliding door of the Heli-Jet.

"It seems that none of us are who we appear to be," Gusto yelled back. "Isn't that right, Manuel?" Jordan looked beside him. Manuel came stumbling out onto the patio, holding his fedora on his head with both hands.

"I didn't tell him a thing, Gusto, I swear!" Manuel yelled back. "No names! This is the policy of El Encantado! No names, no questions asked!"

Gusto laughed at the cowering bartender as some of the Brazilian workers scurried to get the last of the boxes onto the stealth chopper. "That's good enough!" Gusto yelled to them, sliding the door shut as they scurried on board behind him, leaving a pallet of boxes on the dock. Gusto continued to stand on the outside running board as the Heli-Jet began to rise.

Jordan couldn't let Gusto get away—especially not with his grandfather's ring. He climbed up onto the patio railing and readied himself to leap toward the rising aircraft.

Unfortunately, Gusto leaped first.

"*Cannonball!*" Gusto backflipped off the rising chopper and plunged into the Amazon River. The murky water grew oddly still, sinking in the spot where he disappeared like a funnel, pulling in the water around it like a sinkhole.

"TAKE COVER!" Jordan leaped onto the patio as the river exploded.

FLOOOOSH! The Amazon blasted into the air, upending the dock, sending the pallet of boxes flying into the trees, and demolishing many of the buildings in its wake, including the patio of El Encantado. Jordan

and Manuel fell into the suddenly churning water,
along with tons of wood and debris.

Jordan came up for air and grabbed hold of a piece
of dock floating in the violently roiling waters. He saw
the powerful rotors on the Heli-Jet lift it over the chaos,
away from the river. Once it cleared the tree line, the
enormous thruster jets blasted thick orange flames.
KRRRGGGGSSSHHHH! It zoomed off, disappearing
in a fiery explosion of rocket trail.

The Amazon River continued to thrash and churn,
pulling Jordan under. He bobbed up again and made
his way through the debris, trying to reach the shore.
Something grabbed his foot. He looked down and saw
Gusto swirling around him in his Hydro-Hide, trying

to pull him down. Jordan took a deep breath and let himself be taken under.

As soon as he saw Gusto swirl past, Jordan readied himself. He reached out and grabbed Gusto by the neck. Gusto thrashed like a giant fish, diving and bucking trying to get Jordan off. He reached back and tried to hit Jordan, but Jordan grabbed his arm and bent it behind him. Gusto reacted violently, twisting and surging out of the water, flinging Jordan toward the shore. *WUMP!* Jordan fell hard onto the shore, slamming into the muddy debris that was scattered everywhere.

SPLASH! Gusto landed back in the water, peeked at Jordan lying on the shore, then shot like a bullet away from the scene with incredible speed, forcing a wall of water in his wake, which rose up and toppled straight toward Jordan.

Jordan opened his eyes just in time to see the wave full of sharp shards of broken wood and glass about to crash over his head. He closed his eyes—

WHOOSH! Jordan felt something grab him. His stomach dropped, and he opened his eyes. A familiar gray, furry arm was wrapped securely around him. Jordan looked up at Kriss, then down at the rollicking Amazon and the horrible destruction Gusto had left in his awful wake. He spotted Manuel's fedora bobbing amid the debris and farther out, a flash of pink.

He heard a loud *SQUONK!* Jordan couldn't believe his eyes, but he spotted one of Boto's rare pink dolphins diving beneath the Amazon River. Jordan felt something in his hand. He looked down and carefully opened his palm. He was holding Grampa Grimsley's clear, crystal ring.

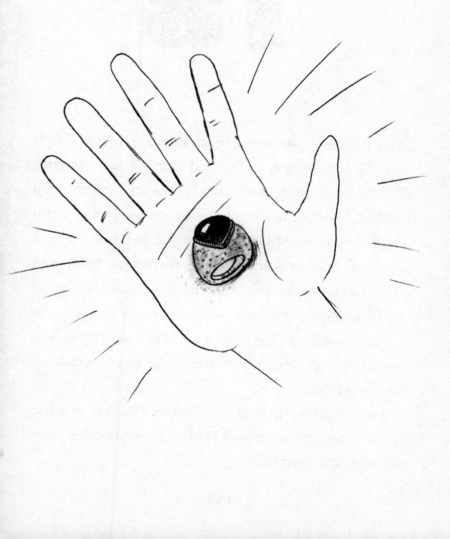

18

After carefully securing the rope ladder to Syd's deck and climbing down, Abbie and Doris hiked the trail descending Mount Breakenridge to the water, then paddled together in one of the two goose boats, south along the shoreline of Harrison Lake. They stopped along the way to search for the footprints Abbie and Kriss had found, filling in the ones that hadn't already been washed away by the water. It was clear where the tracks headed. As the afternoon wore on, Abbie and Doris paddled straight for the docks near Sasquatch Provincial Park.

Doris walked through the crowd of BuckHeads and Bigfoot-costumed Squatch freaks, showing little time or patience for either group.

"Excuse me," she asked a middle-aged man wrapped in what looked like an oversized brown shag rug. "We're searching for a friend—tall, furry, apelike, might be lurking somewhere in this wooded area."

The man stared at her. "Aren't we all, lady. But let me know if you spot him, okay?" She watched as he joined a group of fellow human-carpet hybrid pals.

"This could be harder than I thought," Doris said. "Maybe we were wrong. Maybe even Syd wouldn't expose himself to a crowd like this."

"ATTENTION, FELLOW SQUATCH-WATCHERS!" A loud announcement echoed over the park. "BUCK WILDE'S SHOW STARTS IN FIFTEEN MINUTES! SO COME ON DOWN TO THE BUCK WILDE PAVIL- ION, AND *GIT YER SQUATCH ON!*"

"No, he's here," Abbie said.

155

"Well, let's just hope we find him before they do," Doris said.

The crowd began moving as one through the field, toward Buck's RV porch setup. Abbie and Doris kept a sharp eye out as they went with the flow, and were soon standing with the fans, packed tightly in front of the stage, gazing up at the big-screen TVs mounted on trees on either side.

Cheers exploded as Buck's huge face appeared on the screens. He was in full Squatchin' gear, complete with face paint, his signature trucker hat, and night-vision goggles. He clearly had a cameraman following closely as he trudged through the woods.

"Okay, folks," he whispered dramatically. "We're about a half mile into Squatch central here, and there's some pretty strong evidence that we're closing in on that mangy mountain mongrel. Just look at this!"

A collective gasp went up from the crowd as Buck held up a small, broken twig. Doris rolled her eyes. "This guy's such a noodlehead," she whispered.

"Maybe we should get out of here, and keep looking," Abbie whispered back.

"Shh!" A Squatch fan stood directly in front of Abbie, dressed in yet another horribly fake, black shaggy costume.

"Why do I always get stuck behind the behinds?" she said.

Up on the twin jumbo screens, Buck continued to build the suspense. "Sticks don't just break themselves, Squatch-Watchers. Not out here . . ."

"Oh brother," Doris said. "This dingbat is twice as annoying on two TVs. . . ."

"SHHH!" The hulking fake-furred fan let them have it again.

"Oh, shush yourself," Abbie shot back. "What are you supposed to be, anyway, a gorilla? You wouldn't know the Sasquatch if he walked up and introduced himself."

The fan turned around. "C'mon! Rule number two— no talking during my favorite show!"

Abbie's eyes went wide. "Syd?" She looked down. She recognized Jordan's sneakers. "It *is* you! But . . . where are your Soil-Soles? She looked around anxiously.

"You grub-brained furball," Doris said. "What are you think-ing coming here?"

Abbie noticed a few fans glancing at them. "Okay, let's move. This isn't cool."

"Are you crazy?" Syd said. "This is just getting good—look!"

On the screens, Buck was quietly pushing his way through the woods. He moved a bush out of the way and stopped suddenly. He looked back at the camera. "Are we rolling, Bob? You're getting this, right?"

He moved out of the way of the camera. On the ground was a footprint. It was huge, the same as the ones left along the lakeshore.

"You see that?" Buck whispered into the camera.

"You see that?" Syd whispered into Abbie's ear. Abbie and Doris shared a confused glance, then looked back at the screen along with everyone else.

On TV, Buck crouched down. He touched the soil inside the huge print, then tasted the mud with the tip of his tongue. "Just as I thought," he said. "Fresh tracks."

"Oh, man," Syd whispered. "This is so awesome. . . ."

Buck followed the footprints into a bunch of tall bushes. He stopped. He glanced back at the camera, suddenly with a look of fear in his eyes. Even Doris believed something real was happening. She and Abbie pushed in closer to Syd.

Sticking out of the bottom of the brush were ten large toes.

"The Soil-Soles!" Abbie gasped.

The camera panned up slowly to reveal a tall, dark figure standing inside the bushes, as if it had found a hiding spot, but forgot to hide its big feet. Buck's eyes were wide. He stepped toward the shadowy figure. He reached out his arm. . . .

In the picnic area, Abbie, Doris, and Syd stared in rapt attention, waiting with everyone else to see what would happen next.

Buck put a hand on his lasso. "Spotlight!" he suddenly ordered. A bright light blasted the bushes. The giant Soil-Soles stepped out into the light. Filling them, there in front of Buck, on television before the BuckHeads and the Squatch freaks in the park and all the people watching in their living rooms—stood Señor Areck Gusto, dressed in a black trench coat.

"Hello, Mr. Wilde," he said as if they'd casually bumped into each other in the cat-food aisle at the market. "So glad you were finally able to find me. I was beginning to wonder if I'd have to send up flares."

19

Abbie, Doris, and Syd stood along with the rest of the crowd of onlookers, confused and helpless as they watched Gusto school Buck Wilde on his own show.

RUN.

Buck looked embarrassed. And angry. And stupid. He pointed a trembling finger at Gusto. "You're not the Sasquatch! You're just some dude with his feet!"

"Very observant, Mr. Wilde," Gusto purred. "And this is precisely your problem. But do not worry—I'm here to help."

"All right, mister," Buck said in a sad attempt to save face. "I don't know who you are, but you got about ten seconds to explain what you've done with the real Sasquatch!"

"I'll take only two. I caught the Sasquatch. I destroyed the Sasquatch. And I had his feet made into these boots. Do you like them?"

The camera swung down and zoomed in on Gusto's feet. There was no doubt that these were no ordinary boots, or fake bedroom slippers. The Soil-Soles were on Gusto's feet, and they were very convincing. Buck crouched down and inspected them. He tugged on the toes, and poked at the fleshy, matted fur. He looked into the camera. His lips trembled; his eyes began to water up. He looked lost for a moment.

"Folks . . . I'm afraid the search for the Squatch . . . is over," he whispered.

A collective gasp rose from the crowd. Fans yelled out things that were not very nice, or appropriate. A few, possibly overheated in their costumes, fainted.

"Aw," Syd whispered sincerely. "Just when he was getting so close."

"What is that slimeball up to?" Doris wondered aloud.

"Indeed it is over, Mr. Wilde." Gusto helped Buck to his feet. "But every end brings new beginnings. And that is why I'm here. To offer you a proposal."

"You . . . want to marry me?" Buck said, still stunned.

"Uh, no. My card—" He flipped a business card out of his trench coat.

Buck took it and read it. "'Señor Areck Gusto. Businessman, entrepreneur, and expert . . . *cryptozoologist*?'"

"Just a fancy word that means I'm an authority on mysterious creatures. I have experience in tracking them, in hunting them, and obviously"—he gestured toward his feet—"in catching them. And where I am uniquely successful, you have been, frankly, a miserable failure. But that is all about to change."

Buck glanced at the camera. "Okay! We're gonna go to commercial—"

"Wait, Mr. Wilde. Don't you think your audience deserves to at least hear my offer on how I can help you succeed?"

Buck had lost control of his own show. He stared helplessly at Gusto.

"I didn't come onto your fine program just to tell you in front of your entire television audience that your life has been a total and complete waste. In fact, I'm here to offer you—and your devoted fans—what you've always wanted. The unfettered opportunity to hunt, capture, and *own half of all licensing and merchandising rights to* an actual living, breathing, real, live cryptid!"

"'Scuse me?"

"Your search for the Sasquatch was a Buck Wilde goose chase. In the end, I beat you to it. What I'm offering is another creature. A new creature. A creature that has the benefit of not being already caught and de-footed. I know where it lives. I know where it can be hunted. And I know where it can be captured."

"And who's going to be doing this capturing?" Buck said. "You, I suppose?"

"HAHAHA! No. I've bagged the Sasquatch, Mr. Wilde—that is enough for me. Now I'm only interested in bringing the world closer together. No, the job of Creature-Catcher can only be done—on live TV, of course—by the world-famous Mr. Buck Wilde!"

"*YEAAAAAHHHH!*" The crowd around Abbie and Doris burst into cheers. Even Syd was caught up in the frenzy, cheering his hero on. Abbie looked up at him.

"Really, dude?"

As the crowd grew rowdier, Doris grew more nervous. "I don't know what game he's playing, but this could get dangerous. Let's get out of here and figure out a plan."

They cut through the cheering crowd, who seemed to be getting more and more excited about this strange character's offer. Buck was gaining interest, as well. He grinned at Gusto, then turned to the camera.

"That's our show for tonight, folks! Y'all be sure to tune in next time to see me, *Buck Wilde: Squat—*" He stopped and glanced over at his new business partner.

Gusto leaned in and whispered in his ear. Buck grinned, then finished closing out the show. *"Buck Wilde: CREATURE-CATCHER!"*

Abbie and Doris briskly escorted Syd out through the crowd, back toward the camping area. Wearing a fake black-fur costume over his hulking body and Jordan's sneakers on his tiny feet, Syd didn't cause anyone to glance twice at him. Still, they didn't dare speak until they were standing far out of anyone's earshot. Once they were at a safe distance, Doris punched him in the arm.

"Ow!" Syd said.

"That's for being a big lunk-head!" Doris said. "What were you thinking, going out on your own like that?"

"I know," Syd said. "And I'm sorry. But I had to get my Soil-Soles back!"

"Nice job with that. They really looked good on TV," Abbie said.

Syd looked sadly down at Jordan's little sneakers. "I know I shouldn't have come here, but I saw the tracks along the lake, and I thought I could do it on my own. But don't worry, I stayed behind the trees, to keep out of sight."

"Staying hidden on your way to a public park isn't very impressive, I'm afraid," Doris said.

"I guess you're right. Then as I got close to the park, I lost the trail as they went deeper into the woods. That's when I decided to go undercover, and find out whatever I could. So I snuck into someone's tent and got this costume. Then I just, y'know, mingled."

"You mingled," Doris said, shaking her head. "With these people. People who have dedicated their lives—or at least their weekends—to finding and capturing you! Are you out of your walnut-sized mind?"

"I heard that Buck was heading into the deeper woods, which is where I knew the tracks went. I figured Buck is the best Squatch-Seeker on TV—if anyone could track whoever took the Soil-Soles, it'd be him! So I went to watch on the jumbo screens with everyone else."

"Can you hear how crazy your plan sounds?" Abbie said.

"So what do we do now?" Syd said.

"C'mon," Doris said, heading back toward the camping and picnic area. "Stay close to us and keep that ridiculous costume on, whatever you do."

"Wait. We're going back *toward* those weird people?" Abbie asked.

"We're going to get to a transmitter," Doris said. "I've got to find a way to contact the CKCC again. They need to know that Gusto is back, and he has the Soil-Soles. We're gonna need some backup."

RUMBLE! The ground suddenly shook under their feet. Abbie looked up at Syd, her face white with fear. "Syd! Is that—is this—the megathrust quake?"

"No," Syd said. "It's just that thing."

Gusto's Heli-Jet had just landed on the clearing near Buck's RV with a thud, crushing a few tents and some picnic tables, sending BuckHeads and Squatch freaks scurrying.

The door slid open. A few tan-skinned people hopped out and began carrying boxes up to Buck's RV. The boxes were marked, *MADE IN BRAZIL*.

It was nearly night as Kriss swooped low, carrying Jordan over the tops of the giant kapok, Brazil-nut, and bamboo trees. The thick canopy gave a warm, dense quality to the air, and when the Mothman finally dived beneath the tree line and descended into the jungle, Jordan almost felt like he was plunging back underwater again—a feeling that he'd recently become less than fond of. But it didn't matter. He was about to be reunited with his friend Eldon.

Kriss pulled up near the ground and fluttered madly, almost slamming into a thick kapok trunk. He safely dropped Jordan just before wildly tumbling onto the ground. Jordan looked at him. "You really do need to work on your landings," he said. Kriss stood up and shrugged, then pointed Jordan toward a glowing campfire.

Jordan ran past a few trees to a large, cleared area and glanced around in the dim firelight, trying to discern between shadows and objects. Then he heard a voice call out to him weakly.

"Jordan, is that you?"

He found Eldon lying near the fire on a bed of giant palm and banana leaves. Jordan felt a wave of dread replace his excitement as he knelt down beside his friend.

Eldon was older and more mature than Jordan in so many ways. Ever since they'd first met, he'd always been the perfect picture of good manners, good posture, and good health. As not only the leader of the Creature Keepers, but also a First-Class Badger Ranger, Eldon prided himself on being a role model to others, including Jordan. But the Eldon lying before him on the jungle floor was not the same kid he'd come to know.

Even in the dim light he could see that Eldon was very sick—his face was pale, with dark circles under his eyes, lips thin and blue, hands weak and trembling. Jordan had to hold back tears at the sight of his friend like this. "Eldon, what's happened? What do you need?"

Eldon smiled faintly. His voice sounded strained and raspy. "You're here, so everything's going to be okay. Is Abbie with you, too?"

Jordan tried to put on a brave face, but he hadn't expected this. "There's so much to tell you, Eldon, I don't know where to start. I'm just so glad you're . . . okay."

"You mean alive," Eldon said. "I doubt I look okay."

"Well, you've looked better." Jordan smiled.

"I took a foolish risk, trying to do this on my own," Eldon said. "My goal was to find Gusto, and I thought I could handle it all by myself. I tracked him down here, but then I'm afraid my spooring skills failed me. Did you get my postcard?"

"Yes. I was just at El Encantado. Some horrible things have happened, Eldon. But I don't know if you're up for hearing about them. Everything's so messed up."

Eldon turned his head and let out a brittle cough. Jordan could see how weak he was. He reached over and handed him some water in a small wooden cup.

"Thank you," he said as he took a drink. "Kriss told me all about Syd and the missing Soil-Soles. Boy, oh boy, that really stinks."

Jordan smiled. Despite how different he seemed and sounded, that was exactly the type of dorky thing Eldon was prone to saying, and it comforted him.

"Eldon," Jordan said. "I saw Gusto. He was there. At El Encantado."

Eldon's hollow eyes got wider. He tried to sit up. Jordan settled him back again. "He's gone now. He didn't have the Soil-Soles. But he practically blew up the Amazon in front of Palafito. Really made a mess of things."

"So he still has the Hydro-Hide, and it's still intact," Eldon said. "I'd hoped the volcano might have singed it off him, but it's probably what helped him survive."

"There was something else," Jordan said. Eldon looked up at him. Jordan took his trembling hand and dropped his grandfather's ring into it.

"You found it," he said weakly.

"Put it on," Jordan said. "I want you to keep it, at least for now. I don't trust myself with it. I don't want to lose it—not again. Especially while Gusto still thinks I'm my grandfather."

"Thank you," Eldon said, taking it. "I will. Not because you can't be trusted with it, but because I think I do need it more than you do right now." He slipped it on his finger and exhaled deeply. "And as for you and your grandfather, there will come a day when I will give this ring back to you to keep, as its rightful owner. As heir to what he created."

"There's something else," Jordan said. "In the river, just before I pulled the ring off Gusto's finger. He was trying to drown me. He used his Hydro-Hide to make the water pull me down. It was just like in the lake, when I lost the Soil-Soles. I thought it was the weight of Syd's shoes pulling me—but now I fear it may have been something else."

"Gusto?"

"There was a meteorite. It disappeared somewhere over the lake. Then, a second later, there was a green flash. A layer of light that skimmed across the surface of the water."

Eldon had propped his head up on his hands. He was looking stronger and healthier by the second. He stared into the fire, thinking. "There's something that Nessie does sometimes," he said. "Her loch lock. Because she can't patrol all the world's water at once, she'll sometimes release a single scale from her Hydro-Hide into a body of water, usually at sunrise or sunset. It acts as an early warning system, letting her know if anything foreign has entered the ocean, sea, or lake. When the scale is released into the water, it causes a flashing effect similar to what you're describing. I've seen it myself. Many have. It's what people report as a green flash on the horizon at sunset or sunrise."

"Do you think Gusto knows the same trick?"

"I'm sure he's figured out every possible use for that Hydro-Hide. Maybe his plan was to somehow lure Syd into to the lake. A successful loch lock would alert Gusto right away that the Soil-Soles were submerged and ripe for the stealing."

"Great," Jordan said. "I'm glad I made it easier for him."

"Jordan, if Gusto has the Hydro-Hide and the Soil-Soles, he could be more dangerous than ever. We've got to get word back to the CKCC." Eldon sat up and whistled so sharply and loudly, Jordan thought his eardrums would burst.

FLUTTER-FLUTTER-FLAP-FLOP! A few seconds later, Kriss tumbled to the ground in a gray, furry heap. He rolled to his feet and rushed to Eldon's side.

Eldon smiled at him. "Don't worry, my friend, I'm feeling much better, thanks to Jordan here. Thank you for finding him, and for helping me watch Izzy. Where is he?"

Kriss whispered as he pointed toward the dark jungle.

"Gathering food, huh?" Eldon said. "Okay. Listen, as you know we have an emergency on our hands. I need you to fly back to the CKCC, alert Bernard and the others that we need them. Gusto may be planning something big, and we've got to be ready. Have them come down here in the submarine first. We'll rendez-vous at the El Encantado. The three of us will be there tomorrow, waiting to be picked up. Got it?"

Kriss nodded, and gave a nod to Jordan. He fluttered and flapped a few feet off the ground, then suddenly whooshed out of the jungle, into the night sky.

Jordan looked at Eldon. "Three of us? Who's the third?"

"Izzy," Eldon said. "We can't leave him here without a Keeper. She left him shortly before I arrived. I think he drove her away. Something spooked him, and he doesn't trust humans. It's up to you and me to win his trust and get him to come with us, for his own protection."

"Okay," Jordan said. "How hard can that be?"

Eldon looked at him. "He's a Mapinguari. Not the most open-minded cryptid."

A rustle in the brush got both of their attention. Eldon sat up and whispered to Jordan as they stared into the darkness. "Just let me do the talking, 'til he gets to know you. And it might be best not to make eye contact, at least for now."

Jordan nodded, but immediately found that simple instruction impossible to follow as the Mapinguari stepped out of the darkness and into the firelight.

Izzy was a six-foot tall, red-furred, sloth-like crea-ture with long, sharp claws and a gaping, dagger-toothed

mouth. But its mouth wasn't where a mouth should be—
it was in the center of the cryptid's midsection. And
while this was a very odd physical feature, unfortunately
for Jordan, it wasn't the oddest. Instead, Jordan found
himself staring straight into the single, watermelon-
sized eye in the center of Izzy's massive forehead.

21

While Syd and Doris snooped around Gusto's Heli-Jet, Abbie made her way over to Buck's RV. It was late, but there were still some lingering fans murmuring about what they'd seen on Buck's show. From what Abbie could pick up as she worked her way past them, most folks were eager to see if Buck's mysterious guest star would actually come through on his promise. The die-hard Squatch freaks were obviously having a difficult time accepting that Bigfoot might be gone, but even some of them were curious about new creatures Buck might find, if only to fill the large-footed hole in their hearts.

While the fans gossiped and buzzed, Abbie casually stepped closer to the RV, then snuck up onto the side

of the porch-stage, where she quickly slipped through the door. Once inside, she was amazed at what she saw. The space looked like the inside of a completely different vehicle. While the outside of Buck's RV was dirty, dented, rotted, and rusting, the inside looked like a fancy hotel penthouse suite.

She heard a noise, and quickly hid behind a stack of boxes marked *MADE IN BRAZIL*. She peeked out between them and saw the man himself enter through a back door: it was Buck Wilde.

Buck took off his trucker cap and hung it on a golden hook by the door. He kicked off his muddy boots and slipped his feet into a pair of fluffy white slippers with a gold *BW* stitched on them. Then he pulled on a matching terry-cloth bathrobe and crossed the large room, grabbing a handful of shrimp from a tower of shellfish set on a beautifully polished table. He poured himself a freshly blended vitamin-enhanced fruit smoothie and collapsed onto a tufted velvet couch. A short bald man entered, and began massaging his shoulders.

"What a day . . . oh, yeahh . . . that's the spot. Work your magic, Mr. Mojo. . . ."

A member of the Buckaroo Crew, with a clipboard and a headset, rushed in. He whispered in Buck's ear. Buck waved Mr. Mojo away, sat up, and adjusted his robe. "All right," he said. "Send him in."

Abbie strained to look, then her stomach dropped. Areck Gusto ducked through the door and entered. He still had his long trench coat over the Hydro-Hide, although it now came a few feet short of concealing his other stolen item, the Soil-Soles on his feet.

He looked around, taking in the ambience. "Nice place you've got here, Mr. Wilde. I presume the hillbilly personality is just an act. I respect your showmanship."

"The fans love that stuff," Buck said. "But it also means I'm not the hick-fool you probably think I am." He waved his arm toward the seafood buffet. "Help yourself. Probably the last one of those I'll see for a while, now that I'm gonna lose my show."

"I would never think you a fool, Mr. Wilde. And you're not losing your show." Gusto circled the shrimp tower like a shark. "You've created a strong brand and fan following. I know you're not fool enough to squander that. And neither am I."

"Get to it, Gusto. What do you want?"

"I told you, I want to bring the world closer together. By pulling the cryptids out of the shadows. Then letting natural selection take its course." Gusto snatched a shrimp from the tower, popped it into his mouth, and chomped—loudly.

"You also said you're a businessman," Buck said. "So what are you selling?"

"I thought you'd never ask." Gusto stomped over to a table covered with a black cloth, dangerously close to where Abbie was hiding. "*We* will be selling this."

He yanked the cloth off with a grand flourish. It

floated over the stack of boxes and landed on Abbie's head. She peeked out and saw what Gusto had uncovered. There on the table were T-shirts, posters, dolls, pajamas, underwear, bedsheets, all with the same image or likeness—that of a red-furred, sloth-type creature with a mouth on its belly and a single, giant eye in the center of its head.

"Meet the Mapinguari," Gusto said. "Wild cycloptic sloth-man of the Amazon jungle. And I know precisely where to find him."

Buck's face brightened. He stepped up to the table and admired the merchandise. "Not bad," he said. "Love the adult-size onesies! This is quality stuff! So let me guess. I go off and make this jungle beast famous by hunting it on my show, and you clean up when everyone wants their very own Maggypoo—"

"Mapinguari—"

"—bedsheets. Might need to give him an easier name to remember." He picked up a stuffed Izzy. "Bigmouth! No. Eyesquatch! I'm just spitballing here."

"Yes, yes. We'll figure it out. And of course, you'll receive fifty percent of all profit, which will only be icing on top of the hearty boost in television ratings. Well?"

Buck grinned up at Gusto.

"Wonderful. Now here's how it will work. I will fly you, your Buckaroo Crew, and all your broadcasting equipment straight into the Amazon. Mapinguari's backyard. You'll broadcast live, and on the very first show you'll track, hunt, and capture the creature. You'll be an overnight sensation, the Mapinguari will be more famous than Bigfoot ever was, and we will sell billions in merchandise."

"Hold up." Buck shook out of his daze. "I catch him? On the first show?"

"It's called 'Buck Wilde: Creature-*Catcher*.' Is there a problem?"

"Uh, no, no. It's just—see, my show was called 'Buck Wilde: Squatch-*Seeker*!' Never did much catching, I'm afraid. What do I do with him after I've caught him?"

Gusto shrugged. "I don't care. Cage the beast, release him, kill him. I leave it to you. You are an entertainer!

You know when to give the people what they want, and when to leave them wanting." He put his arm around Buck. "You see, the important thing won't be that you will have caught the Mapinguari—what will matter is that you will have hooked *millions* of new fans."

Buck's grin was back. "And on the next show?"

"Believe me, this simple-minded beast is just the beginning," Gusto said. "Consider it a down payment— there will be many more to come. How does a trip down to Fiji to hunt a Mermonkey sound? Or perhaps Buck Wilde in Australia, chasing down the mysterious Tasmanian Globster? We've got to think bigger, Mr. Wilde. Together."

Buck plopped into his chair and took a sip of his vitamin-enhanced fruit smoothie. "Big . . . I'm gonna be bigger than frozen waffles!" he said.

Behind the boxes, Abbie did her best to keep from attacking them both.

"And let me show you just how big," Gusto said. "I'm personally setting up and having built a proper viewing environment for your most ardent fans, with plenty of room for growth." He unrolled a large architectural diagram. On it was an outdoor jumbo-screen event center with boxes marked "food court" and "merchandise booths." In the center was a tall likeness of Buck, and a banner across the top displayed the name of this wonderland. "I call it, *BUCK WILDE'S WILDE ISLE*! It's being set up just outside as we speak, on what is currently referred to as Echo Island. All will be ready for your fans to watch tomorrow night!"

"*PLLLLTTT!*" Buck spit his smoothie all over his robe. "Tomorrow night?"

"Of course," Gusto said. "When you're about to make television history *and* take the first step in bringing the world a little closer together, you want to start as soon as possible. The Mapinguari is scheduled to be running through the jungle tomorrow night. I expect you and your cameras to be running right behind him. Why dillydally?"

"It's just so sudden, and we have to get to—the Amazon, did you say? How will I and my Buckaroo Crew get all our film equipment, my wardrobe, smoothie machine"—he waved his arms around his cushy RV—"all of this down there by tomorrow?"

"Come. I'll show you." Gusto gestured toward the front door. Buck got up as Gusto threw it open. "Behold, my state-of-the-art Heli-Jet!" Buck stepped out and looked at an empty, windy field. A few costumed Buck-Heads waved to him.

"Sorry, I don't see it. What is it, stealth or something?" Buck said.

Gusto rushed outside, his big boots hitting the porch-stage with a rumble. Abbie stood up and peeked out a window. The Heli-Jet was gone.

One of Gusto's Brazilian minions approached, and spoke in a thick Portuguese accent. "Sorry, boss. But somebody borrowed your hellychopper." He pointed and they all looked up. The quiet rotors were lifting the chopper into the night sky—awkwardly. It lurched, buzzed a tree, then swung around violently. *CRASH!* A sliced-off treetop came flying at Gusto and Buck. They dived for cover near the door.

"WHO LET THIS HAPPEN?" Gusto shouted. Out of the corner of his eye, he saw something scurry out the door of the RV. He stomped on the wooden porch-stage with his Soil-Sole. Abbie was flung in the air on the plank, and he caught her.

"Aha . . . ," he said. "I thought I smelled a Grimsley behind all of this."

22

Abbie kicked and punched the air in front of Gusto as he held her high above the ground. "Let me go, you twisted freak!"

Buck wasn't sure what to make of this. "Gusto? Do we have a problem?"

"No, there's no problem, I assure you," he said. "Just a rat. Please, go inside and check to make sure there aren't any other vermin hiding in your camper."

Buck did as he was told. Gusto looked at Abbie. "I heard everything," she said. "I know what you're up to, and you won't get away with it!"

"You didn't hear the half of it, my dear," Gusto purred. "But I'm actually glad you're here. I was beginning to worry we wouldn't have any Creature Keepers to witness our world premiere tomorrow. I mean, how many invitations do I have to send to you people? Rumors that I was coming for Bigfoot's Keeper, stealing the Soil-Soles, turning up on that buffoon's show—" He looked up as Buck returned. "Ah, there you are!" Gusto pulled a thin, black device from under his trench coat.

"All clear in there," Buck said, eyeing Abbie with a slightly concerned look. "Uh, everything all right out here?"

"Yes, yes. She's just a corporate spy, that's all. Let's see, when was the last time our paths crossed, my dear? Hall of the Chupacabra, wasn't it?"

"Wait," Buck said. "You bagged Bigfoot—*and* tracked down the Chupacabra?"

"Tracked him? He and I were partners. But let's just say our little project kind of . . . blew up. In part, thanks to you, Ms. Grimsley, as I recall."

"Wow, Chupacabra!" Buck said. "Hey, what's he like to work with?"

Abbie looked at Buck. "You're an idiot, you know that?"

Syd struggled to keep the Heli-Jet in the air, while also struggling to keep his rather large butt in the pilot's seat. Both were challenging. One because he wasn't a trained pilot, and the other because not only was his butt way too big for the seat, but also he was sitting on the guy who was a trained pilot. The poor man's muffled voice could be heard as Syd did his best to veer the chopper over the treetops, toward Mount Breakenridge.

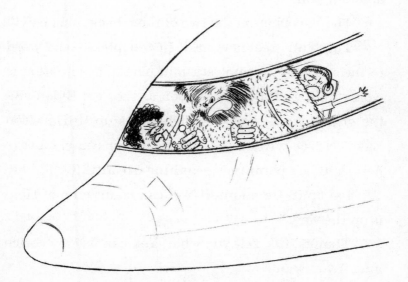

"Tell him to keep it down under there!" Doris yelled, fiddling with the Heli-Jet's control panel. "I'm trying to talk to Ed!" She turned back to the radio microphone in her hand as the Heli-Jet rocked and swayed.

Ed's voice crackled over the airwaves. "Roger that loud and clear, Denmother! You want us to send the recon crew to your current coordinates! One problem—they're not here! Bernard and Mac headed out in the sub with Nessie! Kriss came in with direct orders from Eldon for the team to hightail it down to Brazil to pick him up!"

"Eldon?" Doris said. "Did you say Eldon?"

"Ten-four! The sub's on their way to rendezvous with him and Jordan now."

"Well, I'll be. The little Grimsley did it. I never doubted him."

"They're bringing the two of them back, plus Izzy!"

"That's all great news, Ed! Listen, please send word to the sub crew to come straight here! The situation is worse than we thought. As soon as they get Eldon and the others, have them get their butts up to Harrison Lake! Nessie will know an underwater route. Gusto's here, and he's planning something dreadful!"

"I'm on it, Denmother! You can count on me! Help is on the way!"

"Thanks, Ed. Tell you what. You can use my coffee mug it you want."

"Thank you, Doris. You stay safe, now, okay?"

KA-CHUNK! The Heli-Jet shifted, causing Doris to drop the radio.

"The controls just went dead," Syd said. "This thing is flying itself! Just when I was getting the hang of it, too!"

"Gusto must have engaged some sort of autopilot system," Doris said.

"Denmother!" Ed's voice crackled from the radio. "Are you all right? Come in!" *FRZZZZT!* The radio crackled. Gusto's cold, calm voice replaced Ed's frantic rambling.

"Attention, whomever was idiotic enough to commandeer the private property of Gusto Industries. You are being brought back, by way of remote control. I have the Grimsley girl, so don't try anything stupid. Just sit back and enjoy the view. It will likely be your last. Thank you." *FRZZZZT!*

Doris and Syd looked at each other, then ran to the cargo area of the Heli-Jet and slid open the door. They'd made it a little ways up Mount Breakenridge, but were now being flown back. The tops of the trees swished by just below them.

Doris tore open a few of the MADE IN BRAZIL–marked boxes, hoping for some parachutes. She pulled out a pair of Mapinguari footie pajamas and held them up.

"What in tarnation?" She dropped them and stepped over to Syd, standing in the open doorway. "Okay, plan B! You have to jump! You can't go back, who knows what he'll do to you!"

"No," Syd said. "I don't care if you're in charge, here, Doris. There's no way I'm jumping off this chopper without yoooOOOOOoooooo . . . !"

Doris shoved Syd out of the Heli-Jet. She peered over the side and watched as he bounced off a couple of trees, then grabbed at their branches to stop himself. He looked up at her angrily from a large sequoia.

Doris slid the door closed with a *THUD*. "Dang right I'm in charge, here."

On the ground, the crowd of BuckHeads and Squatch freaks had grown, watching Gusto up on the porch-stage. He had the tiny remote in his hand and was remotely piloting the Heli-Jet.

One of Gusto's Brazilian minions pointed to the sky. "Here comes your hellychopper, boss." he said in a Portuguese accent.

Buck stood near Abbie, who nervously watched as the Heli-Jet descended. Gusto directed the Heli-Jet over the crowd in front of the RV. He clomped down the wooden steps of the porch-stage as the spectators moved back to make room for the landing. Buck and Abbie followed, keeping their eyes on the hovering craft. It was level and centered in the landing space, about a hundred feet off the ground. Gusto grinned devilishly at the others, then suddenly jerked the controller. The Heli-Jet veered violently, hung directly over Buck's RV, and then—*CRASH!*—dropped down on top of it, crunching its runners into the sides of the large camper truck.

"No!" Abbie screamed.

"NO!" Buck screamed even louder.

The crowd cheered at the spectacle of the metal crunching metal, like fans at a demolition derby. Buck

looked at Gusto with tears in his eyes. Gusto was smiling. Abbie stared up at the Heli-Jet's doorway, hoping that Doris and Syd were all right.

"What the heckfire did you do that for?" Buck said. "You ruined my RV!"

"I improved it," Gusto said, "It's now a hybrid." He reached for Buck's microphone lying on the stage. "I also saved you the trouble of packing. Get your Buckaroo Crew together. You depart in two minutes."

Confused and disoriented, Buck stumbled back up the stairs.

"There he goes, folks!" Gusto turned and addressed the crowd with the microphone. "Star of the brand-new show *Buck Wilde: Creature-Catcher*!"

As the crowd's applause grew louder and more energetic, Buck waved and flashed a smile, falling into character for his fans. Gusto continued to sell it. "And to celebrate tomorrow's big premiere, the newest attraction here at Harrison Lake will be opening at noon tomorrow! Come on down to the pier and bring the kiddies! Be the first to enter *BUCK WILDE'S WILDE ISLE!* We'll have food, fun, and lots of merchandise for sale leading up to showtime, when Buck and his fearless Buckaroo Crew will venture into the heart of the dark Amazon jungle to track, hunt, catch, and capture the vicious, freakish, one-eyed, belly-mouthed *MAPINGUARI!*"

He nodded to his Brazilian AV minions, who controlled a laptop just offstage. The jumbo screens next to the trashed RV blinked to life, showing an artist's renditions of a savage-looking Izzy. The crowd let out a symphony of oohs and aahs.

"Now let's all wish Buck and his Buckaroo Crew the best of luck as they head out on their journey into the darkest jungles of South America! Let the countdown begin! *TEN! NINE! EIGHT! SEVEN! . . .*"

Buck looked around, confused and surprised at everything that was happening so suddenly. Gusto's Brazilian minions finished bolting the Heli-Jet's runners to the top of the RV as his Buckaroo Crew scurried aboard.

Abbie noticed Doris being pulled out of the Heli-Jet

on the RV roof, and was relieved to see her doing her best to fight back. She went to run to her, but Gusto grabbed hold of Abbie as he continued counting.

"*SIX! FIVE! FOUR!...*" The crowd was all chanting along now. Buck looked back from the stage-porch as Gusto stood on the ground holding the remote control.

"Wait! You're not coming with us?" Buck yelled.

"Of course not," Gusto yelled back. "This is your show!"

"*THREE! TWO! ONE!...*"

"You just make sure those cameras are running," Gusto yelled. "We don't want to miss a moment as you *CATCH! THAT! CREATURE!*" Gusto hit the controller. The Heli-Jet lifted the RV off the ground, tearing it away from its attached stage-porch. Buck stumbled on the crumbling wooden structure, until his Buckaroo Crew pulled him inside. They all waved and tossed Izzy merchandise down to the crowd as they lifted up over the trees. Gusto hit another button. The jets blasted blue flame, torching a few treetops, and rocketing them out over Harrison Lake, toward the south.

There was a half second of silence, then: "*YEEE-AAAAAAAAHHHH!*"

Over the cheering crowd, Gusto grabbed Abbie's and Doris's arms tightly. "Shall we, ladies?" He smiled at them as he stomp-marched them through

the well-wishing crowd, off toward the docks down by Harrison Lake. As they made their way out through the camping area, Abbie saw a mob of fans practically throwing money at two men behind a booth. Guy and Andre were frantically selling homemade T-shirts. They were old Sasquatch prints, with a twist—as Andre took people's money, Guy used a thick Magic Marker to draw a single eye in the center of Bigfoot's head and a gaping mouth over his belly.

And one was selling them faster than the other could change them.

23

Izzy squatted by the fire, dipped his long claw into a paste he was preparing, and tasted it with his gaping belly-mouth. He grunted, added some mashed-up leaves, and tasted it again. Across the fire, Jordan and Eldon sat watching him, holding empty bowls made from wood bark.

"Remember," Eldon said. "Whatever he serves us, you've gotta act like it's the greatest thing you've ever eaten. We want to win his trust, and not upset him. Izzy's very touchy about his cooking. If he sees we appreciate his food, it'll go a long way in winning him over."

"Okay," Jordan said, repeating this along with his earlier instructions. "So avoid direct eye contact, let you do the talking, and eat his food. I so got this."

"The talking one should be easiest. Izzy doesn't speak English. His Keeper, Silvana, taught him her indigenous Amazon Arawakan language. It's all he knows."

"And let me guess . . ." Jordan looked down at Eldon's Badger Badge sash. "You got one, don't you?"

"As a matter of fact . . ." Eldon located a Badger Badge on the sea of round patches sewn on to his sash that proved Jordan right. "I do. Basic Arawakan."

"Basic? You're not getting lazy on me, are you, Pecone?" Jordan said. He couldn't help but grin. It was good to see his friend more like his old self again.

"*GRUNT!*" They looked up. Izzy stood over them, his massive eye glaring down in the firelight, holding out a crude serving bowl. *PLOP!* The Mapinguari slapped down a heaping helping of thick, lumpy paste in each of their bowls.

"Mm-mm!" Jordan exclaimed excitedly. "Hey! Can I just say, this looks so good! I mean, wowzers!

Yummy-town, here we come, *toot-toot!*"

Both Izzy and Eldon stared at him. Izzy's massive eye blinked, and he emitted a low growl. Eldon leaned over to Jordan. "Don't oversell it," he whispered. "The Mapinguari really doesn't appreciate phonies."

Izzy grunted again, then began speaking in a strange, rapid-fire burst of syllables. Jordan smiled at the beautifully exotic language and wasn't surprised when Eldon began responding just as rapidly to the Mapinguari.

"He says since you're so excited about his cooking, you should be the first to try it," Eldon said.

Jordan stared down at the clumpy paste on his plate. He thought he saw something move in the goo, and hoped it was just the shadow from the fire playing tricks on his eyes. He scooped some up with two fingers, and shivered. *Nope,* he thought. *There's something alive, squirming around in my dinner.*

Another grunt from Izzy followed by a sharp elbow from Eldon forced Jordan to shove his fingers into his mouth. He immediately recognized the sensation. The squirming substance in his mouth was, sadly, something he'd had before. "Hey, grubs," he said through a mouthful of the wiggly glop. "All right. My favorite."

Izzy squinted at him, watching Jordan closely. Eldon leaned over to him again. "He's waiting for you to finish your bite."

Jordan shut his eyes, once again fighting every instinct he had to spit out the writhing goo in his mouth. He bit down. On a grub. Yet again.

The popping sound was horrible, but not as horrible as the juicy, oily burst he felt hit the back of his throat. He swallowed it, paste and all, then weakly forced a smile and gave a thumbs-up. "Hope I'm not overselling it," he muttered, trying not to gag.

Izzy sat back and smiled a little. Eldon whispered, "Nice job. He liked that!" Izzy looked to Eldon. The Badger Ranger smiled and shook his head, then made a rubbing gesture over his belly, and offered a quick series of explanatory syllables. Izzy nodded in understanding and took his plate away.

"Hey! What was that?" Jordan said.

"I told him I was still feeling under the weather," Eldon said. "Now stop talking to me and finish. He'll be upset if you don't clean your plate!"

Later, the three of them sat silently by the fire. Eldon was looking much healthier, Jordan was looking like he might be sick, and Izzy was looking up at the stars.

"He wasn't this quiet when I first got here," Eldon said softly to Jordan. "He was scared, and defensive. It's taken me a lot of time to slowly earn back his trust."

Without looking away from the night sky, Izzy spoke in his native Arawakan.

"What did he say?" Jordan asked.

"He said I still have a long way to go. . . . Well, I'll be a mermaid's mother!" Eldon said. "He understood me! You understand English, don't you?"

Izzy's belly smiled a bit. He looked at them as he chirped something in Arawakan.

"He says he can understand it, but he can't speak it," Eldon said. "His Keeper conversed with him in Arawakan, but would read him bedtime stories in English."

Jordan leaned forward. "Izzy, it sounds like your Keeper took very good care of you. What happened? Why did you send her away?"

Izzy looked back up at the stars for a long while. He

took a deep breath, and began speaking in his strange language.

"The shadow voice made me do it," Eldon quietly translated. "It came like a very bad dream, in that moment between being awake and being asleep. But I knew it was real. I could feel its breath, and hear its words. It whispered to me tales of a human. A powerful, horrible human. A human who kidnapped a great cryptid of the sea, and stole her skin, just to make himself a jacket."

"That was Nessie," Jordan whispered. "He's talking about Areck Gusto."

Izzy's eye suddenly glared at Jordan. It was wide with fear as Eldon continued translating for him. "The shadow told me how this man stole one of the largest, strongest, most powerful and protected cryptids on earth, right out from under the nose of the Creature Keepers. It said if this Gusto could do this, what protection could my Keeper give me from him? It planted horrible thoughts in my head. As my Creature Keeper slept, the shadow would whisper that it wasn't just Gusto, that all humans would eventually grow older, grow to hurt all the cryptids. I was becoming more and more frightened. I had to get rid of my Keeper."

"What . . . what did you do?" Jordan said.

The Mapinguari continued in his indigenous

language. Eldon gasped, then translated for Jordan. "I scared her away. I growled at her. I acted crazy, out of control. I made her think I was going to hurt her. I had to get her to run for her life, in order to save it."

"And after she left," Jordan said. "Did the shadow come back?"

Izzy nodded. "It told me I had done good," Eldon translated. "The shadow told me how the Creature Keepers had lied to me, how they tricked me. The shadow spoke of a dark magic, some potion given secretly to my Keeper, that allowed her to fool me. It taught me that no humans could be trusted, least of all the Creature Keepers. That they were the greatest liars of all."

Izzy looked up from the fire. He stared at Jordan and Eldon. They stared back, unsure what to say. Finally, in strained English, Izzy growled a question on his own.

"Is . . . it . . . true?"

Eldon glanced at Jordan. He thought for a moment. "Izzy," he began. "The one who lied to you, the one who tricked you, was this shadow—whatever it was. You need to know something about us Creature Keepers—"

"Wait," Jordan said, stopping him. "Eldon, I can't let you do this. It's my fault that the elixir was discovered. If anyone's going to tell Izzy the truth and take the blame, it should be me."

"Jordan, that's really not necessary—please, let me talk to him."

"Izzy, listen to me," Jordan said. "Yes. It's true. There was an elixir. And it made old men young. But now it's gone, and it's gone because I was reckless, and—"

"*GRRRR!*" Izzy stood up angrily. He burst out a rapid-fire stream of syllables between growls and grunts.

"What's he saying?" Jordan said. "Is he saying we're cool?"

"*GRRRRRRROAAARR!*" Sparks exploded into the air as Izzy kicked the fire.

"Does it look like we're cool?" Eldon yelled. The two of them were on their feet.

"He's telling us to get out of here! He's calling us liars! Devils! He thinks we're here to hurt him, to capture him and take his coat!"

"No!" Jordan said. "Izzy, let me explain! We're not even men! We're kids! But there are lots of older humans who don't mean you any harm! Let us take you to them! You'll see! If you'll just come with us, you'll see!"

"*GRRRROOOOAAAAARR!*"

"Jordan!" Eldon shouted. "I really must insist you shut up now!"

"Look out!" Jordan tackled Eldon out of the way just as Izzy slashed at them with his large claws. *SWISH!* They both looked up at the tree trunk they'd been standing in front of. Its bark was stripped clean off.

KA-CHUNK! They rolled on the ground as Izzy's claw came down, sinking deep into the gnarled roots on the jungle floor.

"C'mon!" Jordan yelled. "I think we'd better get out of here!" As Izzy struggled to pull his claws out of the ground, Jordan leaped over the fire. He grabbed his backpack, then ran back. He grabbed Eldon, and the two of them ran into the jungle, leaping over brush and ducking under branches.

As they ran blindly through the dark, they could hear growling and yelling, as well as the snapping and slicing of branches closing in on them. They cut left, then right, not knowing where they were or in what direction they were headed. Suddenly, the ground beneath fell away. They tumbled down an overgrown ravine, sliding and rolling until they settled at the bottom. They lay there, listening only to their own breathing, and Izzy's distant growls echoing across the Amazon.

They'd lost the Mapinguari. In more ways than one.

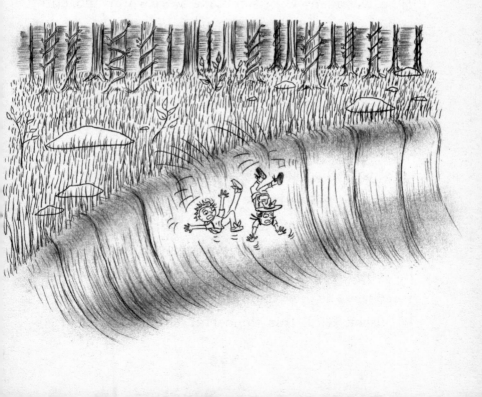

The waters of Harrison Lake were calm and still, reflecting the silvery glow of the moon hanging low in the sky. It was getting close to dawn, but there was a lot of activity down by the dock and out on the water. Gusto's minions were working hard to transport and set up the Buck Wilde mini theme park on nearby Echo Island.

Gusto stood at the bow of a swan paddleboat, his massive Soil-Sole boots taking up the entire front of the boat. He struck a General George Washington crossing the Delaware River pose as Abbie and Doris, his crammed-in paddling prisoners, looked on. He faced them as they approached the shores of the island.

"Look at all this wonderful activity!" he snarled,

waving his hand toward the rafts, small barge, and tugboats. "In less than twenty-four hours, *BUCK WILDE'S WILDE ISLE* will be crawling with fans and tourists— along with plenty of worldwide witnesses watching live on their televisions—as the first of what will be many creatures is hunted down! The news will make its way to all cryptids everywhere, injecting fear into their hearts, instilling a distrust of all men, and feed- ing my legend!"

"Scary speech for a guy standing in a plastic swan," Doris said.

Gusto glared at her, and lifted one of his massive boots. "Don't make me crush you, old woman. I'm counting on you and the rest of your Creature Keepers to help me spread the word. They'll whisper it to their cryptids as they tuck them in at night, unaware of their role in my master plan."

"And what plan is that?" Abbie said. "To be the big- gest jerk, like, ever? I mean, you got the Soil-Soles, why send Buck all the way down to Brazil to hurt another creature? Why lie about Syd? What is it you really want?"

"Me?" Gusto made an innocent face. "Why, I just want to bring the world closer together, that's all." He broke into an evil grin. "And as for the Soil-Soles, I'll put them to good use, don't you worry. I just can't believe how easy it was to get my hands on them. I've got ol' Georgie boy to thank for that."

"Georgie boy?" Doris said.

"This doofus still thinks Jordan's my grandfather."

"He walked right into the lake with them on," Gusto said. "Just minutes after I'd dropped a scale in the water! Such a rookie mistake from a seasoned Creature Keeper. He must be getting rusty in his old age."

"Well, he's twelve, so, yeah . . . his mind's pretty much gone."

"And who said anything about hurting any creatures," Gusto continued. "I'm just looking to open their cages, or at least rattle them. You see, like people, different cryptids respond to different threats. For the poor Mapinguari, it's being hunted by man. For his attention-loving Sasquatch cousin, it's losing the spotlight, and his fans. One by one, I'll get to them, undoing the comfort and care your organization has so carefully constructed. In time, they'll all be running scared. And then they can't be controlled. And without control, they can't be kept. It will be the end of them, and the end of the Creature Keepers."

RUMMMMBBLLE . . . A small, distant tremor shook from Mount Breakenridge. Gusto looked at it along with Abbie and Doris, then smiled down at them. "Hmm," he purred. "Seems the pressure's building around here, wouldn't you say?"

As they drifted onto the beach, Gusto kept his back toward Echo Island. Without turning, he held his arms out wide and grinned at Abbie and Doris, waiting for the reaction on his captives' faces. "That's it, soak it all in," he said. "You are the first visitors to witness the soon-to-be-completed *BUCK WILDE'S WILDE-ISLE!* Is it not fantastic? Tell me what you see!"

"Nice wooden beaver, there," Doris said. "You make that yourself?"

Gusto spun around. Sitting on the beach was the Badger Rangers' completed, towering, unlit Bonding Bonfire Beach Badger—a hodgepodge of logs and sticks and driftwood all bundled together in the rough form of a giant badger, ready for its ceremonial torching.

Gusto stepped out of the boat, splashing through the water, onto the shore. "What—what is this? Where are the food courts? My merchandise booths? WHERE IS MY JUMBO SCREEN?" Abbie and Doris grinned as they stepped out of the swan and joined him on the beach.

One of Gusto's Brazilian minions
(the same one who had the unfortunate
job of telling Gusto that his Heli-Jet had been
stolen) sneaked up and tapped his boss on the shoulder.
Gusto spun around to see all the rafts and boats floating
in the shallows, parked and still loaded up with the gear
for his island. "Sorry, boss," he said. "We couldn't get
started. Because of the natives."

"Natives?" Gusto said. "What natives? Restless
natives?"

"No, boss. Really nice natives. Which makes kicking them off super awkward."

"Howdy!" A friendly voice spun Gusto around
again. He looked onshore and saw Ranger Master Mac-
Inerney standing with Badger Rangers Tommy and

Sinclair. "Welcome to the Forty-Seventh Annual International Badgeroobilee! How can we help you folks?"

Gusto took a bounding step toward them. "You can help me," he seethed, "by getting your tents, your canoes, and your ugly wooden beaver—*OFF MY ISLAND!*" He stomped his massive Soil-Sole, and the entire tiny island shook.

Ranger Master MacInerney squinted as he stared straight at Gusto. "Badger Ranger Tommy, land use documentation, if you please." Badger Ranger Tommy stepped up, pulled out a scroll, unrolled it, and began to read.

"Ahem," he said. "By order of the Canadian Province of British Columbia, the preserved land mass known as Echo Island is hereby granted this weekend to the Badger Rangers' International Association for the exclusive purpose of celebrating their Forty-Seventh Annual Badgeroobilee. Congratulations, and enjoy. Signed, dated, notarized, and authorized, Secretary to the Governor General of Canada."

Gusto sneered. "None of that means anything to me."

"Well, I'll help you," Badger Ranger Sinclair said. "It means unless you're a Badger Ranger, or an invited guest of a Badger Ranger, you'll be getting back into your pretty little swan boat there, and paddling off somewhere else, *sir.*"

Abbie and Doris stepped past Gusto and stood with the Badger Rangers. Behind them, other rangers were coming out of their tents, gathering around the giant wooden badger in the center of the beach, and suddenly looking not so polite.

"Well, Gusto," Abbie said. "You may outpower us, but we have you out-rangered. Why don't you just leave these nice people alone."

Ranger Master MacInerney glanced at Abbie, recognizing her. "Oh, hello," he said. "So nice to see you again. Glad you found your way here."

Gusto nodded, and took a few large steps back, until his Soil-Soles were submerged. He whipped off the coat, exposing his glittering, green-scaled Hydro-Hide beneath. A slow, horrible surging noise sounded on either side of Gusto and his flotilla of supply boats. The lake water rose up like two giant hands on either side of Gusto. He smiled at the fear in the faces of the rangers as they looked up at the towering walls of water hanging over them.

"It is a lovely beaver," Gusto said, nodding at their unlit badger bonfire. "But you might've been better off building an ark."

He clapped his hands together. *BOOM!* The water came together as well, smashing down on both sides

of the little island, instantly washing Abbie and Doris away along with all the Badger Rangers, their tents, canoes, and the official Bonding Bonfire Beach Badger. In seconds, the entire island was cleared off as the crashing water flushed everything up the lake, toward Mount Breakenridge.

When the waters around the island calmed, Gusto turned to the Brazilian workers floating behind him with their unloaded gear. "Well, what are you waiting for?" he said. "Soon the sun will be up, and guests will be arriving! Get to work, and build me my *WILDE ISLE*!"

Farther north, the water surged like white-water rapids, shooting Abbie, Doris, the fifty or so Badger Rangers, and their massive wooden bonfire structure along with it. They all swam and scrambled onto the giant driftwood badger, and Abbie pulled Doris up onto the rickety structure. The Badger Rangers quickly went to work yanking planks off their creation and using them as paddles, then expertly maneuvered the makeshift raft past rocks and through the shoals of Harrison Lake.

Abbie and Doris held on tightly as the giant badger creaked and shifted, riding out the flume of water created by Gusto's tantrum. The Badger Rangers worked as one, navigating and turning each bend of Harrison Lake until they reached the far end—where they met the giant toe boulders at the base of Mount Breakenridge.

SMASH! Their rickety badger-craft slammed into the stone toes, sending rangers flying into the lake and onto the pebbly beach. Abbie clung to one of the boards still connected to the tower, calling out to the dark, sloshing water.

"*Doris!*" she yelled into the darkness. "Doris, where are you?"

"I'm over here, dearie!" Abbie heard Doris's familiar voice behind her. "And look who caught me!" She turned toward the beach. On the rocks, among the strewn boards and chunks of wood, Doris smiled, lying safely in the arms of Syd.

The rising sun cast a pink glow across the Amazon jungle. Jordan and Eldon had been trudging silently through the thick foliage for hours, stopping only so that Eldon could check his compass and adjust their course toward the river.

As the morning light began to break through the darkness, Jordan decided he would try to break through the tension hanging over him and Eldon.

"Eldon, I'm really sorry. I know I should've listened to you. You said to let you do the talking, so of course, I had to open my mouth and ruin everything. Again."

Eldon stopped, checked his compass, and walked on. Jordan continued, "I want to be the best Creature Keeper since my grampa Grimsley. But the harder I try, the more I realize I'm nothing like my grandfather."

Eldon stopped so suddenly that Jordan slammed into him. He spun around and glared, red in the face. "Of course you're nothing like your grandfather, precisely *because* you try so hard! Having Grimsley as a last name doesn't give you the responsibility—or the right—to run around trying to save the entire cryptid world!"

Jordan stared back at Eldon. He'd never seen him this upset, never mind with him. "I—I thought you needed my help," he said.

"I did, you—you nincompoop!" He shouted back. "I needed your help last spring, when I asked you to watch Bernard for me! I needed your help staying with your sister to care for Syd! I needed your help back there with a touchy Brazilian Mapinguari who'd recently lost his keeper! But each time, you refused to help me and decided to go your own way! And each time something disastrous has happened! Yes, your grandfather did great things. But before greatness came patience. Before he learned how to help, hide, or hoax, your grandfather learned how to be humble. He had to teach himself the first lesson in being a Creature Keeper, one that I've been trying to teach you—*how to care for a Creature.*"

Jordan felt a chill down his spine. Eldon looked

down at his compass, then up at the sun in the sky. He spoke without looking back at Jordan. "Your grandfather made plenty of mistakes, too, by the way." He started off again through the jungle. "But he knew he had to learn to crawl before he could try to run."

The sun rose higher in the sky as they continued hiking, and soon they could hear the rushing of the Amazon River. As exhausted as they were, they picked up their pace, excited to see the water, and hopeful to find their friends waiting for them. When they finally broke through the brush, all that was there at the jungle's edge was the ruined remnants of Palafito, the riverside floating village.

The damage was worse than Jordan remembered. The banks of the Amazon were littered with what used to be people's homes, their boats, their livelihoods. It seemed less an act of an angry river and more a violent attack from some evil force. Of course, Jordan and Eldon knew that the cause of this disaster was an unnatural combination of both.

They stood where El Encantado used to be, and picked through the litter that once was the cantina. There wasn't much left.

Jordan stood on a pile of waterlogged scraps of wood that were once Manuel's juice bar. "This is where I saw him," he said.

"Saw who? Gusto?"

"No. Izzy's shadowy stranger."

Eldon looked at Jordan. "You didn't mention that."

"I didn't know who it was at the time. But Izzy's stories last night got me thinking. If that weird bartender was to be believed, the stranger was there to find Gusto. He certainly went crazy when he showed him this." Jordan pulled out the napkin from his backpack. Eldon looked down and read the writing: *G. WAS HERE.*

Eldon looked up at Jordan. "If the *G* is for Gusto, and it's the same figure who was whispering to Izzy about how dangerous Gusto is to cryptids, then it adds up. But Jordan"—Eldon caught Jordan's eye—"how can you be sure the *G* wasn't for Grimsley?"

"I can't be sure," Jordan said.

They both stared out over the water, where the patio to El Encantado used to be. "He ransacked my hut and took my grandfather's journal," Jordan said. "I really wish I had it back. There's something in there I'm dying to read again. It's probably nothing, but he wrote some side notes about something called *cryptosapiens*—creatures who turn from animal form into human form. My grandfather tracked down the myths, and came up with nothing. It was just a bunch of local legends. A dead end."

"So why do you want to read it again?"

"There was something in there, some folklore he came across, having to do with the tears of a cryptosapien, having some powers or something. I was reminded of it the night I was here, and watched the stranger with Manuel. I could be wrong about what I saw, but . . . he may have collected Manuel's tears." He looked at Eldon. "Crazy, right? I mean, Grampa Grimsley decided it was just a myth, local folktales."

"Maybe," Eldon said. "But like I said, your grandfather made mistakes, too."

"SKRONK!"

They both looked toward the water. Jordan knew that sound. He and Eldon ran to the river bank. The Amazon was churning and bubbling in front of them. They backed away slowly, carefully preparing for another possible Gusto attack.

"SKRONK!"

Jordan stepped forward again. "Manuel?" he said.

SPLOOSH! Suddenly, the two of them were doused with river water. They looked up to see Nessie bobbing in the Amazon on her back. She flicked her great flipper and soaked them again.

"Nessie!" Eldon shouted out. "Boy are we glad to see you!"

The Loch Ness Monster responded to this greeting

by diving below. This seemed a bit rude, even for her. A moment passed, and another eruption of water revealed the large submarine belonging to the Creature Keepers. The hatch flew open and a shock of orange curly hair emerged. It was attached to a pudgy boy wearing all plaid. He looked older than last time Jordan saw him, but Jordan still recognized him instantly. Alistair MacAlister, Nessie's Scottish Keeper.

"What are you two doin' way south of the equator?" Alistair shouted. "Don't ya both know there's spiders the size of me buttocks down here?"

"Outta the way!" A large black paw pushed the Scot into the river, where Nessie dived to lift him back up onto the sub. The black paw belonged to Bernard. Most of the Floridian Skunk Ape's black-and-white fur had grown back, and he looked much more dignified without his ill-fitting Badger Ranger uniform. He leaped from the sub onto the shore and scooped up Eldon and Jordan in his big shaggy arms, giving the two of them great hugs.

"Thank goodness you're all right!" he said, staring into Eldon's eyes.

"Yes, I'm fine, Bernard, thank you," Eldon said. "Although there's a good possibility you've cracked two or three of my ribs."

Bernard set the two of them down. He studied Eldon's face. "What is it? What's wrong? There's something wrong. You can't keep it from me, what is it?"

"It's Izzy," Eldon said. "He's frightened away his Keeper, and he didn't take too kindly to us, either. I fear I may have lost him to the wild."

"So he's out there in that tangled mess, all by his lonesome?" Alistair said.

"We have to try to get him back," Bernard said. "Don't we?"

"Jordan reported that Syd may be in danger," Eldon said. "And there's a chance that Gusto may have Syd's Soil-Soles."

"Aye," Mac said. "We received a distress call from CKCC on our way here. Doris and Abbie reported in. Gusto's got them. He's up to something."

"Well, that settles it," Eldon said. "As much as I hate to leave Izzy unattended, Gusto's far too dangerous, especially with those Soil-Soles. I'm gonna need every capable Creature Keeper I have."

Bernard helped Eldon onto the submarine, then turned back. "Perhaps I should stay behind. Once I found him, he and I could sit and chat, get him to reconsider his options."

"That's a nice notion, Bernard," Eldon said. "But Izzy's not really a sit-and-chat kind of creature. Besides, the last thing I need right now is another unsupervised cryptid wandering around the Amazon jungle."

Bernard climbed aboard and looked back at the shore. "You're awful quiet, Jordan."

"Aye!" Alistair chimed in. "You up for battling that Gusto scum-bum again?"

"No."

They all stopped and looked back at Jordan still standing on the shore. "I'll leave the battle to you guys," he said. "I'm going to find Izzy and keep him safe."

Bernard and Alistair both shot Eldon a worried look. "That's a nice gesture, laddie," Alistair said. "But that jungle's huge—how are you gonna search it all by yourself?"

Eldon smiled at Jordan. "I imagine he'll crawl, if he has to."

Jordan smiled back. "Just promise me two things, you guys. Make sure my sister and Doris are safe—"

"You got it," Bernard said.

"—and stop that slimy scum-bum once and for all."

"With great pleasure," Alistair said.

"SKRONK!"

Nessie agreed.

Jordan watched the sub descend into the water as it followed Nessie down the river. He threw on his back-pack and turned toward the jungle. After just a few steps, he noticed something among the wood scraps and rubble of what once was the floating village of Palafito. It was a small wooden crate, marked *MADE IN BRAZIL*. Jordan recognized it as one of the boxes that didn't get loaded onto Gusto's Heli-Jet. He pried open the box. Staring up at him was a single, football-sized eye.

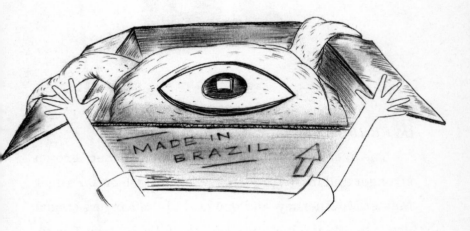

Rrrruuummmmmmble!

The tremors on Mount Breakenridge had grown stronger and more frequent all morning. Doris, Ranger Master MacInerney, and one half of the rangers stayed down by the toe boulders keeping a lookout for Gusto. Meanwhile, Syd and Abbie led the rest of the Badger Rangers up the mountain trail.

RRRRRUUUMMMMMMMMMBLE!

Abbie gave Syd a concerned glance. "Okay. How bad is this?"

"Hard to be sure, but it's been almost three full days now since I walked the fault line. Last megathrust earthquake, the rumblings got more frequent and intense, just like they are now. Great Cascadian quake of 1700. Wasn't as fun as it sounds."

Abbie looked up at Syd. "Dude, how old *are* you?"

Once they reached the plateau, Syd led them over to one of the many spots Abbie recognized from their outing a few days ago.

Abbie cleared the rangers back. Syd breathed in deeply, then squatted even deeper, centering himself over his tiny little feet. He closed his eyes, took one more deep breath, then leaped six feet straight up in the air. His little sneaker-clad feet came stomping back down on the rock, hitting with a pathetic *slap!* Syd fell back on his bottom, rolling on the ground and holding his heels in pain. "Ow," he said. "Okay, that really hurt."

RRRRRUUUMMMMMMMMMBLE!

This tremor was the worst one yet, knocking all the Badger Rangers off their feet. Trees shook, and a large branch of a giant sequoia cracked from above. Syd looked up, and dived to grab a handful of rangers just as the branch hit the ground with a *CRASH!*

"The pressure's really building up," Syd said. "We need to do something."

"Syd," Abbie said. "You can't crack these small rock beds. What if you have to pull the emergency ripcord? What if . . . we have to crack open Roxanne?"

RRRRRUUUMMMMMMMMMBLE!

Another major tumbler shook across Mount Breakenridge. This one uprooted a tree, which fell with a thundering *THUD* nearby.

"Okay, we need a backup plan," Abbie said, turning to the Badger Rangers. "You little dorks are supposed to be resourceful. We need to crack these rock beds open to let out some of the pressure below. Let's see what you got."

The young rangers quickly fell in before her and puffed out their chests to show her. Abbie worked her way down the line, inspecting their Badger Badges. Unlike Jordan, whose sash was filled with the little patches of achievement, these young clan cadets had only one or two badges each. But they were proud of whatever skill they'd mastered, and were eager to offer their services for the cause.

"Woodworking!" said the first Badger Ranger.

"Llama Shaving!" yelled the next. Abbie continued down the line.

"Puppetry!" said another.

"Modern Sculpture!"

"Financial Planning and Portfolio Management!"

"Uh, like . . . Public Speaking?" the next kid mumbled, staring at his feet.

"Medieval Traps and Ballistics!" said another Badger Ranger.

She continued working her way down, hearing dozens more varying, unique, and totally unhelpful skills, until she finally reached the end of the line.

"Trumpet," the small Badger Ranger sighed, sadly lifting his instrument to his lips. He tooted out a deflated *phhrrrrrrrt* . . .

Abbie looked back at the clan. There was an awkward silence. "Really? No 'seismic pressure–relieving rock cracking' badges?" More silence. "Okay, well, why don't you all just grab up some wood and rocks and stuff and . . . do whatever, I guess. . . ."

The Badger Rangers saluted in unison, then quickly scrambled to gather sticks, stones, and logs. They went to work utilizing different leveraging techniques, wedge theories, and finally, sheer brute Badger force, attempting to reopen the tiny crack in the rock. Nothing worked.

RRRRRUUUMMMMMMMMMBLE!

"This isn't safe," Syd said. "We can't even risk hiking back down to the others. Everyone, follow me! We've got to get to the tree house!"

RRRRRUUUMMMMMMMMMBLE!

Abbie led the clan of Badger Rangers across the plateau toward Syd's tree house. The tremors were coming fast and furious now, shaking the ground so violently that Syd had to scoop up stumbling rangers as they ran.

They reached Syd's tree house and looked up. The ladder was still hanging down, but was swaying from the tremors. The massive grove of trees holding up Syd's home was creaking and trembling. No one wanted to go first.

"You want us to climb all the way up there?" Badger Ranger Tommy said.

RRRRRUUUMMMMMMMMMBLE!

The grove of trees shook and shuddered. *CRACK!* A split formed at the base of a mighty sequoia at the far end of the grove, shooting a jagged line up its trunk.

RRRRRUUUMMMMMMMMMBLE!

CRACK! The split grew wider. The sequoia buckled. There was an awful creaking noise from high above. Syd looked up.

"Watch out!" he yelled. He gathered up a few Badger Rangers standing near the grove and shoved others out of the way. Abbie quickly herded them away from the grove, where they dived to safety just as the split sequoia completely gave out.

CRRRRREEEEAAAAACK!

Syd's tree house came crashing down hundreds of feet, blasting through the lower branches of the other support trees, splintering and busting apart as it fell to the earth. It hit the ground with an earsplitting *BOOM!*

Syd stood up and looked at the wreckage as Abbie checked on the Badger Rangers. She stood and joined Syd. The two of them stared at the awful sight. Missing from the pile of debris was Syd's deck. Abbie assumed it was somehow spared, but it was surreal and sad to see Syd's cozy, hidden house in the sky smashed, shattered, and grounded.

Jordan hiked through the jungle with Eldon's compass, and a good sense of which direction they'd come from before. What he didn't have was a lot of confidence that he'd find Izzy in the last place he saw him—or that the Mapinguari would be very happy to be found.

But it was the only direction he knew to go for now, and he'd made a promise to Eldon. He had to find Izzy, and he had to find a way to win back his trust. He only wished that he understood Arawakan. As the hours wore on, he finally reached the ravine where he and Eldon had tumbled. It looked a lot smaller in the daytime, but he could see the broken branches where they'd fallen on the far side, and the path they carved when they climbed out.

The sun was high in the sky and beating down on the jungle canopy. Standing at the edge of the open ravine, Jordan could look up at a large patch of open sky, unblocked by massive treetops. He stared up at the blue space for a moment, resting before he continued on. As he was about to turn away, something caught his eye.

It was another streak of fire, just like the meteorite he saw over Harrison Lake. This one was much closer, however, streaking down across the blue sky, landing in the jungle not too far from where he was.

Jordan headed straight for where he guessed the comet might have landed. As he got closer, he could smell something burning. Then he saw the smoke.

The smoldering streak ran like a scar about a hundred feet across the jungle floor. It was singed black, burning clean through a few trees and bushes, stopping at a still-smoking patch at the end.

There was nothing in the smoldering patch, just a charred circle of fire where whatever landed had come to rest. There was no rock or meteorite there. Whatever it was, it had disintegrated, been taken away, or got up and left on its own.

A noise caught Jordan's ear. It sounded like Izzy, and it sounded close.

Jordan spotted Izzy in a small clearing and began to move closer. His stomach suddenly dropped at the

sight of the hooded stranger Jordan had seen at El
Encantado.

The figure's face was hidden deep within his dark
hood. He was talking low and close to Izzy. Jordan felt
a chill run down his spine. He circled the clearing,
staying hidden in the brush but getting as close as he
could so he could hear what the figure was saying.

"You did very well, chasing off those two Creature Keepers," it said. "It's all right to admit. Chasing
them—*hunting* them—felt good. That's because it's in
your nature. It's the way the world should be. . . ."

The hooded figure inched closer to the Mapinguari.

He stood taller than Izzy and possessed a familiar presence that gave Jordan another chill. But Jordan couldn't place it. "Give in to your natural, savage instincts. Hunting and fighting humans will soon feel like the most normal thing in the world—because it is."

Izzy shook his great, shaggy head back and forth, like he didn't want to hear this.

"You must decide," the stranger continued. "There are hunters coming for you. They were sent by the Creature Keepers you scared off. You'll get no help or protection from them now. You're all alone. You need my protection."

Izzy growled. He looked like he wanted to run away, but couldn't stop listening.

"But this is the day the hunted becomes the hunter! The humans will soon arrive with equipment to find you. Weapons to hurt you. Devices to capture you. And worst of all, the cameras—to show the entire human world just how easy it was to hunt and kill you. I told you this day would come. I whispered in your ear how the Creature Keepers were lying to you. And I was right. Now it's time to trust me again. It's time for creatures like you to stop running, stop hiding, and take your proper place over all humans! Join me!"

Izzy shook his head wildly and growled something in Arawakan. Jordan stepped out into the clearing. "I don't speak Arawakan," Jordan said. "But I can translate body language." The figure spun around as Jordan stepped closer. "Pretty sure he's saying, 'Get away from me, you creepy weirdo.'"

Izzy growled at the sight of Jordan.

"Hmm," the figure purred. "Our mutual friend seems upset to see you here."

"I'm just here as a friend, Izzy," Jordan said. "It's okay."

"You're here as a Creature Keeper. And a *human*!"

Jordan peered at the hooded stranger. "You're right about that. Because unlike you, I'm not hiding who I am. Why are you?"

"*I HIDE FROM NO ONE—ESPECIALLY HUMANS!*"

"Huh," Jordan said calmly. "Well, this is the second time *this* human has seen you, and both times you've had on that goofy, hooded robe. In a tropical jungle. In the summertime. Just sayin'."

"We've met more than twice," the stranger said. "Shall I remind you?"

The familiar chill ran through Jordan's body again, but he shook it off. He couldn't show fear. He glanced past him, at Izzy. He had to try and reach the Mapinguari. "Izzy," Jordan said. "Whoever or whatever this thing claims to be, remember what Eldon told you. It's lying. Lurking in the shadows, it won't even show its face. All it wants is for you to hate humans. Well, Eldon's a human, and he came to see that you were okay. I'm human, and I came back not to hunt you, but to help you. This thing has only made you scare away the one who you cared about the most. The one who cared about you. Your Creature Keeper. And she was human, too."

Izzy whined softly. His great eye blinked. Jordan felt a connection.

"ENOUGH!"

The hooded stranger suddenly leaped at Jordan, tackling him to the ground. It was a violent reflex that Jordan had experienced before. The chill returned, and this time Jordan couldn't shake it. This time, he recognized it.

"You talk too much, Grimsley!" the figure shrieked as he pinned Jordan down.

Jordan writhed beneath the stranger and managed to get an arm free. He reached up. "You know my face— time to see yours!" He grabbed its hood and yanked it back—but Jordan already knew what he would find underneath.

Staring down at him with its horrible red glowing eyes, doglike snout, and snapping jaws was the face of Chupacabra.

28

Chupacabra was unique, even among cryptids. He was the very first creature Jordan's grandfather had encountered, and was the reason George Grimsley decided to seek out others and create a secret society to protect them. The irony was that of all the cryptids he discovered, Chupacabra was the one who wanted nothing from Jordan's grandfather—except revenge.

Jordan had learned how his Grampa Grimsley had photographed Chupacabra while traveling as a young man, and sold the pictures for money. This exposure caused the cryptid to be hunted down like a dog. Jordan's grandfather regretted what he had done, and wanted to make it right. He formed the Creature Keepers, then sought to find Chupacabra again so he could offer him protection and a safe haven. That was the first time the angry cryptid tried to kill him. But it wouldn't be the last.

Like Gusto, Chupacabra was under the impression that Jordan was his grandfather. He knew about the Fountain of Youth elixir the Creature Keepers had used to stay young. He was convinced George Grimsley had taken it, too, and was now passing himself off as Jordan. And so, along with inheriting the legacy of the Creature Keepers from his grandfather, Jordan had also inherited a very dangerous enemy.

"Surprised, Grimsley?" The doglike creature's hot breath blasted Jordan in the face, its glowing eyes boring into his.

"Only that you can speak." Jordan struggled beneath him. "I see Gusto, your human master, taught his old dog a new trick!"

Chupacabra's eyes glowed brighter as he trembled with rage. "Gusto is not my master! I am his!" He tossed Jordan across the clearing. Jordan glanced up at Izzy, who was watching, looking frightened and unsure what to do.

"You see?" Jordan shouted to Izzy. "This traitor

worked with Gusto, to kidnap Nessie and steal her coat! He's a fraud! He's been filling you with lies to confuse you! You've got to believe me, before he—*oof!*" Jordan was suddenly lifted into the air by Chupacabra again. The beast held him up and looked at him closely.

"You should know about being a traitor, George! You lied to these poor cryptids, made them think their Keepers were young, when actually you were giving them some magical potion to trick them all! And now your secret's exposed! But you selfishly kept enough elixir for yourself to stay a boy, didn't you?"

"You stupid mongrel, how many times have I told you—I'M NOT GEORGE GRIMSLEY! GEORGE GRIMSLEY IS MY GRANDFATHER, AND HE'S DEAD!"

Chupacabra tossed Jordan to the ground again and pulled out a familiar book from his robe. "If you're not George Grimsley then why did you have his journal?"

"Give that back! It belongs to me!"

"Exactly," Chupacabra snarled. "Finally, you admit it." He tossed the journal aside, and looked over at Jordan's backpack lying on the ground. "Now let's see what other keepsakes you have in here, Georgie boy. This should prove to Izzy once and for all what liars you and all your followers are. . . ."

Weary and in pain, Jordan pulled himself up and stumbled to his feet. He couldn't give up. Not after his promise to Eldon.

"HAHAHAHAHA!" Chupacabra's horrible laugh echoed through the jungle. Jordan looked over to see him pull out Syd's Teddy Squatch. Jordan was confused, until he realized Abbie must've slipped it into his backpack. For good luck. *So much for that,* he thought.

"A stuffed toy, in honor of one of your most beloved cryptids, for when you're far away from him," Chupacabra snarled. "How touching. And typical, *George.*"

He stepped closer to Izzy and showed him Teddy Squatch. "You see? It has a leash around its neck. Man's pet. This is what they want to do to you. But you're not a pet. You are special. Superior. And it's time we creatures come out from the shadows and stand up to humans everywhere!"

Izzy backed away a bit, looking frightened and confused as Chupacabra held up the stuffed Sasquatch. "This is the clown cryptid the humans call Bigfoot, the one they put on T-shirts and coffee mugs and watch on their televisions. He deserves the same fate as his beloved human fans. And that's what he'll get!"

In one quick snap of his powerful jaws, Chupacabra bit the doll's head off, swallowing it whole, and then tossed the rest of it to the ground.

"You nasty old goat!" Jordan charged, slamming into Chupacabra's midsection. The two of them rolled and scuffled on the jungle floor as Izzy watched from the rock.

Chupacabra quickly got the better of Jordan, rolling on top of him, pinning him to the ground again. "So, we are back where we started, Georgie," he sneered. "This time I won't fail. You were the reason I became hated and feared and hunted throughout the world. And now I finally have the chance to thank you properly. Good-bye, George Grimsley. I hope this hurts."

He raised his sharp claws—

WUMP! A log bashed Chupacabra in the side of the head, sending him fly-ing across the jungle floor. Jordan looked up, stunned to see Izzy standing over him, holding a good chunk of tree. In his other hand, he held the journal.

The Mapinguari pointed to Grampa Grimsley's

initials on the cover of the journal, then to Jordan. He opened his belly-mouth and uttered the same three English words he'd uttered before—perhaps the only ones he knew.

"Is . . . it . . . true?"

Jordan stood up and looked Izzy in the eye. "No," he said. "I'm not George Grimsley. I know he was probably the first human you trusted, and I know I could lie to you to make you trust me, too. But I wouldn't do that. George Grimsley was my grandfather, and I am not him. But I am a friend. And I'm very grateful to you for saving my life."

The Mapinguari tossed the hunk of tree and handed Jordan the journal. It immediately blew open in Jordan's hands as a strong gust of wind began whipping around them.

They looked up. A large, junky-looking RV was descending into the jungle nearby. Atop it, gripping the truck like a white falcon holding its prey, was Gusto's Heli-Jet. Its near-silent rotors violently shook and sliced the jungle leaves and treetops as it landed.

"I warned you," a voice spoke up weakly. Jordan and Izzy spun around.

Chupacabra limped toward the fire, staring daggers at the two of them. "I warned you that the men were coming to hunt you. And so, here they are."

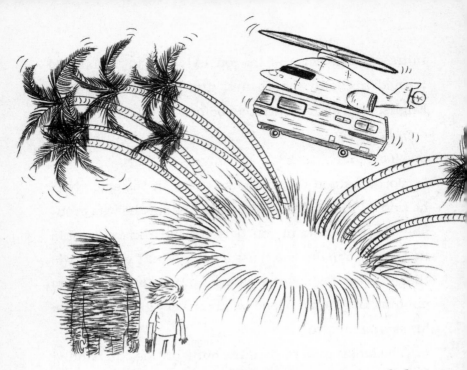

Izzy stepped in front of Jordan and growled at Chupacabra.

"I could've protected you if you'd joined me," the injured creature continued. "But you chose to stand on the side of men. You'll see how they treat you, how your Creature Keeper will fail to protect you from his own kind. And so will the entire world."

Chupacabra stepped into the fire. His robe turned to flame, swirling around his body, but he smiled calmly. "Good luck, cryptid," Chupacabra snarled. "You'll need it."

FWOOSH! He suddenly blasted into a streak of flame, shooting past the tree canopy like a meteorite returning to the heavens. Izzy looked more spooked than ever. His big eye took in the RV touching ground nearby, then glanced at Jordan. Then Izzy turned to run.

"Izzy, wait!" Jordan yelled. "That beast was right about one thing—you can't run and hide from those men." Izzy stopped, and stared at Jordan. "With the equipment they have, they will hunt you down. But he's wrong about having to fight them. There's a third option to fighting or fleeing." He picked up his backpack and slung it over his shoulder. "You have to trust me, Izzy. Let me be your Creature Keeper. Let me do what Creature Keepers do best—help, hide . . . and hoax."

The hike back down Mount Breakenridge was a slow and dangerous slog. Every few minutes, another pressure-rumbler would shake the side of the mountain. All the Badger Rangers would lie on the ground, while Syd hovered over them, watching for any loose rocks or landslides. When the tremors stopped, they'd carefully continue along the trail, which was broken and uneven from the seismic disruptions. As they finally reached the rocky shoreline of Harrison Lake and caught sight of the rest of the rangers standing near the toe boulders along with Doris and Ranger Master MacInerney, both parties let out a loud cheer.

But it didn't last long.

RRRRRUUUMMMMMMMMMBLE!

"All right," Abbie said. "Listen up, everybody. We've got a twice-in-a-millennium megathrust earthquake that's about to blow, with the potential of breaking at least the west coast of this continent off its mantle, or something." She glanced at Syd. He gave her a thumbs-up and nodded for her to keep going.

"All we have to do to stop it is crack open a very large, very deeply embedded rock, affectionately named Roxanne, up on that mountain. And the only way to do that is by using Syd's giant Soil-Soles, which have been stolen by the crazy, evil dude who blasted us off the island last night."

"Gosh," Doris said. "When you put it that way, the situation sounds *so bad*."

"And I've thought of a *really bad plan* to try and stop it," Abbie said. "It's going to require all of you to use whatever dorky skills you have, and it's a long shot that's probably doomed to fail. But it's all I've got, so unless anyone else has any ideas, let's get busy before we find ourselves buried under a nice-sized chunk of North America."

The others looked at one another. No one had any ideas.

"Okay, then. The basic idea is simple—since we can't go and take the Soil-Soles back from Gusto and crack open Roxanne ourselves, we're gonna trick Gusto into bringing them over here and cracking her open for us!"

They all stared at her with blank looks on their little Badger Ranger faces. Doris leaned in to Abbie and whispered, "Maybe you should just skip to the part where you tell everyone what you need them to do, dearie."

"Right. Little dorks with badges in carpentry, sculpture, medieval traps, and puppetry, come see me. The rest of you little dorks start disassembling what's left of the giant wooden badger. Syd, start loosening up those toe boulders—we're gonna need 'em. Doris, you prepare the other paddle-goose. You and I are going to do a little spying mission. Let's pull it together people, we don't have much time!"

RRRRRUUUMMMMMMMMMMBLE!

Abbie put everyone to work, but the tremor really got them moving.

Moments later, Abbie and Doris were paddling out on Harrison Lake, hugging the bend in the coast that led southward toward Echo Island. Before they turned the corner, they looked back at their troops at the bottom of Mount Breakenridge. The rangers were busy dismantling and repurposing the parts that once made up the giant wooden badger, while Syd was rocking the toe boulders back and forth, loosening them and rolling them toward the work area.

"I hope you know what you're doing," Doris said.

They quietly paddled within a good distance of the little island. Doris pulled out Ranger Master MacInerney's binoculars for a closer look.

"Well, Gusto's open for business," she said. "Plenty of people already there. It looks more like a theme park."

"Theme park?" Abbie said. "Eight hours ago it was a beach with nothing on it but a bunch of canvas tents and a giant driftwood badger!"

"It's more than that now," Doris said. "See for yourself."

She handed Abbie the binoculars. Abbie saw what was formerly Echo Island, now known by the enormous banner above a giant movie screen as *BUCK WILDE'S WILDE ISLE!* The outdoor screen reminded Abbie of an old-time drive-in movie theater her parents used to drag her and her brother to. It had a big crack in it, likely from all the seismic rattling, but it was otherwise intact, showcasing a fancy new logo for Buck and Gusto's new show: *Buck Wilde: CREATURE-CATCHER!*

To one side of the screen was a large statue of the man himself, Buck Wilde, striking a manly pose with his lasso. One of his arms had broken off, no doubt also thanks to the seismic shakes. In front of the movie screen, among toppled food-court carts and disheveled merchandise booths, the BuckHeads were milling about. And they didn't seem very happy to be there.

"They look scared," Abbie said.

"See Gusto anywhere?" Doris said.

"Not yet."

RRRRRUUUMMMMMMMMMBLE!

The distant tremor from Mount Breakenridge shook the island. The crowd reacted in panic, and many of the BuckHeads rushed toward the small docking area where the ferryboats were tied off, only to be stopped by Gusto's men. "They're not being let off the island," she said. "What a psycho this guy is. But where is he?"

"He's got to be there. He wouldn't miss his own big premiere."

"Okay. Let's get back, and let's hope our team has finished." As they turned the ugly black goose around and headed back toward the others, something caught Abbie's eye. She thought she saw a falling star descend from the sky and disappear somewhere behind the giant movie screen on Wilde-Isle.

"Hey, you little dorks did a pretty good job!" Abbie addressed the proud but exhausted Badger Rangers as they all stood at the base of Mount Breakenridge, looking out on the water at a fifty-foot-tall driftwood sculpture floating on a wooden platform. It was a very rough likeness of Syd, standing tall with his giant feet. His arms were raised over his head, and he held a large sign that spelled out over his head in pieces of driftwood, *BIGFOOT LIVES!* They all watched as Syd launched it, sending it drifting out into the center of the lake. Where the toe boulders used to be, there were now just five divots in the shoreline.

"I have to say," Syd said, "I really don't care for that name."

"Sorry," Badger Ranger Sinclair said. "We didn't have enough planks for all the letters needed to spell out *Sasquatch*."

"Yeah," Tommy said. "It was either this or *Sasquat*. We went with this."

"Get over it, you big lummox," Doris said. "Great work, rangers. Nice to see you kept the bonding part of your exercise intact."

RRRRRUUUMMMMMMMMMMBLE!

"Okay," Abbie said. "Time for phase two of my really bad plan." She turned to Syd. "I need you to start climbing. Halfway up the trail, at the first overlook. Stand as big as you can, so Gusto can see you from the water."

"Okay," Syd said. "What'll I do when he comes after me?"

"You're One-Step-Ahead Syd," she smiled. "You stay one step ahead."

30

Abbie and Doris sat in their paddle-goose, spying on Buck Wilde's Wilde-Isle with the binoculars again, but this time from a closer spot. They could see that the BuckHeads and the former Squatch freaks had grown quite vocal—and angry.

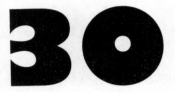

RRRRRUUUMMMMMMMMMBLE! Another tremor shook the island, toppling over more of the merchandise carts and sending the mass of spectators into more of a frenzy.

"LET US OFF! LET US OFF!" the mob chanted. The crowd near the tiny ferryboats that had brought everyone over was pushing against Gusto's Brazilian friends, who were nervously holding them back, and steadily losing the battle.

Abbie watched as a few stragglers decided to swim for it. As they jumped into the water to swim for the mainland, a small wave rose up, and toppled them back onto the island. The wave then crashed on the beach, and left standing in its wake Señor Areck Gusto.

The crowd fell silent and parted, staring at the massive Squatch feet at the bottom of his black trench coat. The Soil-Soles plodded straight up the center of the island, where he took a bounding leap and launched himself in the air, landing with at loud *THUD!* on the stage apron in front of the movie screen. He turned and addressed the crowd.

"No one is going ANYWHERE!" he bellowed so loudly that Abbie and Doris could easily hear him from their paddle-goose, clear across the lake. "We stand together today on the edge of history! Regardless of what happens to us, come earthquake, tsunami, or fire from the skies, the broadcast premiere of Buck Wilde's new show will reach the masses! And it will change the course of mankind!"

"Look! It's the curse of the Bigfoot!" shouted a Squatch freak. "He's back for revenge!"

"*SILENCE!*" Gusto stomped a foot, shaking the island. "There is no curse!"

"Then what is that?" yelled another voice in the crowd. "Out on the water!"

RRRRRUUUMMMMMMMMMMBLE!

The distant tremble offered a nice, dramatic effect to what they all saw as they looked across the water. Gusto's eyes grew wide, and the crowd gasped. There, floating around the bend in the center of Harrison Lake, was a fifty-foot wooden Sasquatch, holding up a simple message: *BIGFOOT LIVES!*

The crowd began a chant that grew louder. "*BIG-FOOT . . . BIGFOOT! BIGFOOT!*"

"QUIET! ALL OF YOU!" Gusto stared out at the water and thought for a moment. He suddenly smiled at the crowd, turning on the charm. "My friends, please! Don't you get it? This is all part of *BUCK WILDE'S WILDE ISLE* experience! We planned this for your entertainment!"

"No! It's the curse!" Someone yelled from the crowd. "Bigfoot is back, to take what is rightfully his!"

"Nonsense!" Gusto chuckled. "It's all part of the show! A theatrical re-creation of how I, Areck Gusto, bravely fought and defeated the vicious creature known as Sasquatch! Consider it a warm-up to the *real* creature-catching Buck will be doing! Now watch as I reenact my daring clash with this formidable beast, or a loosely constructed representation thereof! Ha-HA!"

Gusto hopped back down onto the beach. The crowd parted again, creating a direct path toward the wooden Squatch. *BOOM! BOOM! BOOM!* He bounded in his Soil-Soles down the path, then took a flying leap at the water's edge and went soaring through the air, feet-first, straight for the floating statue.

SMASH! It was a direct hit. Gusto instantly turned

the Badger Rangers' driftwood Squatch sculpture into a shower of splinters. Gusto fell through the underlying raft it was floating on, and felt something tug at him. He jerked his head around underwater. The raft had held up the hollow Squatch, but also the different-sized toe boulders. They were connected by handmade twine and sequoia bark, and when Gusto crushed the raft, the great round rocks collapsed around him, dragging him down toward the bottom of the lake.

Nearby, Abbie and Doris watched in awe from their lookout goose. "I cannot believe that worked," Abbie said. "Okay! Start paddling in for phase three of the very bad plan!" She and Doris pointed their goose for Mount Breakenridge.

"You keep this up and we might just have to rename this the 'Not-So-Very-Bad-Plan-After-All Plan'!" Doris yelled.

RRRRRUUUMMMMMMMMMBLE!

Beneath the lake, Gusto thrashed around in his Soil-Soles, weighted down by the five toe boulders entangling him. He wriggled out of his trench coat. The Hydro-Hide sparkled in the waters of Harrison Lake and its scales began flapping as if coming to life.

Abbie and Doris paddled to the spot where the toe boulders were once wedged into the shoreline. They leaped out of their goose boat and darted toward the Badger Rangers.

"Everyone, quickly, into the trees!" Doris ushered them inland to a grove of sequoias just off the small beach. As they scrambled off, Abbie stood looking up at Mount Breakenridge. She spotted Syd climbing straight up the mountainside rather than zigzagging back and forth along the trail. He was nearly to the lookout point, when another rumbling tremor hit.

RRRRRUUUMMMMMMMMMBLE!

"Syd!" Abbie watched as he slipped off the rock he was climbing. He dangled there, just below the vista, hanging on by one hand. She watched helplessly as he struggled to get his other hand up onto the ledge of the vista, then heard something else behind her—a roaring, thunderous noise. She turned to see a tower of water approaching, with Gusto riding its crest.

Gusto stood atop the giant wave, his arms crossed, riding it straight toward the mountainside. She looked back at Syd, and was relieved to see he'd reached the top of the ledge. He was hopping up and down, waving his arms and making obscene gestures toward the oncoming wall of water. He pulled out the Badger Ranger's trumpet and blew an obscene-sounding *phhrrrrrrrrt!*

Gusto saw him. He bore down and whooshed faster and higher atop his wave, straight toward Syd. Syd turned and ran farther up the mountain trail for the flat plateau.

"Abbie!" Doris yelled. "Take cover!"

Abbie turned and saw the wall of water looming over her. The wave broke, catapulting Gusto up the mountain in wet pursuit of Syd. Down below, Abbie shut her eyes and prepared to be pummeled by the wave—then felt something grab her and pull her skyward.

She opened her eyes. Once again, the furry gray arms of Kriss had swooped in to the rescue. Kriss soared up toward the flat plateau area, where he and Abbie saw Syd standing in the center of Roxanne, hopping up and down the large stone floor. Gusto had soared high in the air on the crest of the wave and was now free-falling straight at Syd, Soil-Soles first, eager to stomp him with his own swindled shoes.

At the very last second, Syd dived out of the way, into the bushes, as Gusto slammed his Soil-Soles onto the stone-slab surface of Roxanne—a direct hit.

BOOM! CRACK! HISSSSSSSSSSSSSHHHHHHH!

A deep crack in Roxanne broke open, releasing a blast of steam and pressure. Gusto shot out of the crack like a pellet from an air-powered rifle. Abbie watched him soar lifelessly, his rag-doll body spinning and twirling out of control across Harrison Lake.

Doris and the others heard the loud crack from the trees they'd taken cover in, down below. As the water subsided, they climbed down out of the trees and noticed something. There was a calm to the ground, and a sudden stillness in the air. All was quiet. The rumbling had stopped. Mount Breakenridge was still again. Then they looked up.

Syd was running down the trail in Jordan's sneakers, holding Abbie in his arms. Kriss was flying alongside them. And they were all yelling something. Even Kriss. Something that became clearer to Doris and the others as they approached the bottom of the trail.

"The very bad plan worked perfectly," Abbie

yelled. "Great job, everybody! NOW SWIM FOR YOUR LIVES!"

A loud thunder-like CRACK! echoed down from the mountain. It was the sound of solid rock—Roxanne's sheer cliff—splitting like timber, tumbling in great chunks onto the shore of Mount Breakenridge and into Harrison Lake.

"Swim for it, everyone!" Abbie yelled as she herded them toward the water. "Swim as fast and as far away as you can! GO! GO!" Syd ran past Doris and Abbie toward the shore, grabbing the littler Badger Rangers and flinging them as far out into the lake as he could. Kriss took to the air, grabbing Doris and flying her out over the lake.

The Badger Rangers were in the water, swimming for their lives along with Abbie and Syd, while Kriss and Doris flew overhead. Behind them, the sheer cliff slowly toppled into the water like a glacier peeling off into the sea. Syd glanced back. He knew they weren't nearly far enough out, and he knew what was coming their way. He remembered the Great Cascadian quake of 1700, and reached for Abbie's hand. She gripped it tightly.

Something stirred beneath them. Something big. It lifted them up. Syd and Abbie stopped swimming and looked ahead at the others—they were being raised, too.

The Creature Keepers' submarine breached, lifting the swimmers like a platform. As it surfaced, they found themselves on its metal deck. The hatch opened. Eldon popped out and his eyes went wide. The chunks of cliff forced a mini tsunami out from the base of Mount Breakenridge—and it was barreling directly toward them.

"Quick!" Eldon yelled. "Everybody in!" They scrambled into the hatch. He slammed and sealed the submarine door just as the water tossed the vessel, violently flinging around the people—and the creatures—inside.

As the surging wave carried the submarine straight toward Buck Wilde's Wilde Isle, a flash of sparkling green leaped out of the water ahead of it, racing to reach the tiny island first. Nessie cut across the front of the mini tsunami like a bodysurfer, her Hydro-Hide scales flickering and fluttering, working to stop it. As she weaved in and out of the wall of water, it slowed, then rolled back, finally leveling off, sloshing back to normal.

The momentum of the lake water caused the submarine to continue to drift forward, even as it stabilized. When it finally rolled to a stop under the water, the sub righted itself and breached—just off the coast of Buck Wilde's Wilde Isle.

"Is everyone all right?" Eldon yelled to the crew inside. They stumbled around, dizzy and disoriented, as if they'd just gone through the tumble cycle in a giant clothes dryer. There were a lot of bumps and bruises, and more than a few seasick stomachs. But more than anything, they were happy to all be together, and honored to meet the young Badger Rangers who'd helped save the entire region from a megathrust earthquake.

Doris ran to Eldon and squeezed him tightly. Abbie was glad to see Eldon, too, and immediately asked about her brother. Eldon explained to them both what had happened with Izzy, and how Jordan had chosen to stay behind.

"I can't believe he sat out a world-saving mission to babysit a cryptid instead," Abbie said. "Do you think he'll be okay?"

"I wouldn't have let him go if I didn't," Eldon said. He smiled at the seasick crew all around them. "You, on the other hand, seem to have Ranger Master potential. This is a fine-looking unit you have here."

Abbie scowled, then dragged Eldon over to Ranger

Master MacInerney, who was trying not to throw up on his Badger Badge sash. "Young dork, meet old dork," she said, shoving them together. "You two have a lot in common, I'm guessing."

Alistair had opened the hatch and peeked out. He gestured to Eldon, Abbie, and Doris to come with him.

"Oi! You're gonna wanna see this!"

Eldon ordered the cryptids onboard—Syd, Bernard, and Kriss—to stay below and out of sight, and to help Ranger Master MacInerney tend to the younger Badger Rangers.

"And keep them wee Badger lads quiet," Alistair added. "Ol' Haggis-Breath took care of that tsunami, but that don't mean we're not still in dangerous waters!"

Standing atop the submarine, Abbie, Doris, Eldon, and Alistair had front-row seats to a chaotic scene happening on Buck Wilde's Wilde Isle.

This was not the fun-for-the-whole-family gathering that Gusto had promised. After being rocked by tremors for most of the day, many of the fans on the island had just seen a massive rogue wave nearly wipe them out, only to subside at the last second by some miracle. There were still mumblings about the ghost of Bigfoot that had appeared on the haunted waters, and their host Areck Gusto might have been swallowed whole by the Sasquatch Spirit, depending on who you asked. The natives were officially restless.

Gusto suddenly came streaming out of the sky, crashing feetfirst through the floor of the movie-screen stage, disappearing inside it.

Gusto's arm reached out of the hole he'd punched through the stage. He wearily pulled himself out and stood with some difficulty. He scanned his island creation and the crowd gathered within it, taking in the aftermath of what looked like a small riot. T-shirts and merchandise were piled up like rags, food carts were tipped over, and the crowd was ready to revolt. Gusto looked like a shell of himself. He bent down and picked up a microphone from the stage. He held it extremely close to his mouth and blew heavily into it. *"CHHHHHHH-GGHH . . . CHHHHHHGGHH . . ."*

His breathing blasted over the speakers. He stared out at the silent crowd.

"Y'know folks, sometimes you gotta fight for your rights."

They all stared at him in silence.

"And today, you all did that. You survived everything we threw at you—the simulated earthquake machine, a tidal-wave special effect, and even our one-of-a-kind Battle of Bigfoot reenactment extravaganza! You stuck it out and made it through opening day at the craziest adventure park ever built, the only park wild enough to have the original wild man's name on it—*BUCK WILDE'S WILDE ISLE!*"

A few hoots and hollers went up. People began to cheer. Gusto was picking up steam.

Just offshore, atop the deck of the submarine, Abbie was struck by the gullibility of the masses. "He's got to be kidding! Are those BuckHeads really buying this crud?"

"What're we waitin' for?" Alistair said. "Let's go and finish him!"

Eldon shook his head. "He's got the Hydro-Hide and the Soil-Soles. We can't be reckless with so many people around. Let's see where he's going with this."

Onstage, Gusto continued winning over the crowd. "And now that you've all proven yourselves worthy, I can finally present to you the moment you've all been waiting for! The world premiere of Buck Wilde's brand-new live TV show, *BUCK WILDE: CREATURE-CATCHER!*"

The crowd burst into cheers. The BuckHeads were back. Gusto grinned out at the mass of humans he now had eating out of the palm of his hand.

32

"*WE WANT BUCK! WE WANT BUCK! WE WANT BUCK!*"

Any worry the crowd had about earthquakes or tsunamis had vanished as they chanted louder and louder for their hero. Gusto beamed at them, watching them whipping themselves into a frenzy. Then, finally, he let them have it.

"Ladies and gentlemen gathered here at *WILDE ISLE*! . . . Folks out there in TV land! You know him! You love him! The one . . . the only . . . *MR. BUCK WILDE!*"

The lights cut out, and the screen lit up with Buck's face. His voice blared out over Harrison Lake. "*All right, all right, all right! How's everybody doin' out there!*"

The cheer of the crowd erupted, echoing past Abbie and the others aboard the deck of the submarine, and across Harrison Lake, bouncing off the avalanche-buried shores of Mount Breakenridge.

Buck's smiling face filled the movie screen, and he spoke to his devoted fans through a headset microphone attached to his trademark trucker cap, which sported his new logo.

"I'm down here in South America, ready to wrangle up a brand-new varmint! You Creature-Catchers back at home keep your eyes peeled, 'cause my infrared thermomolecular night-sensor goggles work just as well in the jungles of the Amazon, where me and the Buckaroo Crew are getting ready to catch us a real, live, uh"—Buck glanced down. His lips moved as he read a scribble on his hand—"uh, Mapinguari!"

As the crowd erupted again, Buck moved so his face wasn't filling the entire screen, giving a first glimpse of where he was simulcasting from. It was dark in the Amazon, but the crew's TV klieg lights lit up the thick jungle brush. The RV and Heli-Jet could be seen parked in the distance as Buck and his crew began tracking through the bush.

They hadn't gone five steps when Buck suddenly spotted something. He turned to face the camera, excitedly letting the folks at home know what was going on.

"Look there! I see him!" He pointed to a thicket a hundred yards away. The lights and camera jerked, focusing on the spot where he was pointing. A blur of a large, one-eyed hairy head ducked out of the glare, and ran deeper into the jungle.

"Didja see that? That was him! C'mon, boys!" The camera jostled as they all gave chase, sprinting after the shadowy figure.

A massive gasp went up among the crowd watching from Wilde Isle. People yelled at the screen, egging Buck and his Buckaroo Crew on.

"Go get him, Buck!"

"Catch that one-eyed critter, Bucky boy!"

Atop the Creature Keeper submarine, Abbie felt dread in the pit of her stomach. She thought about her brother, and she thought about the poor creature being hunted down. She shared a worried glance with Doris and put her arm around her. Eldon and Alistair stared at the screen with a look of concern. They all felt helpless as they watched.

SPLASH! A wave suddenly washed over the deck behind them, dousing them with cold water. Equally cold and shocking was the voice they heard a second later.

"I just love good reality television, don't you?"

Gusto stood on the turret-like sail of the submarine in his Soil-Soles and freshly wet Hydro-Hide, watching the show and munching popcorn out of a souvenir Izzy cup.

"Lemme at him!" Alistair tried to scramble up the steep sail, but slid down.

"Uh-uh-uh," Gusto said, shifting his Soil-Soles atop the metal platform he was standing on. "Let's see. . . . I'm picking up some vibrations. . . . Yes, it feels like you've got some young stowaways below, along with a cryptid or two, perhaps."

"Ya bowfing tattyboggle!" Alistair leaped up again. "I'll gie ye a skelpit lug!"

Eldon pulled Alistair back. "I don't know what you just said, but best if we calm down. We can't endanger the crew below. Not 'til we know what's up his sleeve."

"My sleeve?" Gusto pretended to admire his sparkling Hydro-Hide. "This old thing? Just something I threw on—really goes with the shoes, dontcha think?" He threw back his head and laughed from his perch, then looked around. "And speaking of old things, isn't this my old submarine? I love what you've done with the place."

Abbie glanced across the water, back at the screen. Buck and his crew were gaining on the hairy one-eyed creature. "Gusto. You have to stop this."

"What can I do?" Gusto said, faking concern. "They're so far away!" He looked down at Eldon. "Which reminds me—why are your people all gathered *here*, when one of your cryptids is all alone and in danger, way down *there*? I thought it was your job to protect these poor, defenseless creatures. Or did I have that wrong?"

"You filthy mongrel!" Doris said.

Gusto pretended to gasp. "Oh, no! Don't tell me the Creature Keepers—the great protectors of all cryptids everywhere—abandoned one of their most vulnerable creatures just because their most popular cryptid *couldn't find his shoes one morning*!" He cackled again, sending a chill down Abbie's spine. She stepped forward.

"You stole the Soil-Soles to cause all this destruction just so Izzy would be abandoned and make easy prey for that bogus bounty hunter?"

"That was just one of many reasons, my dear," Gusto said. "Another is much more straightforward—as of tonight, with the launch of this show, I have declared a war between us humans and your cryptids. And when one is at war, it is always good strategy to disarm the enemy of its most effective weapons." He looked down and admired his sparkling Hydro-Hide and enormous Soil-Soles. "All the better if you can use your opponents' weapons against them on the battlefield." He tapped his foot on the platform. *CLANG!* The sub vibrated, shaking and creaking for an uncomfortably long time. "Also,

I won't lie. These puppies are a lot of fun."

"You forgot one thing, Gusto," Abbie said. "Izzy isn't alone in that jungle."

"That's right," Doris said. "He has a Creature Keeper with him."

"A *great* Keeper," Eldon added.

"Aye. The best!" Alistair whispered to Abbie, "We're talking about Jordan, right?"

"Ah, yes!" Gusto smiled. "Grimsley! You think the old man still has it, eh?"

"For the last time, he's my brother, not my grandfather!" Abbie snapped.

"Ooh, everyone quiet!" Gusto looked across at the screen on Wilde Isle. "I don't want to miss the best part!"

33

Gusto kept an eye on Abbie, Eldon, Doris, and Alistair as they turned to watch along with the rest of the crowd on the island.

Onscreen, Buck was closing in on the one-eyed creature he'd been chasing through the jungle. He glanced at the camera, sweat beading up on his brow.

"Folks, this is like nothing I've ever encountered in all my years hunting the Squatch," Buck whispered. "The jungle is alive all around me. I can sense the savage beast's heat, I can smell its breath. I can see its— *HOLY SMOKIES, I CAN SEE IT!*"

Buck pointed. The spotlight shone on a large log. Sitting there perfectly still was a brown, furry apelike figure, with a single eye on its forehead and an enormous mouth on its torso. Buck approached. He could see it breathing heavily as he reached down for his lasso. He began to swing the lasso over his head as he continued to move in.

WHOOSH! He flung it around the creature's body and yanked it back, pinning the creature's arms to its sides. It jerked a bit but didn't fight. It sat perfectly still.

Buck tossed his head back. "*YEEEEHAWWWWW!* Didja see that? I caught something! I did it! I really, actually caught a real, live creature! *ON LIVE TV!*"

The crowd watching on Buck's Wilde Isle went berserk. They let out a cheer that drowned out even Buck's amplified voice. They hugged and high-fived one another, jumping up and down in ecstasy. This was a first for them, too.

Atop the submarine, Gusto was still standing on the sail. He let out a loud, cruel laugh. "Oops! Looks like Grimsley wasn't quite ready for prime time!"

"You monster!" Abbie lunged for Gusto's feet. Doris grabbed her and pulled her back. "We can't let him get away with this!" Abbie yelled at Eldon, who was still staring at the screen. She thought he was in shock, but then she noticed a smile spread across his face. He started giggling. Then he burst out laughing.

"What's so funny, boy?" Gusto sneered. "You lost! Your Creature Keeper ran away in fear, while my Creature-*Catcher* exposed what will be the first of many of your precious cryptids—in front of millions of witnesses, on live television! The war has begun! You're right, that *is* hilarious!"

"I don't know much about television," Eldon said, still smiling. "But is it true what they say? That the camera adds ten pounds? Because I've met the Mapinguari, and watching him on your show right now, it looks to me like he *lost about two hundred.*"

Gusto snapped his head toward the screen. Buck was showing off for the camera, pretending to reel in the creature with his lasso, then posing heroically with it.

Abbie noticed something else. As the camera moved in closer, she saw that the Mapinguari's skin looked loose and frumpy. Its eye didn't blink. It's mouth didn't move.

Abbie smiled, too. "Jordan," she whispered to herself.

Gusto peered closer at the screen. He'd gone silent suddenly.

Buck put a foot up on the log and posed next to the lassoed creature. "This one sure didn't put up too much of a fight, did he, folks?" He put his arm around its furry shoulders and grinned at the creature sitting perfectly still in his lasso.

"What's this?" He looked behind the creature, his smile fading. He stood it up and turned it around and around, unwinding his lasso.

On the back of the creature's head was a white label pinned to a small zipper. Buck read it, on live TV. "'G. was here' . . . ?" he read into the camera, then looked at the creature. "Who in the world is 'G' . . . ?"

Buck's trembling fingers took hold of the zipper and slowly began to pull it down the center of the creature's head, all the way down its back. The two fuzzy halves of the creature dropped away.

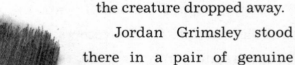

Jordan Grimsley stood there in a pair of genuine Mapinguari adult-sized footie pajamas. He grinned at Buck. "Smile, Mr. Wilde. You've just been Gusto-Gagged!"

Buck's eyes went wide. He stumbled back and bumped into the camera. He pointed a trembling finger at Jordan. "Y-you're not a creature! You're just some kid in a costume!"

"Technically, they're adult-sized footie PJs. Great idea, dontcha think?"

"*WHAT IS THIS?*" Buck yelled into the camera.

"*WHAT IS THIS?*" Gusto yelled back at the screen.

"*NOW!*" Eldon yelled to the Keepers.

He and the others charged. Alistair heaved Doris up toward Gusto's feet, while Abbie scaled the ladder on the far side of the sail. They both grabbed at Gusto's Soil-Soles, and tugged with all their might. Eldon ran to the hatch and opened it. "Bernard!" he yelled down.

"Open the left forward trim tank! NOW!"

Gusto struggled to keep his balance with Abbie and Doris hanging off his massive feet. Suddenly, the submarine tilted hard to one side. Gusto stumbled. Abbie and Doris let go to avoid tumbling with him.

CLANG! SPLOOSH! Gusto hit the side of the submarine and plunged into the water, disappearing into the dark depths of Harrison Lake.

"Where is he?" a voice boomed out from behind. Bernard, Syd, Kriss, and the Badger Rangers climbed out of the hatch to lend a hand.

"No!" Eldon shouted. "Get back below! Gusto's in the water! It's not safe up here! Everyone, back into the—"

The submarine suddenly jolted, sending them all scrambling to hold on to the deck.

Abbie pulled herself up and looked around. Although it was dark, she could see that the submarine was no longer in the lake. It was balancing on a fountain of water, fifty feet above the surface.

"Oh, no . . ."

"I HAVE JUST ABOUT HAD ENOUGH OF YOU PEOPLE!"

Gusto's low voice called out from the port side of the submarine. Like the sub, he was suspended by a thin spout of water, both of which he was controlling with his Hydro-Hide. "You ruined my debut, and you let down all those poor people on Wilde-Isle! So now I'm going to let you down—right on top of them!"

The fountain moved through the water, tilting back to toss the sub onto the island, where the confused, innocent, clueless crowd was still staring up at the screen.

"If any of you have any last words, now would be the time to—"

"*SKRONK!*"

"*Skronk?*" Gusto looked over, confused. "Who says 'skronk' as a last word?"

A flash of green exploded out of the water. Nessie flew through the air, extending her long tail. It sliced through the stream holding Gusto like a samurai sword, cutting off his contact with the lake.

The submarine immediately dropped onto the surface with a *CRASH!*

Gusto tumbled back into the lake, and Nessie wasted no time diving after him. The others ran to the side of the sub and stared down at the spot where they disappeared. All was quiet for a moment. The water began to roil and bubble up. *SPLOOSH! SPLOSH! KABOOM!* Every few seconds, a massive burst of water would blow out of the surface, as if a depth charge had gone off. There was a major burst from deep below the surface, then nothing. The water got very still again. Abbie scanned the dark surface of the lake. She heard Alistair's Scottish voice to her right, quietly muttering to himself.

"C'mon, Haggis-Breath. C'mon, girl . . ."

FLOOOOOSH! Suddenly, Gusto blasted out of the lake like a cannonball, soaring far and fast across the night sky. *"SKRONK!"* Nessie's head had popped out, watching Gusto as she water-blasted him away. She turned to her audience aboard the submarine, looking very pleased with herself.

The Badger Rangers let out a cheer. Abbie heard a sniffling to her right, followed by a loud *HONK!*—as Alistair MacAlister blew his nose and pulled himself together.

"Whaddya think yer doin', ya' lazy sea cow?" the Scottish Keeper yelled down to her. "Go an' get him, girl! Bring him back—and bring back those Soil-Soles! Go on, now!"

"*SKRONK!*" Nessie dived below the surface and shot off toward the far end of Harrison Lake.

The others turned to face the island, a little surprised to see the crowd of BuckHeads oblivious to what had just happened out on the water. They were all still glued to the screen, shocked and unable to turn away from their hero, who seemed to be having a major meltdown.

"I don't understand," Buck muttered. The Creature-Catcher was near tears.

"It isn't complicated," Jordan said. "You got scammed. That Gusto is a royal creep. Did you see his moustache and goatee? You can't trust a guy with facial hair like that."

"I—I just thought he was *European* . . . ," Buck's lip began to tremble "B-but the Mappygoo"—he looked down at the word written on his hand again—"Mapinguari. Gusto said he was just the first of many cryptid creatures I'd get to . . ."

"The *what*?" Jordan broke in, glancing at the camera. "The Maggiechoo? What are you talking about? Look, I don't know anything about any cryptical creatures. All I know is you got punked! Gusto-Gagged! That's what his show's all about!"

"But—the island, the Heli-Jet, all that merchandise . . ."

"All part of the prank. See, while you were here running around the jungle making a fool of yourself, he was making a killing—selling T-shirts and underwear! It's the oldest scam in the book! I just can't believe you"—he glanced at the camera again—"*and your fans* fell for it!"

Buck Wilde glared at the camera. A strange look came over him, the cold-blooded stare of a true hunter. "All right, Buckaroo Crew," he said in a serious-sounding voice. "Everyone back to the Heli-Jet. This Gusto likes pranks. We're gonna hit him where it hurts." He looked at the camera and made a slicing motion across his neck. *"Cut."*

On Wilde Isle, the screen went dark. And the people gathered before it were about to go even darker. *"GUSTO . . . GUSTO . . . GUSTO . . ."* The BuckHeads were chanting a different name, and for a very different reason—not to praise their hero but to find their swindler. The fickle fans had quickly turned back into an angry mob again. As their fury boiled over, they surged—screaming horrible names at Gusto, overturning more food carts, pulling down Buck's statue, and setting a massive pile of T-shirts, pajamas, and other Izzy merchandise ablaze on the beach.

Atop the submarine, Ranger Master MacInerney approached First-Class Badger Ranger Eldon. His clan of rangers was lined up in formation behind him, many with bandages and slings on their arms from their

earlier tumbling. They all gave Eldon the Badger claw salute in unison. Eldon saluted back.

"Ranger Pecone," the Ranger Master said. "Requesting permission to go ashore with the mission of teaching an angry mob proper fire safety precautions."

"Permission granted, Ranger Master MacInerney," Eldon said. "And regarding what you and your rangers may or may not have seen in the last twenty-four hours—"

Ranger Master MacInerney nodded. "Just a nice group of somewhat odd-looking citizens, in need of Badger assistance." He winked and saluted again, then turned to his clan of rangers, lined up along the deck, ready to dive in.

"Wait," Abbie said from behind. The rangers turned to face her and Doris. "I wanted to say that, uh, for a bunch of little dorks, you guys did a good job, and you, y'know, kinda made me proud. For a buncha little dorks, I mean."

"She's trying to say you kicked butt, dearies!" Doris added.

The Badger Rangers gave them both a Badger claw salute, then turned and leaped into the water in perfect formation.

Eldon, Abbie, and Doris watched carefully as they made it the short distance to the island, then stormed the beach armed with lectures on proper fire safety protocol.

"How nice," Doris said. "See? They got their bonding *and* their bonfire."

The Buckaroo Crew tried to keep up with their leader, Buck Wilde, as he raced like a crazy person back through the Amazon jungle toward Gusto's Heli-Jet.

Jordan watched them go, then stood alone in the dark, with his Izzy pajamas in a pile at his ankles. He took a deep breath of the moist night air, sat back down on the log, and listened to the jungle sounds all around him. A snicker from above caught his attention. Jordan looked up. "Izzy, quiet!" Jordan smiled. "They still might be close by!"

Perched on a branch overhead, Izzy giggled so hard he nearly fell out of the tree he'd been hiding in.

Jordan and Izzy were still laughing about the look on Buck Wilde's face when they reached the Mapinguari's jungle den. Izzy suddenly stopped. He sniffed at the air, then peered into the darkness.

"What is it?" Jordan said, glancing around. "Is it Chupacabra? Is he back?"

Izzy rushed toward the entrance to his den. Jordan followed, but stopped short at the sight of a young, dark-haired woman. She stepped out and smiled. Then she opened her arms to Izzy.

The Mapinguari and the woman hugged. Jordan thought he heard the formerly ferocious cryptid purring in her arms. She looked past his furry arms at Jordan.

"You must be Silvana," Jordan said. "Izzy's Creature Keeper."

The woman nodded, closing her eyes tightly as she held Izzy. She pulled back and looked into his one gigantic eye. "I am so sorry, *filho*," she said gently in a thick Portuguese accent. "I will never leave you again, I promise." Izzy smiled back at her, and she stepped up to Jordan. "And thank you, for taking care of him while I was away. But I am back now. Please tell Eldon and the others I am so sorry, and I am willing to accept whatever consequences the CKCC decides to assign me."

"Sure," Jordan said. "But can I just ask you, I mean, from one Creature Keeper to another, how could you just leave?"

She looked at him sadly. "I was frightened, and confused. So I ran. But I quickly realized that the world is a much more confusing and frightening place. I met a man, on the river. He was handsome and charming. He said he would help me find a home, a new life. And I believed him. But he did not turn out to be who I thought he was."

"You mean . . . he hurt you?"

"No. I mean . . . he was a dolphin."

"Oh." Jordan thought for a moment. He suddenly remembered something. He opened his backpack and pulled out his grandfather's journal. He flipped through it and found the entry he was looking for.

"Yes! My grandfather's search for creatures like that—it was in this part of the world! He called them *cryptosapiens*. But he dismissed them as myth."

She nodded her head. "There are many myths here in the Amazon, and the Boto Encantado is one of them. But he is real. I met him."

Jordan looked at her. "Silvana. This man, did he wear a fedora? White suit, really into fruit smoothies?"

"Ay! Yes! What was with all the smoothies? Day and night, the smoothies! I tell him, enough already with the smoothies!"

"It's Manuel," Jordan said. "I knew there was something fishy about him."

"You mean 'mammally,'" Silvana said. "Dolphins are mammals. Not fish."

"Right. I knew that."

"He kept trying to make me drink a special smoothie," Silvana said. "Made with his sweat or his teardrops or something nasty like that. He said it had special powers. He wanted to turn me into a dolphin-person, like him. He said it would be safer for me, that soon the special creatures of the earth would rise up and take over from the humans, or something. He said he already used his powers to help the leader of these creatures disguise himself as a man, and it might work on me, too. Ay, crazy. That's when I got scared. Scared for me, but more scared for my Izzy. That's when I ran from the nasty dolphin-man and came home. And when I found my Izzy was not here . . ."

She began to cry. Izzy put his arm around her.

Jordan's head was spinning. "Silvana. Please think. The nasty dolphin-man. Where did you last see him?"

"He lives by the river, near the place where the village was destroyed."

"Thank you, Silvana," he said. "And welcome home. I know you'll take good care of Izzy. I'll put in a good word with Eldon and the CKCC. Don't worry, it'll be okay—I'm a Grimsley, I have some pull." She wiped a tear and smiled at him.

Jordan stepped up to Izzy. "You'll be okay now," he said. "You have someone who's going to grow old with you. Take care of each other, okay?" Jordan stuck out his hand.

Izzy looked at Jordan's hand. He grunted and slapped it away, then gave Jordan a very tight hug. It was slobbery, too—especially because Izzy's belly-mouth lined up with Jordan's head.

BANG! CLANG! SMASH!

The metal crashing and crunching noises sounded foreign among the natural chirping and squeaking sounds of the jungle at night. And as Jordan ran toward where the RV and Heli-Jet touched down, they grew louder.

CLANG! CLONG! CRASH!

Jordan was relieved to see the piggybacked vehicles still parked where they had landed, but confused by what else he saw. Buck Wilde and his Buckaroo Crew were standing atop the RV, kicking and beating on the Heli-Jet with camera equipment, baseball bats, and small appliances they'd pulled out of Buck's RV kitchenette. *CRUNCH! BONG! SMASH!*

"STOP IT!" Jordan yelled up to them. "What are you guys doing?"

Buck held up a hand. The Buckaroo Crew stopped.

"Well, well, well. Look who it is, boys—Gusto's little trickster buddy. What do you want, pajama boy?"

"What? I'm not with Gusto! I hate that guy!"

"Oh, yeah?" Buck tossed an aluminum baseball bat. "Prove it."

Jordan looked at the bat.

"This is Gusto's private property," one of the Buckaroo Crew said. "We're hitting him where it hurts!" *CLANG!* He kicked the door, denting it a bit.

"Hey, guys, I have an idea," Jordan said. "How about instead of beating up our ride home, we actually *ride it home*—then when we get there, we beat up Gusto, instead?"

They all glanced at one another. Buck turned to his

crew. "Why didn't any of you think of that? Seriously, sometimes I wonder what I'm paying you guys for."

Jordan sat in the pilot's seat of the Heli-Jet, fiddling with switches, quickly figuring out the operating system. He switched over to manual control and slowly pulled back on the throttle. The Heli-Jet lurched into a tree. He tried again, and this time it lifted clumsily off the ground. Buck sat next to him, sadly staring out the window as they began to rise above the thick jungle.

"The whole wild ride is over," he said.

Jordan glanced at Buck. He actually felt a little bad for him. "C'mon. Nothing's over. There must be something else you can do."

"Squatch-searchin' was my life," Buck said. "And all that time I was chasing a creature that had already been caught, and had his feet made into trophy-boots. Man, I'd give anything to get a pair of those puppies."

Jordan was tempted to tell Buck that Syd was alive and well and wearing his sneakers but decided to stay true to the Creature Keeper code of silence. He listened as Buck continued.

"So what do I do? I go off and make a horse's patootie of myself on national television. All I had was my reputation, and now I ain't even got that. I'm just a big phony." He sighed. "You know my name ain't even Buck Wilde? I changed it. For TV."

"What's your real name?"

"Glen," he said. "Glen Savage."

Jordan was really starting to feel guilty as he steered the Heli-Jet–RV combo low and slow over the treetops. "Let me ask you something, Buck," he said. "What will you miss more—being a hunter or being on TV?"

Buck looked at him. "Is this a trick question? I'm really not in the mood to be tricked again, Jordan."

"If there weren't any cameras, if there wasn't an audience, if there weren't any fans, would Buck Wilde still want to be part of catching a very rare creature?"

Buck sat up in his seat. "You better not be messin' with me, man."

Jordan smiled. "You ever heard of the pink Amazon river dolphin, Buck?"

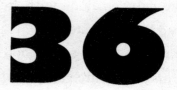

36

*G*RRRRRRRZZZZ . . . The grinding sound wasn't coming from the Heli-Jet's near-silent rotors. The aircraft hovered low over the Amazon jungle, where a member of the Buckaroo Crew reached out of the RV door and picked fruit from the trees. The sound was coming from inside the RV. Specifically, from Buck's RV kitchenette. Even more specifically, it was coming from the industrial-sized frozen-drink machine he negotiated for when he signed his last TV contract.

Buck stepped out of his walk-in closet dressed in his best angling outfit—waders with suspenders, tackle vest, and floppy hat. But instead of a fishing pole, he had his trusty lasso at his side.

"How we doing, Buckaroo Crew?" he said.

"Coming along all right?"

His cohorts looked up from their project, but kept working. One dumped the fruit he'd gathered onto the counter. Another chopped up the fresh guava, mocambo, and passion fruit, while a third tossed the chunks into the grinder along with fresh acai berries. A fourth offered Buck a taste.

"Mmm-mm! Boy, that's some good smoothie, right there! Okay, finish that batch and fill them chum buckets. I'll let Jordan know we're ready to rock!" He pulled out his lasso and hollered up toward the Heli-Jet.

"Okay, Jordan! Let's go fishin'!"

Up in the cockpit, Jordan maneuvered them over the

Amazon River, slowly crisscrossing the wide expanse of murky water near where the little village of Palafito had been destroyed. He looked down and saw the Buckaroo Crew dumping buckets of brightly colored fruit smoothies from the RV into the river below. The thick liquid hit the river like technicolor vomit, then floated along on the water's surface.

Buck climbed out of the RV and made his way to the ladder attached to the back of his camper. He swung his lasso as he stared down at the fruit-splattered water below.

"Here, pinky, pinky . . . c'mon, now . . . come and get your daily vitamins. . . ."

"There!" Jordan yelled, pointing to the river water up ahead. A flash of pink broke through the surface, then dived again. Jordan banked the aircraft slowly, and the Buckaroo Crew carpet bombed the area with the smoothie chum.

Then they waited.

"*SQUONK!*"

The pink Amazon river dolphin surfaced, gobbling up the delicious puree of mocambo and passion fruit. It happily rolled in the sludge, seemingly unable to control itself in the presence of such a delicious and natural source of vitamins and antioxidants. It broke through the water, flipping in the air in a burst of smoothie-fueled bliss.

SWISH! Buck snagged the large pink mammal in his lasso. "Gotcha!"

Buck was nearly yanked off the RV, but quickly looped his rope around the ladder, securing it tightly. The Buckaroo Crew scrambled to the back of the RV and began carefully hauling the rare creature out of the river. As Jordan hovered low, they used a large net to capture it and pull it into Buck's trailer.

"*YEEEEEE-HAAAAWWWW!*" Buck let out a yelp that let Jordan know they had their creature. Jordan set the navigation system for Canada, shifted the

Heli-Jet to autopilot, and climbed down to check it out. The Heli-Jet's rotors lifted the RV/airship hybrid high above the jungle, then its rocket thrusters engaged, blasting them northwest across South America.

Down in the RV, Jordan, Buck, and the Buckaroo Crew gathered around the pink Amazon river dolphin flopping on the floor of Buck's mobile living room.

"Man, I just had these carpets cleaned," Buck said, suddenly busting into a grin. "But who cares? It was totally worth it! Boys, did you see me pull this big fish in?"

"Big *mammal*," a Buckaroo Crew member said. "Dolphins are mammals."

"Phil, please," Buck said. "Not now, okay?"

"Oh, he's a mammal, all right." Jordan stepped inside and stood over the giant freshwater dolphin. "You're *all* mammal, aren't you, *Manuel?*"

"*Squeak! SQUONK!*" The creature's eyes met Jordan's stare. Jordan recognized a familiar twinkle. There was no doubt in his mind—they had their dolphin.

"I know it's you, Boto. Now I want you to shapeshift or switchify or Freaky Friday yourself, right now. I have a few questions I'd like to ask you, person-to-person."

Buck leaned over to Jordan. "Uh, hey, Jordan, I know they say dolphins are as smart as people and all, but I'm not so sure they can answer people questions like people do."

"I bet it can answer this one." Jordan scooped a big glass of fruit smoothie out of the power blender and held it in front of the dolphin's beak. "Mmmmmm . . . Does Boto want some more smoothie? Hmmm? Does he? Does he?"

The pink Amazon river dolphin stared at the glass. He stopped flopping.

"*SQUONK!*"

"All you can drink, big fella. But you're gonna need more than flippers to take this glass from me. C'mon now. A nice, delicious fruit smoothie . . . should I throw it away?"

The pink dolphin's flipper slapped at the glass awkwardly. "*SQUONK!*" It flailed around a bit, then went still. It began to shudder.

Then it began to change.

Its tail flukes formed into human feet. Its thick, muscular tail divided into two legs. Its flippers morphed into arms and hands, and its thick, smooth pink torso sprouted black hair as it turned into the unmistakably manly chest . . . of Señor Manuel Boto.

The Buckaroo Crew had hidden behind the couch. Buck stood staring in awe.

The very wet, very naked Manuel Boto sat up and

took the smoothie from Jordan. He took a deep sip, licking the extra juice from his bushy black moustache. "Mmmm . . . that's a good smoothie," he said. "Do I detect a touch of acai berry?"

"Dry him off," Jordan said. "I'll be right back to interrogate him. And for goodness' sake, give him some clothes!"

Their flight path had them clearing Central America in no time, and they were soon zooming north over the South Pacific, heading toward the equator. Jordan programmed the autopilot to fly low to the water to stay off radar. He didn't have exact coordinates yet, and he needed them. He'd put out a signal to the CKCC and asked Buck to stay in the copilot's chair in case there was a response.

Jordan climbed back down into the RV. He needed information, and knew that Manuel could be slipperier than, well, a wet dolphin. He found the bronze-skinned bartender relaxing with a smoothie, kicking back in Buck's robe, wearing a *Buck Wilde* trucker cap over his bald spot and blowhole.

"I know it was Chupacabra you were talking to that night at El Encantado," Jordan began.

"Such a smart boy!" Manuel's bronze face flashed a perfectly white smile.

Jordan held up his grandfather's journal. "I've also figured out what it is he was after. Your tears. You're a cryptosapien. You can change from creature to man at will."

"HAHAHAHA—*squonk*! Another win for the smart boy! So. You know who I am, and you figured out my secret. And in return, I am eternally grateful for the delicious smoothie. Now may I go, please?"

"Not 'til you tell me what your tears do," Jordan said.

"Ah, so the smart boy does not know everything, no?" Manuel said. He suddenly spoke in a low voice. "All I can say is this, senhor—the tears of a cryptosapien can be, for some, *transformative*."

"How? Like change-into-animals transformative?" Jordan said. "And what do you mean, 'for some'? Like who? Men? Women?"

"Unfortunately, not women, no. If they were, I would now have a half-dolphin, half-lady girlfriend. Sadly, I do not."

"Silvana told me about your creepy teardrop concoction. Kind of a turnoff, crying in a girl's drink on the first date, dude."

Manuel shrugged. "There are plenty of fish in the sea. HAHAHA—*squonk*!" He covered his mouth. "I beg your pardon. But you got my joke, no?"

"What did Chupacabra want with your tears? I need answers, Manuel."

"Trust me, smart boy. There are some answers that may be too dangerous for you to know. Or for me to tell."

Jordan stared at Manuel. "You're scared. You're afraid of Chupacabra." Boto shot Jordan a glance. "You and he made a deal that night. What did you get in exchange for giving him your tears?"

"A promise! That when the time came—when it was time to choose sides—I would be looked upon as a creature. Not a man!"

Something about the way this conversation turned sent a chill down Jordan's spine. "And what did you give him in exchange?"

"You already know the answer to that."

"Your tears. So he ensures you will be seen as a

creature rather than a human . . . and what exactly do your tears do for him?"

Manuel thought about this for a moment. Then he smiled. "Exactly the opposite."

BLAM! WHOOOSH! The RV door suddenly slammed opened, sending a blast of cold ocean air whipping around the trailer. Buck climbed in from above.

"Jordan! Someone's on the radio! Name's Ed—says he'll only talk to you!"

Jordan got up. "Watch Manuel," he said to the Buckaroo Crew. "Don't let him out of your sight. Not even for a second."

37

The dawn spread across Sasquatch Provincial Park, over Echo Island (formerly and briefly known as Wilde-Isle), all the way across the waters of Harrison Lake until it reached the foot of Mount Breakenridge. With the new sunlight came a clear view of the aftermath of all that had happened the night before.

The Badger Rangers had spent the rest of the night helping the disheveled and disoriented ex-BuckHeads off the island and back to the mainland, where they packed up their cars, campers, and tents and silently rode off in the chilly dawn.

Then, once the bonfires were extinguished and all the trash gathered and separated for responsible recycling, the Badger Rangers held a brief closing ceremony for the Forty-Seventh Annual International Badgeroobilee. They said farewell to Echo Island, boarded their bus, and rode silently back to Vancouver Airport.

Long after everyone had left, when there wasn't a soul to be seen or heard, a slight ripple disrupted the glass-like surface of Harrison Lake. The Creature Keepers' submarine broke through the water, slowly gliding northward toward Mount Breakenridge. In its wake, a green head bobbed up and down.

The Loch Ness Monster and the submarine both slowed to a stop near the end of the lake. The submarine's hatch opened. The crew, weary from searching for Gusto all night, climbed out slowly.

"You think he might be dead?" Abbie said, stretching and yawning.

"We can't assume that, I'm afraid," Eldon said.

"Maybe he never came down to earth at all," Bernard said hopefully. "What if he just shot into the atmosphere, and exploded somewhere in space?"

"That would be so awesome," Doris said.

"SKRONK!"

"Well, wherever that howfin galoot is, Haggis-Breath says he ain't in the lake. She's checked every nook an' cranny."

FLUTTER-FLUTTER-FLOP-SPLOOSH!

Kriss attempted landing on the deck but flitted about at the last second and slipped off the edge of the submarine. Nessie lifted him up and dropped him in a soggy puddle onto the deck. Abbie couldn't help but giggle.

"Nothing from the air, either, I take it?" Eldon said. Kriss shyly shook his soggy, waterlogged head.

Eldon looked off at the sunlight slowly creeping its way up the dark mountainside. "Well, that settles it. It'll be broad daylight soon. With all the commotion and television coverage last night, I expect this place won't stay this quiet for long." He turned to the others. "I'm not comfortable having this many cryptids out and about. Wherever Gusto is, he's likely injured and lying low. When he makes a move, we'll find him. Until then, I'm calling off the search." He turned to Alistair. "Mac, could you ask Nessie for one of her scales, please? This lake may be Gusto-free for now, but I want to know if that changes."

"Aye." Alistair plopped down on the bow of the submarine and whistled. Nessie floated over and gave him a look. "Knock it off, willya? I know you don't like this, but it has to be done." She let out a *"humph!"* and flopped her head upside down on his lap.

Abbie noticed something on Nessie's underside. There was a large patch of pink skin, completely unprotected by the Hydro-Hide. "Alistair, what's that bald patch on Nessie?"

Nessie popped her head up. She snorted and ducked underwater. Alistair turned to Abbie. "Wish ya hadn't pointed that out. She's pretty prideful about her looks. That's a patch that didn't grow back after—y'know, what happened."

"Oh, I'm sorry," Abbie said. "I didn't mean to upset her."

"No one ever does," Alistair said. "But it never keeps her from overreactin'."

316

Nessie popped her head up again, but refused to look in either Alistair's or Abbie's direction. She made a tense face and emitted what Abbie thought was a very unladylike grunt. *Clink!* A single shiny, sparkling scale popped off her neck and flew through the air. Alistair caught it and smiled at his cryptid. Then he got up and handed it to Eldon.

Eldon took off his Badger Ranger hat, placed the scale inside, and pulled his hat tightly back on his head. "Thanks, Mac," he said. "And please let her know we appreciate the donation."

"Nah," he said. "She don't deserve it, the big baby. I'll go below and sync up the sub's navigation system to her tracker collar so she can at least lead us home."

"Sounds good," Eldon said. "Abbie, Syd, and I will see you there in a few days."

"You're not coming?" Alistair said.

"We're not coming?" Abbie and Syd said.

"We've got a homeless Creature," Eldon said. "There's a protocol when this happens. We've got to get up on that mountain, assess the damage to Syd's house, destroy any evidence, and figure out a relocation strategy."

"Speaking of relocation, what's the plan for my brother?" Abbie said.

"I'm sure he's enjoying his well-deserved post-hoax leisure time getting to know Izzy. The Amazon's a beautiful place, if you're not being chased through it by an angry Mapinguari. Once Kriss gets a day or two of rest, I'll have him fly down and bring Jordan back."

Abbie smiled. "Hey, Eldon, you're still a dork and all, but I appreciate you letting me stay behind to tag along with you and Syd."

"Tag along?" Eldon looked genuinely surprised. "You're Syd's Creature Keeper. You're leading this trip. Let me know what I can do to help."

"And I'll let the both of you know," Doris said from behind them. "If you think I'm not coming with you, you better think again."

Roxanne's fallen cliff had buried the smooth-stoned beach, covering it with craggy, jagged rocks that stretched much farther out into the lake and creating a new, much less welcoming coastline.

Bernard steered the submarine as close to the mountain as he could without running aground. Abbie, Eldon, Doris, and Syd said their good-byes to Bernard, Kriss, Mac, and Nessie, and jumped in the deep water.

They watched the submarine glide away and submerge beneath the surface of Harrison Lake. Eldon carefully removed his hat and handed something to Abbie. She looked down at the sparkling green scale in the palm of her hand. "Go on," Eldon said. "Toss it."

Abbie tossed the scale high like a coin. It shimmered in the sunlight as it flipped through the air, then hit the water with a soft *plunk!*

SWOOF! A wave of green immediately blasted out in every direction, flashing the surface of the water. It left a salty film on Abbie's skin and a briny taste on her tongue.

They swam toward the mountain until the water grew too shallow. Abbie felt the sharp, sheared rocks that had tumbled off the mountain and carefully waded toward the craggy, defensive barrier onshore. The base of Mount Breakenridge looked completely different buried under the fallen cliff. They climbed over the pointed crags, searching for the trailhead, or anything at all that seemed familiar.

"Over here!" Abbie was crouched atop a jagged chunk of cliff, where she poked at something green snagged on the rock. The thin, flesh-like clump had a spongy feel to it, and sparkled in the sunlight. Abbie scraped at it, and held a small, sparkling object up to the sunlight. It was a scale. Gusto had passed through here, and torn a bit of his Hydro-Hide on the rock.

"And look at this," Doris said. Lying on a flat stone was a tiny black cork surrounded by bits of broken glass. The rounded bottom of a vial was still intact, but whatever it had held was gone.

The four of them stood and turned to face Mount Breakenridge. Directly beneath where Roxanne's cliff had fallen, a jagged pile of spiky rocks towered up the mountainside. Hidden in the shadows of the large slabs was an opening, like a cave entrance, but cracked and smashed inward, as if by a battering ram or wrecking ball. The stone on the ground near the entrance was broken into bits, and there in the pulverized powder of the crushed rock was a famously familiar set of footprints.

"Soil-Sole tracks," said Doris.

"Gusto," said Eldon. "He must be inside."

"Well," said Syd. "Shall we knock first, or just pop in on him?"

38

Climbing out of the RV and up into the Heli-Jet was a bit more challenging while rocketing over the North Atlantic Ocean. Jordan carefully clambered into the cargo space cluttered with MADE IN BRAZIL–marked boxes, then sat down in the pilot's seat, and grabbed the radio microphone.

"This is Jordan Grimsley, OVER!" Jordan said loudly. "Creature Keeper Jordan Grimsley here. CKCC do you read me, OVER!"

"Jeez Louise! You don't have to yell!" Ed's voice crackled back over the radio. "I'm not deaf! And you don't have to say 'over,' either. I'll know you're done talking when you stop. . . . See? I didn't say over, and you knew I was done, 'cause I stopped. Over."

"Ed! I need your help! What's going on up in Canada?"

"I just got a status report from the recon group," Ed said. "They're all fine, and heading back to base in the sub. A few of 'em are going up to Syd's place to examine the wreckage, destroy evidence, you know, the usual cryptid relocation protocol."

"Wreckage? Ed, what's going on up there? Is everyone all right?"

"Yeah! Like I told ya, most of 'em are heading back as we speak. Eldon stayed up there with Doris, Syd, and your sister to tie up some loose ends, that's all."

"What about Gusto? And the Soil-Soles?" Jordan noticed Buck climb into the cockpit and sit in the copilot's seat. Buck gazed out the window at the ocean whizzing by below.

"No sign of either, I'm afraid," Ed's voice crackled back. "Gusto's gone, and they weren't able to find him. The lake's been sealed, and the Sasquatch perimeter's secure enough that Eldon decided to send the recon team back to base."

Buck looked up. He'd been casually listening until he heard the word *Sasquatch*.

"With Gusto still at large?" Jordan was growing more anxious by the second.

"Report said Nessie blasted him clear across the

lake," Ed said. "Eldon's assuming Gusto's been injured or worse. He's only human."

Buck looked up again. *Nessie?*

"Listen to me, Ed," Jordan said. "I've got a bad feeling about this. Gusto survived getting blown out of a volcano, so I highly doubt we've seen the last of him. I need to get to Syd and the others, ASAP. I need the coordinates to where they are. We have a cryptid who could be in danger, do you read me?"

"Loud and clear, Jordan. Let's see . . . Sasquatch. I've got 'em right here. Forty-nine degrees, forty-one minutes, ten seconds north latitude, one hundred twenty-one degrees, fifty-four minutes, six seconds west longitude! Lead you right to Syd! Didja get all that?"

Jordan leaned over in front of Buck and punched the coordinates into the navigational system on the console as Buck stared wide-eyed. Jordan went to hit Enter, then stopped.

"Wait. Ed, what are these coordinates?"

"You should know, it's your invention! The Global Cryptid Positioning System coordinates for the Sasquatch. Take you right to him!"

"No, Ed," Jordan said. "Listen to me. That won't work. Syd doesn't wear his GCPS collar. It's on his Teddy Squatch."

There was a long silence. "His Teddy what, now?"

"His Teddy Squatch. Which is back in the Amazon. Those coordinates are useless."

Buck looked disappointed. He stared down at the navigational control panel in front of him as Jordan sat back down in his seat.

"I don't know what in tarnation you're talking about, Jordan," Ed said. "But I'm checking out these coordinates, and they drop you smack-dab in the middle of Mount Breakenridge."

Jordan's mind was reeling. This was impossible. He kept playing over in his head what had happened in the jungle, the place where he last saw Teddy Squatch—or what was left of him—after Chupacabra bit his head off and swallowed it whole.

"But the only way that collar could lead us to Canada is if—"

CLICK. A soothing computerized voice spoke from the terminal. *"Congratulations. You've successfully entered your destination. Autopilot engaging now."*

Jordan looked up. Buck stared at Jordan from his seat in front of the navigation console. Then he reached over in front of Jordan and cut the radio transmission. "We're on our way," Buck said. "Over and out."

"Buck, what are you doing?"

"You made me look like a fool," Buck began in a low, angry tone. "You let me believe the only thing I ever lived for—catching the Squatch—had been a waste of time. When all along you knew he was alive—you even had a *homing device on him!*"

"Listen, Buck, let me explain."

"There's nothing to explain," Buck said. "If these coordinates are right, we're now flying straight for the Squatch. When we get to him, he's mine. He's finally all mine."

Jordan didn't have time to fight or argue or even

explain the situation to Buck. He needed to get to Syd, too, now more than ever. There was something strange going on. He needed to ask Manuel one simple question. Even if he refused to answer, the look on the crypto-sapien's face would tell Jordan what he needed to know.

He climbed out of the Heli-Jet and carefully made his way down toward the RV door. He swung himself inside and found Buck's Buckaroo Crew tied up together in a circle on the floor, each of them gagged with a passion fruit jammed in his mouth.

"Manuel! Where is he?"

They all nodded toward the door. Jordan spun around to see a naked Manuel standing in the open doorway, his bare backside facing Jordan.

"So long, amigo! Thanks for all the smoothies." Manuel prepared to jump.

"Wait!" Jordan cried out. "I just have one question for you! You have to tell me, when he took your tears, who did Chupacabra transform into? Please!"

"HAHAHAHA—*squonk!*" Manuel laughed. "You forget the one house rule of El Encantado, smart boy! No names!"

Manuel flashed a grin, then leaped out of the RV. Jordan ran to the door, and saw Manuel's naked backside turn pink in midair, his arms and legs form into

flippers and a tail, and his backside morph into a dorsal fin.

SPLASH! Manuel Boto entered the water the same way he was scooped out of it—as Boto Encantado, the rare pink Amazon river dolphin.

The smashed opening in the rubble at the base of Mount Breakenridge led to a labyrinth of giant stone pillars. Formed from the crumbled cliff, it was like a forest of jagged rock.

Abbie, Eldon, Syd, and Doris made their way along a pulverized path that had been formed by Gusto and his Soil-Soles. He'd obviously kicked and stomped his way through the rock, tunneling a pathway with his feet into the heart of the mountain—and leaving only one way out, as well.

With each step, Abbie, Eldon, Syd, and Doris went deeper beneath Mount Breakenridge. Each step brought more darkness, too, as they moved farther away from the entrance. The last thing Abbie noticed

before plunging into total blackness were the walls of the long, small passageway. No longer formed from the shards of Roxanne's cliff, the walls they were passing through now were solid rock.

They felt their way along a steady decline, running deeper and deeper underground. Ahead of them Abbie saw a light. The dark, narrow path opened suddenly into a narrow, dimly lit cavern. Abbie looked up. High overhead, a jagged line of sunlight streamed down. They were standing at the bottom of a massive crevasse. The same crevasse Gusto had split in the surface of Mount Breakenridge.

Syd looked at Abbie. "We're inside Roxanne," he whispered.

The cavern was long and narrow, with walls shooting up hundreds of feet—a giant split in the rock with a solid stone floor beneath their feet. Dark cracks and grooves in the base of the walls, where the stretch of sunlight could not reach, were filled with shadow. It was from one of these dark spaces that Abbie heard a terrible sound—a heavy, raspy breathing.

"There's someone in the dark over there!" Abbie blurted out in a frightened whisper.

"All right, Gusto," Eldon said. "Come out and let's have a look at you."

Gusto stepped into the dim light. As he did, his Soil-Soles shook the entire cavern. Chunks of rock rattled loose from the walls, crashing all around them. Steam seeped up from cracks in the floor, and the rumbling beneath continued, even after Gusto stood still.

"Nice place you got here," Abbie said. "It really suits you."

Gusto looked as rough and craggy as the cavern they found him in. Ragged and bruised, his Hydro-Hide torn, he stood tall in his Soil-Soles, grinning down at his guests.

"This place was all a mistake," Gusto croaked, turning to Syd. "Thanks to the little trick you played on

me up on the surface, my grand plan was completely averted."

"Grand plan?" Doris said. "You got Syd's Soil-Soles!"

"His fancy footwork atop that rock up there caused me to release the pressure beneath this mountain. Pressure I was counting on to build toward its natural outcome."

"The natural outcome would've been complete disaster," Syd said, pointing at a wide swath of smooth rock running through the center of the cavity floor. "That's the tip of the Cascadia Subduction Zone!" Syd turned to the others. "The pressure was building in this chamber, pushing down on that area, causing the quakes. It was released when Gusto cracked open Roxanne. But from down here, direct impact from the Soil-Soles could trigger a megathrust earthquake that could shake the continent off its mantle."

"This is a dangerous place to mess around in, Gusto," Eldon said. "Even for you."

"You twisted old goat," Doris yelled. "What is it you want? Out with it!"

"I told you, back at the lake, remember? I just want to bring the world closer together, that's all." Gusto grinned as he eyed the strip of smooth stone running through the center of the floor. "And now, with all of you here as my witnesses, it's time I do just that—"

Suddenly, a vibration from above shook the cavern, causing small rocks to tumble from the walls. Gusto toppled backward, into the shadows. Abbie, Syd, Eldon, and Doris stumbled as they took cover from the falling stone. Abbie peered upward. Something eclipsed the sliver of light at the surface. The cavern went pitch-black.

"Congratulations. You've reached your destination." The Heli-Jet and the RV attached to it had parked directly on top of Roxanne, covering her deep crevasse. Jordan and Buck climbed out of the cockpit and stepped onto the forest floor to look around.

"All right, so where is he?" Buck hollered. "We were locked into the Squatch's critter GPS device, and it brought us here. But I don't see no Squatch!"

"You want us to keep filming you, boss?" a Buckaroo Crew member hollered from the RV.

"Yes, yes! Keep filming!" Buck called back.

Buck had his lasso at the ready and was tiptoeing around the parked vehicle, searching for Sasquatch. Jordan scanned the forest in search of another cryptid. He took in the uprooted trees as well as the rubble and rock that had rolled down from farther up the mountain. Something had gone down here, and he had a terrible feeling about it.

Jordan suddenly recalled a word Ed had mentioned: "relocation." His stomach dropped, and he turned to

Buck. "He isn't here, but he lives nearby! I can take you there—you wanna see where Bigfoot sleeps, dontcha?"

"Heck yeah!" Buck exclaimed. "Let's GIT OUR SQUATCH ON!"

Buck and his crew piled back inside the RV. Jordan climbed up and into the Heli-Jet. He lifted the RV up over the treetops. As he zoomed silently over to where Syd's tree house used to be, Jordan fought to push down the fear and anger he felt growing stronger in his belly.

The moment the light returned to the cavern, Abbie scanned the area for Gusto. Fallen rubble was everywhere, and the steam seeping up from the floor made it difficult to see.

"Everyone okay?" she heard Eldon's voice echo from somewhere behind her.

"I'm all right," she heard Syd say off to her left.

"I'm good," Abbie said. She waited a moment. "Doris? Where are you?"

"*Here I am!*" a shrieking voice screeched out from before them. It was Gusto. He stood on a rock jutting out of the floor, mocking Doris's voice. He laughed as he looked down. Abbie looked down, too, and caught her breath. Lying there on the floor was Doris. She wasn't moving.

"NO!" Abbie got up and ran to her friend.

"Aw, you see? Bringing people together is what I do!" Gusto went into a crouch. "And now it's time to take that concept to a global level, and begin phase one of Operation Pangaea!" He leaped into the air, his Soil-Soles ready to land directly on the swath of stone cutting through the center of the cavern floor. Syd dived out from behind a rock and suddenly side-tackled Gusto, intercepting the earth-shattering stomp. The two of them rolled onto a nearby rock shelf, where Syd wrestled Gusto as he struggled to stand. Gusto kicked

and screamed in Syd's strong arms. "Let go of me!" he shrieked. "Put me down!"

Abbie knelt beside Doris. She was lying on the stone floor, her leg wedged between two rocks. "Doris! Are you all right? Say something!"

Doris opened her eyes and smiled. "Oh, hello, dearie. There's goat's milk in the icebox and honey in the cupboard. How do you like your chamomile tea?"

Doris was dazed. Abbie noticed she had a lump on her head. Eldon rushed over. He moved the rocks to free her leg as he inspected her.

"She's sprained her ankle and taken a knock on the noggin," he said. "She'll be okay, but she needs to ice that concussion right away. We've gotta get her out of here."

"I'll carry her out the way we came in," Syd said. He was still bear-hugging the lanky, wriggling Gusto, holding him up and keeping him—and the Soil-Soles— from the touching the treacherous fault line below.

"Yes!" Gusto suddenly cried out. "You must help your friend! Set me down and carry her to safety! It's the only way, or she'll die!"

"If I set you down, we all die." Syd turned to Abbie. "What do we do?"

She glanced at Eldon. "Don't look at me," he said. "He asked his Keeper."

Abbie imagined herself trying to carry Doris out,

remembering the long way in. She looked up at the crack in the ceiling. She saw the sunlight. Then she looked down at the steaming cracks along the upper ridge of the cavern. "Syd," she said. "Remember that first night, how you got Jordan and me up into your tree house?"

Syd's eyes grew wide as he remembered. He looked up at the crack overhead, then down at the nearby ridge. He hauled the Soil-Sole-wearing Gusto away from the fault line, over to an area beneath the opening in the ceiling. He kicked away some of the rubble to expose the dusty rock floor. He slipped off Jordan's sneakers and stood barefoot. Then he closed his eyes.

Gusto squirmed in Syd's arms like a cranky infant trying to get free from a baby harness. "What are you doing? Put me down!"

BONK! Syd head-butted Gusto. "Shh. I'm trying to hear what Roxanne is telling me." Syd opened his eyes and used his heel to scrape an *X* in the dust. He looked over at Abbie. "Ready when you are," he said. "*X* marks the spot."

Jordan couldn't believe his eyes. Syd's tree house was gone.

He hovered over the sequoia grove that had held

it up, and saw that the last tree, the one that had supported Syd's bedroom, had split and fallen, pulling the rest of the house down with it. The other trees still stood strong, but the house they once cradled in their branches was lying in pieces on the forest floor. The beautiful deck remained intact, but it was little comfort.

"Hey!" Buck's voice called up to Jordan from the open RV door below. "I thought you were taking us to Bigfoot's house! This is a nice deck and all, but c'mon! Is this dump really where he slept? No more tricks, now!"

The combination of seeing Syd's destroyed house and hearing Buck's voice caused something inside of Jordan to snap. He felt a rage come over him he'd never felt before. Suddenly, all he wanted to do was teach Buck and his Buckaroo Crew a lesson. He leaned out the window of the Heli-Jet cockpit. "You wanna see where Bigfoot slept? Okay, then! Next stop, Bigfoot's bedroom!" He swung the Heli-Jet clear of the deck and looked down. He could see the wreckage of Syd's house on the ground, hundreds of feet below. Then he cut the engine, and they all dropped like a stone.

"*Aahhhhh!*" Buck and his Buckaroo Crew's screams cut through the whooshing wind.

CRASH! The RV slammed into the pile of wood that was once Syd's house. The tires of the truck broke the impact somewhat, but Jordan could hear Buck and his crew yelling and moaning beneath him. He smiled and yelled out the Heli-Jet window to them.

"There you go!" Jordan said. "Bigfoot's bedroom! Next stop, the kitchen!"

He fired up the rotors and jammed the controls. The craft shot straight up into the air. Jordan was about to slam them back down again when he suddenly heard a *SNAP!* The Heli-Jet jerked. Buck and his crew screamed. Jordan looked down. The RV had broken loose on one side and was dangling from the Heli-Jet. Jordan's rage suddenly disappeared. "What am I doing?" he said aloud.

SNAP! CRRRREEEEAAAAK! The RV broke free from the Heli-Jet in another spot. As it swung treacherously over Syd's deck, Jordan looked out his side window at the empty-armed sequoias that had held Syd's house. He thrust and banked hard, swinging the RV over the deck.

BOOM! The RV's flat tires slammed into the branches and held firm. The back and front of the massive camper wedged between two sequoias with a *CRUNCH!*

The unhinged RV door slowly fell off, landing with a rattle on the deck. Buck stumbled out first, and fell to his knees. He looked up at Jordan, who was still hovering overhead in the Heli-Jet.

"Everyone all right?" Jordan yelled down. The Buckaroo Crew tumbled out behind Buck. Jordan saw one of the crew shuffle over to the railing and throw up over the side. He studied the navigation console. It was still showing the coordinates for Syd's GCPS tracking device. Jordan lifted the Heli-Jet over the treetops and headed back toward Roxanne.

Abbie helped Doris up onto Eldon's back. "Oh, hello, dearie," the old woman said in a singsongy voice. "Are we going on a trip?"

"Yes, you are," Abbie said. She glanced at Eldon, who didn't look at all comfortable with this plan. "Don't worry," she said. "There's nothing to this. I've done it myself."

"There is no Badger Ranger Badge for this," Eldon

said. "For good reason."

Eldon carried Doris piggyback over to the center of the *X*. Abbie nodded to Syd. The Sasquatch lifted the screaming Gusto up over his head. Syd looked for a second like he might hurl Gusto across the cavern, but instead he brought him straight down forcefully, feetfirst, onto the floor of the ridge. Gusto's Soil-Soles banged the *X*—cracking it open.

HISSSSSSS! A strong blast of steam shot into the air. It thrust Eldon and Doris straight up and toward the sunlight-filled fissure cut into the ceiling.

"Aaaaaahhhh!" Eldon yelled as they disappeared into the ceiling crack.

"Wheeeeeeee!" Doris's giddy voice echoed throughout the cavern.

41

"*Congratulations. You've reached your destination.*"

Jordan switched to manual and parked the Heli-Jet not directly on top of Roxanne but on the forest floor nearby. He looked at the navigation console, then out the window, trying to make sense of the situation. "Why?" he asked himself. "Why would the GCPS system tell me a homing device I know I last saw in the Amazon jungle is actually here—sixty-five hundred miles away from Brazil, on top of a big rock?" Jordan peered out at Roxanne. "A big rock with a large crack in it." He squinted. "A large crack with a tiny hand sticking out of it. . . ." Jordan leaped out of his seat. "Oh my gosh! A hand!"

Jordan ran from the Heli-Jet to Roxanne. Eldon

was gripping the edge of the fissure, Doris still clinging to his back. Jordan grabbed hold of them and tugged with all his might, pulling them both up and out of the crevasse.

"Jordan! Boy Howdy, am I glad to see you," Eldon said. "Doris took a knock on the head. We need to get ice on that concussion of hers right away."

"I know just the place," Jordan said. "We've even got our own personal medevac!"

Doris looked at the Heli-Jet. "That's some sweet *techspertise* you got there, dearie!"

"Her condition is worsening," Eldon said. "She's making up words now."

In the short time it took Jordan to fly Eldon and Doris back up to Buck and his Buckaroo Crew on

Syd's deck, Eldon quickly filled Jordan in on all that had happened in and around Harrison Lake. From the tsunami wave caused by the cascading cliff to Buck Wilde's Wilde Isle (where hundreds of BuckHeads had witnessed Jordan's Izzy-hoax) to Nessie blasting Gusto clear across the lake, Jordan was amazed at all that had gone down. By the time Eldon got to the part about being trapped deep beneath Mount Breakenridge with an evil madman trying to set off a megathrust earthquake that could send the entire continent of North America adrift, Jordan had the Heli-Jet hovering over the deck. He put the chopper in autopilot mode and turned to Eldon.

"I have one question," he said. "And it's going to sound crazy. Down in that hole, is there any chance—any chance at all—that Chupacabra was there with you?"

"Chupacabra? He's alive?"

"He's more than alive. He's our mysterious cryptid-whisperer who freaked out Izzy. And now he's trying to recruit creatures to join him in a war against humans."

"Well, he wasn't down there with us. I think I would've noticed!"

"Not if he disguised himself," Jordan said. "And that's what I'm most afraid of."

The two of them carefully lowered Doris onto the deck and handed her off to a confused-looking Buck Wilde. As Eldon dumped the stray boxes marked MADE IN BRAZIL onto the deck and gathered the tree-house rope ladder onboard, Buck confronted Jordan. "Hey, newsflash, fellahs," he said. "This ain't Bigfoot."

"You wouldn't know Bigfoot if he stepped on your toe, sonny boy," Doris said.

"Listen, Buck," Jordan said. "Doris is a very old and dear friend of ours, and she needs your help. You take care of her and I promise I'll see that you get to meet Sasquatch, face-to-face. You have my word on that."

Buck looked at Doris for a moment, then back at Jordan. "Okay. What's she need?"

"Is your frozen drink machine on the RV still operational?"

As Jordan and Eldon lifted away from the deck in the Heli-Jet, they could hear the grinding sound of the industrial smoothie machine. They looked down and saw Doris waving happily to them with a fruit smoothie in her hand, a big bag of ice on her head.

"Do you think she'll be okay?" Jordan asked.

"Okay?" Eldon was triple–square knotting one end of the rope ladder to the eyehooks mounted to the cargo floor of the Heli-Jet. "She thinks she's on a tropical vacation!"

"Now we've got to get Abbie and Syd outta that hole," Jordan said. "They're in a lot of danger. The situation is worse than you know."

"What's worse than standing on an underground fault line that could break apart the whole continent with a guy who's got the proper footwear to make it happen?"

"If that guy isn't a guy at all," Jordan said. "But Chupacabra, in disguise."

"HAHAHAHAHA!" Gusto's awful laughter echoed through the cavern.

"You're a monster," Abbie said. "And a real jerk."

"You have no idea." Gusto suddenly jolted, trying to wiggle free. Syd struggled to retighten his grip. Gusto smiled up at his captor. "Your arms must be getting awful tired, *Littlefoot*," he teased. "Why don't you set me down for a minute? Go on. Take a break."

"I don't think so," Syd strained as he gripped Gusto even tighter. "I'm not letting you near that Subduction Zone trigger. I'll hold you 'til my arms fall off."

"All right." Gusto sighed. "I can wait. Sooner or later, though, even the mighty Sasquatch will need to rest."

Abbie studied Gusto's feet. "There must be a way to get those Soil-Soles off."

"They only come off if the wearer willingly lets them go," Syd said.

"Then why did Jordan lose them? He never would have given them up."

Gusto snickered. "Simple. It was either give them up or drown. Choices become clear very quickly when you value your own skin over your cause. That's the difference between your kind and mine. You see, I care about no one, including myself. There is only my master plan."

"So if you could crack open that fault line, what's your 'master plan' on getting out alive?" Abbie said.

"That's just it. *When* I crack open the earth, Señor Areck Gusto will cease to be. But from the flames . . . Who knows who or what will be reborn?"

"Okay," Syd said, adjusting his grip. "He's officially lost it."

"I've lost nothing," Gusto said. "Because I have nothing to lose."

A tiny rock suddenly bounced off Gusto's head. Another fell nearby, then another. There was a rumbling from above. The cavern rattled. The Heli-Jet was back.

The ground shook and Abbie lost her balance. She stumbled backward over a rock.

"Abbie!" Syd released Gusto as he lunged to help her.

"*HA!*" Gusto took a few bounding steps off the ridge. Abbie and Syd watched in horror as he leaped feetfirst toward the center of the cavern, straight at the smooth strip of rock running through the floor below: the Cascadia Subduction Zone fault line.

SPROING! Something from above suddenly dropped in front of Gusto, catching one of his Soil-Soles like a fish in a net. Gusto jerked to a stop in midair, and hung upside down above the fault line. His great foot was tangled in a long rope ladder dangling down from the open crack in the ceiling. Gusto kicked and jerked wildly, which only caused the strong rope rung to coil even tighter around his right Soil-Sole.

Aboveground, Eldon saw the rope ladder pull taut. He turned and gave the thumbs-up to Jordan, sitting in the cockpit. The Heli-Jet began to lift, pulling the ladder up with it.

"AAAARRRGGGH!" Gusto yelled as he rose above the cavern floor. *"WHAT IS THIS? WHAT'S GOING ON?"*

"C'mon, that's our ride!" In a flash, Syd scooped Abbie up in his arms and leaped off the ridge, straight at the bottom of the rope ladder, just catching a rung. As he grabbed it, Abbie slipped from Syd's grip and fell a short distance before quickly clutching Syd's thin ankle.

Gusto hung upside down about a dozen rungs above them, writhing and shrieking in frustration.

Abbie noticed Gusto relax his body and hang limp from the ladder. The snagged Soil-Sole suddenly opened up. Gusto had released one of the Soil-Soles so he could use the other to accomplish his master plan.

He dropped, sailing past Syd toward the fault line below. Thinking quickly, Abbie grabbed Gusto's skinny, bare ankle, stopping him with a mighty yank. As the ladder pulled the three of them out of the crevasse, Abbie strained to keep her grip on both Syd's and Gusto's ankles. She shut her eyes and focused, and didn't open them until she felt the cool, fresh air of Mount Breakenridge on her face.

42

Once clear of the open crack in the earth, Abbie let go of Syd's ankle. She and Gusto dropped a few feet to the ground. Gusto wriggled free of her grip and frantically rolled toward the fissure, trying to worm his way back into the cavern. He got to the edge and was suddenly stopped cold by a large, strong force pinning him to the ground.

Planted firmly on Gusto's puny chest was a Soil-Sole. And planted firmly inside that Soil-Sole was Syd's foot. The Sasquatch loomed over Gusto. "I'd like the other one back, please. To complete the pair."

As soon as Jordan landed the Heli-Jet, Abbie quickly used its attached rope ladder to wrap Gusto from head to toe. Syd pulled the bindings as tight as

he could until it squeezed Gusto like an anaconda, and Eldon quadruple–square knotted the ends of it. Once Gusto stood bound and leashed to the Heli-Jet, they all breathed easier.

"See?" Eldon said. "Nothing beats a grade-A rope and solid knot-tying know-how."

Jordan yelled from the Heli-Jet cockpit window. "Your rope wouldn't have done much good pulling them out of that rock if it weren't anchored to this XU-57 Heli-Jet. Score one for top-of-the-line modern technology."

"You're both top-of-the-line, grade-A dorks," Abbie said. "Although on this one, I think maybe you're both right."

"Yes, I couldn't agree more," Gusto said. "A hybrid of old and new really is the best option—it offers strength, power, and most importantly, *an element of surprise*."

Eh-eh!

The chirp of a remote sounded behind them. The Heli-Jet's rotors suddenly whirred to life. Through the cockpit window, Jordan looked confused and frightened. Abbie glanced back at Gusto. His hands were tied behind his back, but she recognized what he had in his bound hands: the thin, black Heli-Jet remote.

"Syd! He has the controller! Grab him!"

Syd dived to tackle Gusto, but he was too late.

FWOOSH! The Heli-Jet shot straight up into the air, pulling the rope ladder leash, yanking Gusto off the ground.

Inside the Heli-Jet, Jordan frantically punched at the cockpit controls. Nothing worked. They'd been overridden by the remote, and he was powerless to do anything. Swinging from his leash outside, Gusto randomly stabbed at the buttons on the remote behind his back. The chopper jerked in the air, dropping and soaring erratically, tossing Jordan around inside the Heli-Jet, and whipping Gusto around outside.

The others watched helplessly from the ground as the Heli-Jet zigged and zagged overhead. It suddenly lurched forward, and Abbie, Eldon, and Syd ran to keep up, following as the chopper dragged Gusto through the treetops. Something small and black caught Abbie's eye as it tumbled down through the branches. Gusto had dropped the remote.

In the cockpit, Jordan noticed that the control panel had come back online. He crawled to the pilot's seat and quickly stopped the Heli-Jet, steadying it in a hover. As he prepared to take it down for a landing, a strong hand suddenly gripped his wrist from behind.

Jordan spun around. Gusto had bits of the shredded rope ladder hanging off his tattered Hydro-Hide. His face was cut and scraped, and he had chunks of tree bark and branch jutting out of his thick black hair. Despite all this, he looked very pleased with himself as he stood grinning over Jordan.

"This is the property of Gusto Industries," he snarled. "Get off my Heli-Jet, Grimsley." Gusto yanked Jordan out of the pilot's seat and tossed him across the cargo floor.

Jordan slid to a stop just before the open doorway. He glanced down at the ground far below the hovering Heli-Jet and thought he spotted Abbie and the others. Then he stood up and bounded back toward Gusto.

"You can quit pretending," Jordan said. "Your name isn't Areck Gusto. I know who you are—or rather, *what* you are."

"Oh?" Gusto stepped toward Jordan. "And who—or what—would that be?"

"You've used cryptosapien tears to hide your true identity—*Chupacabra*."

"Ah. Has someone been listening to magical myths and dolphin tales?"

"Boto didn't tell me anything I didn't already suspect. Remember when you bit that stuffed animal's head off in the jungle? Well, you also swallowed a tracking device, which led me right to you. It was just before Izzy clocked your ugly head with a log."

Gusto laid a hand on the side of his head. His grin began to fade.

"Still hurt? Good," Jordan said. "Izzy sends his best, by the way. He *and* Silvana."

Gusto glared at Jordan. "You've gotten so smart in your old age, haven't you, Georgie boy? You want to see my true face again? Fine. But only if you show me yours—*George*." He glanced at Jordan's hand. "Lost your ring again, I see. You stole it back from me in the river, but you seem to have misplaced it. Without the elixir that runs through that ring, you're defenseless against your true age. So show me, George. I want to see that wrinkly old human face before I kill you. In return, I'll allow you the pleasure of gazing upon my exquisite creature form."

Jordan's mind was racing. He got an idea. "Okay," he said. "But you go first."

"Beauty before age. Got a light?" He grinned at Jordan. "Never mind." He snapped his fingers. A small flame appeared on the tip of his thumb. He held it to his lips and blew. The spark burst into a flame, engulfing his body. It swirled around him, then disappeared, burning away all that was Gusto, revealing Chupacabra.

The doglike cryptid looked the same as he had in

the jungle. But without his robe, Jordan could now see that the Hydro-Hide had become part of his skin. It had melded onto him like a natural set of scales. The single Soil-Sole on his left foot looked strange, but it too blended onto his calf like it was part of him.

He burst out laughing. "YOUR TURN, GEORGIE!"

Jordan took a deep breath. He shut his eyes. He twitched and winced as if in pain, then buried his face in his hands. Chupacabra stepped back as Jordan hunched over, then jerked his body and stumbled around the cargo area. They circled each other until Jordan stood with his back to the cockpit, Gusto staring excitedly from the center of the cargo floor. Suddenly, Jordan dropped his hands, raised his head, and smiled.

"Hoogly-magoogly!" Jordan shouted, grinning at the startled Chupacabra.

"What is this?" The confused cryptid barked. "You're not George Grimsley!"

"Finally! It's about time you got that through your thick skull! No, I'm not! But what I am is a dedicated Creature Keeper—and your worst nightmare!"

Jordan leaped backward and grabbed the controls to drop the Heli-Jet down to the forest floor. Chupacabra lunged at him. "YOU TRICKED ME!"

The creature slammed them both into the control

panel. The Heli-Jet tilted violently. Jordan gripped the back of the pilot's seat. Chupacabra tried to clutch at Jordan with his sharp claws, but Jordan lifted a bunny-slippered foot and kicked him in the head—squarely in the same spot where Izzy had clunked him with a log.

"AAAARRRGGGH!" Chupacabra tumbled backward, sliding across the tilted cargo floor and out the open doorway of the Heli-Jet.

Jordan quickly pulled himself into the pilot's seat and righted the chopper.

On the ground, Abbie, Eldon, and Syd had watched the hovering Heli-Jet high above them bank sideways. As it straightened out again, they could see a lanky figure hanging from its side. Eldon peered through his Badger Ranger binoculars. "I'll be a skunk ape's sister, Jordan was right!" he exclaimed. "Gusto *is* Chupacabra!"

"What?" Syd gazed up at the kicking beast scrambling to climb back into the Heli-Jet. "We've got to stop that thing before it gets back in there with Jordan! Somebody hand me a boulder!"

Abbie looked down at the remote in her hand. "I got this," she said. She hit a random button, and the Heli-Jet suddenly lurched, sending Chupacabra tumbling along the outside of the ship, frantically trying to grab hold of something. His claws dug in, scraping the side of the Heli-Jet, until he stopped himself. Chupacabra was clinging to a rear rocket, staring straight into the mouth of the massive jet thruster.

Abbie squinted up at him and placed her thumb on a button marked Thrust.

"This is for Doris, you two-faced creep." *Click.*

KRRRGGGGSSSHHHH! The thick explosion of orange flame blasted Chupacabra.

In an instant, he was gone—and so was the Heli-Jet. The thruster sent the airship zooming across the forest, smashing through treetops, careening straight for Syd's newly refurbished RV-based tree house and deck.

Branches and tree trunks broke, bounced, and bashed off the cockpit window as Jordan stared wide-eyed at what was dead ahead. He saw Doris, Buck, and the Buckaroo Crew dive out of the way on the deck, spilling their smoothies as they took cover. He clutched the controls of the Heli-Jet and yanked back as hard as he could.

The aircraft veered straight upward, just missing the edge of the deck, climbing and bursting through the treetops into the blue sky. Jordan cut the rockets, leveled off the Heli-Jet, and began to slowly descend back into the forest. Just before reentering the tree-tops, Jordan looked through the cracked window out at Harrison Lake spreading peacefully away from Mount Breakenridge. Far beyond the distant mountains on the other side of the lake, Jordan caught a glimpse of a thin, fading red trail of what looked like a meteorite vanishing over the horizon.

The Heli-Jet touched down on the wreckage of Syd's fallen house. Jordan was greeted by Abbie, Eldon, and Syd on the ground and by Doris, Buck, and his crew up on the deck. As cheers and hellos greeted him from above and below, Jordan stepped out of the Heli-Jet, stumbled onto the ground, and promptly passed out.

Syd noticed Jordan's feet. "Is he wearing my bunny slippers?"

Jordan wasn't running away from anything. He was walking through a thick jungle in his pajamas. He immediately realized that this was a dream. He was able to recognize this because his mind wasn't clouded with fear. He could think clearly. Also, he was walking through a jungle in his pajamas.

What he couldn't recall was who he was walking toward, or why. He knew it was someone he was happy to see, and he knew whoever it was would be happy to see him. And that was a good feeling.

He came to a small clearing with a single, simple hut. There was a smoldering campfire that had recently been put out. Jordan poked his head inside the hut. It was dark and empty. A panic began to overtake him.

Had the fire been put out suddenly? Was whoever he'd come to see in danger and had to flee? Jordan's good feelings were quickly smothered by a horrible fear. His mind was racing when something directly behind him tapped him on the shoulder.

"*AAAAHHH!*" Jordan spun around—and saw a great big eye staring at him. "Izzy!" The Mapinguari's enormous belly-mouth smiled at Jordan, and the two of them hugged. Jordan shut his eyes tightly and squeezed as hard as he could, as the happiness came rushing back in again. And that was a good feeling.

"Uh, Jordan?"

The voice was not in Arawakan. And it was not Izzy's. Jordan opened his eyes. He was awake, sitting up in a strange bed. He pulled back from the furry, one-eyed creature he was hugging. Sitting there on the edge of the bed, wearing a pair of officially trademarked Mapinguari footie pajamas, was Eldon. "Er, welcome back," he said. "You were out for a while. How're you feeling?"

Jordan looked around the tiny bedroom. The walls were adorned with framed Buck Wilde posters, and the bedsheets were *Buck Wilde: Squatch-Seeker!*—branded.

"You just needed some rest. You've been through

quite a lot. Come on out when you're ready. There are a few folks there who are gonna be happy to see you."

A moment later, Jordan stepped out of the bedroom. A cheer went up in the main cabin of Buck's RV. The first thing Jordan saw was the entire Buckaroo Crew fixing smoothies in the kitchen—all dressed in Izzy footie pajamas.

"If I'm still dreaming," Jordan said at the odd sight. "I'd like to wake up now."

"Haw!" Buck stepped up to him, sporting Izzy pajamas, too. "We couldn't wait all night for you to wake up, so we started without ya! Welcome to Syd's official RV-Tree-House-Warming-Welcome-Home-Hap-Bon-Voyage-Pretty-Much-Everybody-Else Pajama Party!" He held out a glass of some frosty, neon-green concoction. "Smoothie?"

Jordan took the smoothie. "Did you call him 'Syd'?"

"Yeah! Y'know Bigfoot! I finally met him!" Buck leaned in closer. "Although it turns out he doesn't like that name. But hey—I really appreciate you keeping your promise to me." He yelled across the cabin. "Yo, Syd! Git yer hairy butt over here!"

Syd bounded over and lifted Jordan up with a big hug. He had a pair of Izzy pajamas stretched over his great, wide shoulders. "Isn't this great? This is the actual RV! From the TV show!" Jordan and Buck traded a smile. "This is a piece of television history— his show isn't on anymore, y'know!"

"Yeah, yeah," Buck said. "We know." He threw his arm around Syd's shoulders like they were old buddies. "My man Syd told some stories about your first coupla days on the job!" He elbowed Jordan in the ribs. "And I thought I had a rough time making a Sasquatch connection! Haw!"

"Don't listen to him, man." A voice caught Jordan's ear. He turned around to see Hap Cooperdock standing there, looking more than a little silly in his Izzy pajamas.

"Hap?" Jordan said. "Okay, now I know I must be dreaming."

"Nah," Hap said. "This is as real as it gets, man! And don't you listen to that blowhard—you and your sister did a great job taking care of Syd."

"Thanks, but . . . what are you doing here?"

"I had road-tripped all the way down to Mexico when I found out about Buck's last show. When I heard about Gusto turning up, I realized I didn't do a very good job luring him away from here. So I turned around and started heading back."

"Well, welcome home. Sorry about your house."

"It's cool! I'd gotten used to living in the back of the VW bus, so this is like a perfect step up—but with that awesome view! Man, I really missed that."

Jordan looked across the RV cabin to the door leading out onto the deck. He saw Doris, Eldon, and Abbie standing outside. His sister was the only person, besides himself, not wearing footie pajamas. Jordan smiled at this.

The sun was setting behind the trees, casting a beautiful golden glow on the forest all around the deck. Doris grinned as she saw Jordan approach.

"Jordan! How's your head, dearie?" she asked.

"Fine." Jordan smiled at her. "How's yours?"

"My head's fine!" She held up her empty glass. "Thanks to these. Be right back."

Jordan watched Doris step into the party, and noticed Syd's single Soil-Sole parked in its spot on the deck just outside the door. It was a sad sight.

"Gusto," Jordan said. "He's—"

"He's Chupacabra," Abbie said. "Nice work putting that together, little bro."

"Thanks. Good job jet-blasting him and saving my life," Jordan said. "But he's still out there. He can manipulate fire. It's kind of his thing."

"He might be out there," Eldon said. "But we sure slowed him down, at least for a while. It'll hopefully give us some time to figure out what his next move might be."

"Us?" Jordan shook his head. "Not me. You were right. Finding Izzy, winning back his trust, reuniting him with Silvana, that's what being a Creature Keeper is all about. I learned how much I have to learn. And I'm done trying to save the world."

Eldon glanced at Abbie. The two of them burst out laughing. "What?" Jordan said. "What's so funny?"

"It's too late," Abbie said. "We're official." She pointed to a pin on her shirt. It looked like a small golden shield and had the letters CK engraved on it.

"What's that?" Jordan said.

Eldon stepped up to him and pinned the same shield on his shirt. "I'm making you and Abbie Elite Keepers. If we're going to war, I want the best I have to help lead."

"But we're interns, remember? What happened to crawling before running?"

"Pff—speak for yourself," Abbie said. She walked off to join Doris inside.

"Your sister led an entire clan of young Badger Rangers," Eldon said. "She learned how to lock down a loch and sacrificed her own safety to get Doris and me out of a dangerous situation. But most important, she got her creature home safely. She's ready."

"Well, I'm still learning to crawl. Help, hide, and hoax, remember?"

"Like you said, you went back into that jungle and found Izzy. You helped him and hid him—and you pulled off one of the finest hoaxes I've ever witnessed in all my days as a keeper. You're ready enough."

Jordan looked down at his shield, then back up at Eldon. He had a gleam in his eye. He held up his hand to his forehead in a Badger Claw salute.

"Elite Keeper Jordan Grimsley, reporting for duty," he said.

As the moon rose above Harrison Lake, Jordan, Abbie, Eldon, Doris, and Syd lay out on the deck in their footie pajamas, staring up at the star-filled patches of sky between the crisscrossing branches of the towering sequoias. They laughed and shared stories from all they'd seen and done, both together and apart. The four humans were sad that they had to leave Mount Breakenridge the next morning, and Syd was sad that he'd have to see them go. But they all agreed that it was a very good thing that Syd wouldn't have to be relocated from such a peaceful, beautiful place.

One by one, they soon drifted off to sleep. First, Doris's gibberish about *techspertise* faded into a dreamy mumble. Next, Syd's great, snorty snoring echoed off the trees. Then Eldon's Badger Ranger hat slowly slipped down over his eyes. Jordan and Abbie were the last souls stirring on Mount Breakenridge. They whispered to each other about what they'd need to do to prepare for what was coming, and they admitted to each other that they were both a little anxious about what might happen next. What they didn't have to say was how happy they were to be in it together. There was no need to mention that.

Just before they drifted off to sleep, they were able to agree on one last thing—of all the Annual International Badgeroobilees they'd ever attended, this one had definitely been the wildest.

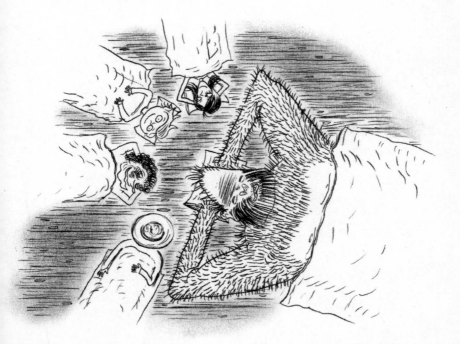